THOSE WHO LIVE IN
THE SHADOW OF
THE ULTIMATE WEAPON.

TEPLOV. The KGB executioner. Colder than death, he lusts after Black Magic.

BELIK. Black Magic's military director. Awed by Jamshid's incredible powers.

WINTER. Ex-CIA. Only he grasps the full horror of Black Magic, the true nature of the weapon.

CATHERINE HARRIS. A beautiful actress, a rising star. Destined for torture because she is Paul Winter's new lover.

PAKRAVAN. Winter's old friend, but in the magic-mirror world of Black Magic he becomes Winter's most dangerous enemy.

JAMSHID ROSTRAM. The mysterious one. Deeply wounded by a life of injustice, he has vowed revenge. His secret god is Black Magic.

BLACK MAGIC
**A terrifying novel of evil impulse—
and the dark side of the heart.**

Books by Whitley Strieber

The Hunger
Black Magic

Published by POCKET BOOKS

WHITLEY STRIEBER

BLACK MAGIC

PUBLISHED BY POCKET BOOKS NEW YORK

POCKET BOOKS, a division of Simon & Schuster, Inc.
1230 Avenue of the Americas, New York, N.Y. 10020

ISBN: 0-671-46084-6

First Pocket Books printing February, 1984

10 9 8 7 6 5 4 3 2 1

POCKET and colophon are registered trademarks
of Simon & Schuster, Inc.

Printed in the U.S.A.

Many scientists and military personnel from various nations aided me in the preparation of this book. I dedicate it especially to those who took risks to do so.

The bulk of recent telepathy research in the USSR is concerned with the transmission of behavior impulses—or the subliminal control of an individual's conduct.

—DR. MILAN RYZL,
Psychic 1, nos. 1–2 (1969)

"Apparent psi phenomena may be mediated by ELF (Extra-Low Frequency) electromagnetic waves."

—CHARLES T. TART, HAROLD
PUTOFF AND RUSSELL TARG,
Mind at Large, Praeger, 1979

There are weapons systems that operate on the power of the mind and whose lethal capacity has already been demonstrated.

—COLONEL JOHN ALEXANDER,
Military Review, December 1980

Prologue

THE PRESENT

SECOND LIEUTENANT RICHARD PETERS, USAF, sealed the door of the Launch Control Capsule. The locking pins secured themselves with a high-pitched whining sound, then stopped. The red indicator light on the Capsule Status Panel winked out.

"We're sealed, Ford," Richard said to First Lieutenant Ford Cox, the Combat Crew commander. His eyes ran up and down the Communications Console that was his responsibility. Nothing wrong—as usual. He glanced at the massive door that had just shut them off from the outside world. At their departure briefing he and Cox had been informed that crew R-022 had identified a defective memory chip in the onboard computer of one of the flight of ten missiles controlled by this launch capsule. A repair team was due out to replace the chip and would need to be cycled in and out of the missile's silo.

Aside from routine training and maintenance, that was all they had to look forward to for the next twelve hours. Or days. Or eons. Crewing missiles was one of the most difficult jobs in the Air Force, an exercise in will and sheer endurance. Boredom was the enemy, and you fought it all the time.

The USAF helped out with the Minuteman Educational Program. You could get an M.B.A. while doing a tour on Missiles if you made the effort.

A tour always started easily. There was little real work, or so it seemed at first. The tedium was almost welcome, like something stolen. Unnoticed at first, the pressure mounted. Finally, after about two months, a man asked the deadly question of himself: "How the hell am I going to stand this?" It was fatal because it opened the floodgates of truth: sitting in an air-conditioned hole doing nothing was a very special level of hell, one that Dante hadn't mentioned in the *Inferno*.

An extremely high degree of technical proficiency was required. That meant constant training alerts, constant simulations, and constant evaluations. Boredom alone would have been all but unendurable, but this was much worse. To the dull, repetitive routine was added complexity and a need for absolute perfection in every tiny detail. It didn't take long to discover why this was a soldier's job. There were severe challenges to a man's or woman's endurance.

One grew horribly fascinated by time. Each day became something to be borne. The hours and then the minutes grew relentless, slower and slower until even the smallest chip of time seemed to contain eternity. They hadn't been sealed ten of those minutes and Richard was already staring at the clock above Ford's console, facing the mystery of time, trapped.

"Let's start looking for 022's cache," he said.

Cox sighed. His way was to numb himself. Richard knew that his own increasing nervousness was beginning to rankle his commanding officer.

"You want to get into that now? The repair team's due at silo four at 0800."

Richard wanted to. Each crew had a cache of magazines and other time-passing paraphernalia hidden somewhere in the capsule. Traditionally crews sought one another's caches. Sharp competitions had developed. No crew had ever survived a full tour without losing a cache. "We oughta get started on the obvious places at least. We've got three up on them now. Their stuff is gonna be well hidden this time."

Cox said nothing. Richard looked across the small room at him, at the neatly trimmed back of his head. Cox was the perfect missile crewman—quiet, calm, intelligent. Moderate in all things. Impervious to boredom despite his keen mind. Yet he was no robot. Cox was a warm and decent man. Sometimes Richard secretly enjoyed tormenting him.

Richard was smarter than Cox—too smart even for missiles, if the truth be told.

In the first few months down here he had completed his degree in cybernetic engineering. After that he had tackled particle physics, but he didn't have the patience for it. Now he just sat, counting needles of time. Twelve hours added up to 43,200 seconds. Eighteen minutes had now passed —1,080 seconds, less than three percent of the total.

"My orders include a security perimeter violation drill, if that makes you any happier," Cox said suddenly. Richard's problem was no secret to him.

"When's it coming down?"

"I don't know. We're being rated on it."

"Great."

"I thought you'd be happy. Something to look forward to. A little fun."

"About the smallest amount of fun a human being can have and survive."

Richard glanced again at the clock over Cox's console, which turned out to be a mistake. He almost saw a face; the illusion made him snort and shake his head. Ford turned around and looked at him.

"You OK, Dick?"

"Yeah." But he was far from it; he was sweating, suddenly freezing cold. His flesh crawled. Beneath his tight

3

uniform shirt muscles were knotting. His stomach felt like it had the time he had gotten a wormy salad during basic at Lackland AFB in Texas.

His eyes returned to the clock. The face was gone, and Richard knew why. It was in him, swimming like an eel in a fresh river.

He drove his mind in other directions. Looking at clocks in his present state clearly caused symptoms. OK, so much for looking at clocks.

Time to force the old mind down a more familiar path. Lately he had been reading some of the newsmagazines, hunting for some sign of impending nuclear crisis. Morbid as hell. Even neurotic. But he didn't actually want war. Just something that would make the job matter a little.

The newsmagazines did not speak of war. Far from it; all the talk was of the troubled Soviet empire. The Russian decline that had started in the late seventies was becoming an outright collapse. The birthrate was dropping; people were dying younger. There was a plague of alcoholism. Strikes were frequent, unofficial work stoppages a way of life. Food supplies were sporadic. And the army was threatening to execute men found drunk on duty.

Although the Soviets were desperate enough to resort to war, they appeared to have lost their will along with their faith in Marxism. The great storm was dying.

"I'm gonna just eliminate the obvious places," Richard said. "I've got money riding on this." He did indeed. Too much money—on purpose. He had made bets with fourteen people, bets he could not cover, just to create a sense of urgency.

He didn't wait for Cox's approval, but rather began his search. First he took care of the usual places: taped under the consoles or behind the equipment racks. Next he had a look in the topside vent shaft.

The end started there. He had the agonizing sensation that something uncurled inside him, something like a huge black worm. His hands shot down to his sides and he dropped

4

from the shaft. Ford was standing in the middle of the capsule, his face distended and pouring sweat. Richard wanted to say something to his crew mate, but his throat was closed as if by the clutch of a monstrous fist. He felt himself walking, returning to his console, dropping with a jarring thud into his chair.

His hands went to the Launch Control Panel, hovered over the switches. Richard tried to remove his hands. They kept going on their own. His mind spoke calmly at first, then more frantically as Richard realized what he and Ford were doing.

Wait a minute, hold it.

His hands got his manual, opened to the day's codes.

No!

Behind him he heard Cox moan. He couldn't even look in that direction. When he tried he was conscious of some physical presence preventing him, a dark half-visible shroud of a thing so big that it jammed the capsule, but at the same time was something else . . . almost a child.

"DEFCON One alert," Richard's voice said. "Prepare for launch."

NO!

"Check," Cox said. He activated the Missile Status Indicator Panel. "Alert status confirmed."

"Check." Help us. Please, somebody help us!

"POC launch option select."

"Select ten."

"Initiating selection."

"Initiated. Light on. Light off." The missiles were now prepared for launch. Richard sat like a stone doll. His mind rushed with desperate attempts to regain control of his body while he watched his hands do their work.

Air hissed between Cox's teeth, the only sound of the commander's own struggle.

"Insert unlock code."

Richard input the day's code into his console and lifted the cover on the keyhole. "Unlock code inserted." He tried to grab his own wrist, watched the fingers of his left hand flutter inches from their object. Then the fingers bent back until they cracked with a blinding burst of pain. His right hand continued its work.

"Enable switch to enable."

"OK."

The Launch Console now lit up, a row of red gleaming lights, a row of switches ready to turn. Richard heard Ford's voice as if it were at the end of a long tunnel: "No—God—nnnn . . ." Then the voice changed abruptly to its usual crisp tones. "Key insert time."

"Check." Richard's own voice was normal.

Simultaneously they inserted their launch keys into the keyholes.

"Key turn in ten seconds."

"I agree." Richard tried to pray. God help us, we're about to launch the whole wing!

"Key turn."

There was no sound. Far above them, though, the plains must be echoing with the thunder of the fifty-ton blast doors flying off the silos with explosive force.

"Confirm key turn."

Richard's finger went to his launch button. He tried to shut his eyes, couldn't even do that. There was a five-second window during which both men's launch buttons must be pressed or the launch automatically aborted. With each second a bell sounded. Through three of the bells Richard's finger did not move. The urge to press that button built until he thought he would catch fire from the inside out if he hesitated another moment.

Then the claxon indicating launch abort blared.

Richard had won.

Blood was pouring off his body in place of sweat, soaking his uniform. There was a searing pain, as if he were boiling hot.

He might have won part of the battle, but it very clearly was not over. He began to concentrate on moving his hand to the emergency call switch. Nothing—then a bare inch. Another! Please!

Something inside him was growing frantic.

There was a crackling sound—Ford had his hands around his own head. As he snapped his neck, his feet kicked against his console and he made a sharp whistling sound.

Richard could not scream, not even when Cox shot up out of his chair and slammed with a horrible clatter of fluorescent panels against the ceiling. Then his dead body, the head lying on one shoulder, sank to the floor.

Richard looked at Cox's body. It was *sitting,* the head lolling back so far it stared at him upside down.

With Ford dead, Richard's tiny germ of self-control was swept away. In him there appeared raw hate that was not his own, vindictive and furious. His death agony began.

Richard's hands came up around his throat. The fingers jabbed and pinched and tore, finally in scrabbling eagerness breaking through, ripping his breath and blood away.

Dark.

It takes a good team fifteen minutes to execute the emergency procedures necessary to penetrate a sealed Minuteman Launch Control Capsule from the outside.

Peters and Cox were both dead. The crew commander's neck was broken, the comm officer's throat torn out.

The capsule's controls indicated that the ten Minuteman missiles were ready to launch. Ford Cox's launch button was depressed. Peters's was not. It had been that close: but for the pressing of one small white button the flight would now be on its way across the Pole.

1
1979

IMMEDIATELY AFTER THE ABDICATION of the Shah, Paul Winter attempted a mission of deliverance deep in Iran. In the company of his SAVAK contact, Amir Pakravan, he drove south to Khurramabad, then on into the wild Zagros Mountains.

The only car he had been able to sign out of the embassy motor pool was an old Buick, and his silk shirt was wet from negotiating the difficult roads.

As they climbed higher into the mountains, the wind rose to brutal intensity, screaming down the rough gorges and buffeting the car violently. They had been listening to Radio Tehran, but now even that faded away. The radio offered only static here. There was no link to the outside.

The brown, tortured earth, the rushing gray sky, the crags and gorges, all confirmed the isolation of this place. Although the thought of meeting a band of Lur tribesmen appalled him, Paul took inordinate pleasure in the emptiness. He had been too long in Tehran, too long slaving over the reports of his field agents, trying and trying to put together a coherent picture of what was happening to the country.

Beside him Pakravan twisted the dial of the radio, then angrily flipped it off.

Paul said nothing. He lived alone and usually worked alone; he did not often speak. Inside him there were gray skies parallel to this, and similarly empty lands, the desolate scape of sad remembrance. Add a sense of *déjà vu;* he had been in situations like this before. He remembered the falls of Havana and Saigon, and the subtle abdication of Vientiane.

Perhaps because he viewed his as an imperial nation, he affected elegance of manner and dress. He wore silk and maintained a beautiful home on Lavi Avenue in Tehran. There was more than just the salary; General Dong had rewarded him handsomely for the year of hell he had spent in Laos providing the general's private army with professional intelligence advice.

An imperial man. The long, hard days of empire, the declines, and the spreading wings of the furies . . . he fancied that he shared much with the last Romans.

"How much farther, Amir?"

"Another valley."

Amir had promised Paul a major coup. The moment the abdication had occurred, he had said, "I'll give you the most valuable thing in Iran and let you take it out."

Duty had seemed clear. But Amir played a crooked game of cards; could something of such great value really be hidden in the Zagros? Paul watched an eagle spiral down past the car. Below them were blue reaches sweeping down to the fertile Susiana, plain of peace and slow summers, where people smiled often and the wind was not so cruel as here.

The car ground fierce protest as it climbed; it was not adjusted for high altitudes.

"There it is, Paul, the Institute for Bioenergy Studies."

A cluster of buildings was huddled against the granite shoulder of a mountain. As they approached, Paul saw in the main building a bloated copy of the ethereal Ali Kapu Palace in Isfahan. There was the same broad portico—but this one

9

was too broad; and the same tall columns—but these were too tall. They looked like toothpicks.

Dim light shone from the windows. When Paul cut the engine, he could hear the whine of a generator even over the ocean of wind. As they got out, Paul saw Amir make a furtive sign with his left hand.

"Jinn bothering you?"

Amir laughed a little too loudly. "Force of habit."

Paul looked around, at the huge building and the even more massive mountain rising behind it . . . at the seething, formless clouds that swept past not a hundred feet overhead. "I wouldn't be surprised if there weren't a few *jinn* around here, Amir."

Pakravan made another sign. "Drop it, Paul."

Paul slipped his left hand beneath his jacket, felt the pistol nestled there. It was the finest of a fine collection, a carefully remachined .38 capable in skilled hands of extraordinary range and accuracy. Paul's hands were certainly skillful. He loved pistols, the look and feel of them. Their implications he accepted—or had convinced himself that he did.

"You won't need your gun. These people are friendlies."

"What about the *jinn?*"

Pakravan lowered his head, a certain sign that he had taken as much needling as he could. "Let's go in," he muttered.

Paul followed him to the big carved door. His knocking gave a hollow return, but was answered in a surprisingly short time. "I am Hassan," said the shaking, ancient man who appeared. His beard was matted, his eyes were red. Paul remembered the radio: "The evil genius of the Shah's CIA clique, the poisoner of children, the foulest of the foul abominations."

This man?

He took them both by the wrists and pulled them inside. "Come, come there are planes about. The air force has given itself over to Khomeini!"

10

Paul could not disagree. The fantastic truth was that the most thoroughly westernized of the Shah's services was the most fanatically pro-Imam. When he had seen men who had been trained at Kelly AFB in San Antonio, men he had played golf with, screaming and hurling the insignia from their uniforms, he had known both that the Shah was lost and that nobody in the West would ever really understand why.

He was among those closest to the situation, and he didn't know.

"There is little time! Where are the helicopters?"

Memories of Vientiane, men going to their knees: "Paul, please, you must bring in helicopters. Paul, please . . ."

Old hands, shaking, grabbing in the half-light for his lapels, brown eyes misting, lips working. "American! Do you know they call us sorcerers?"

"No, I hadn't been aware of that."

"I have thirty-three people here. All will be sentenced as sorcerers if they cannot get out." He was trembling so badly that Paul's impulse was to embrace him, to cradle him as he had his own father in the last, sunken days of his life. "Do you know, American, the penalty for sorcery?"

He could guess. "Death?"

"By living burial!"

He said it as if revealing something shameful about himself, some ugly sore he preferred to hide.

"I don't have helicopters. First I must find out what you're doing here. Show me why this place is so important."

"He doesn't know this, Captain Pakravan?"

"His Majesty would not allow us to show your reports to the Americans. They have no idea what you have accomplished."

"Come then, we waste time!"

Hassan turned and swept down a long concrete corridor. Paul saw that the facade of the building had been a lie. Behind that benign portico was a concrete-and-steel fortress.

11

Paul became aware of the weight of his pistol. He did not like bunkers. As he had gotten older, he had become increasingly nervous about windowless rooms and dark hallways. Like many of his co-workers, he could no longer keep track of the enemies he had made. Betrayal was part of the routine. And retribution, also? One tried to avoid places from which there was no escape.

The corridor ended at a spiral stairway. It led down to a heavy steel door, the kind weapons designers always seem to use to shut away devices they claim that they trust.

Beyond the door was a shockingly bright, modern room. All the foreboding of the half-lit corridor evaporated in a flood of brilliant blue light. Even for the Shah the equipment was modern. Paul's practiced eyes saw the very latest in computers, high-speed, high-density systems, as well as dozens of instruments even he did not recognize. Young men and women—lab coats, glasses, clipboards—moved purposefully about. This lab could have been at Langley or in some American university.

Then Paul's eyes traveled up. The ceiling at the rear of the room was raised easily forty feet and the floor sunken ten. All was covered in white tile, as a swimming pool might be. Here the light was even brighter, and here also was one of the most remarkable and mysterious structures Paul had ever seen. From the ceiling was suspended a huge web of thread-thin wires hung with leaves of gold so finely hammered that they appeared to be translucent. It was unlike anything Paul had encountered before. As he walked slowly toward it, he realized how really large it was, and how very strange.

A rattling sound drew his eyes away from the antenna. Beneath the array there was of all things a little boy playing Parcheesi by himself, busily rattling his dice and tossing them from his cup.

Paul stopped. Amir's hand for an instant touched his own. The boy was stunningly unusual-looking. His eyes were flecked with gold; his hair was dusty red. His skin had the olive warmth one associated with the southern Mediterranean, not Persia. His full lips hung slack with concentration as he played his game. Paul realized that he was playing at least four positions at once. How odd, to play a game of chance against yourself.

When the boy heard them, he looked up. A literal shock, as if of electric current, passed through Paul when the boy's eyes found his own.

In some ways the face was just that of a child. In others it was quite simply horrible. The eyes were soft but not gentle; they looked as if they concealed a long habit of anger, much too long for a child. The sensual lips were damp in a way that a boy's lips should not be; the face was excruciatingly delicate.

"I have succeeded in combining modern physics with the ancient magic of my people," Hassan said. His voice trembled, the aged hands again touching Paul's lapels.

"Magic?"

"Control of the mind from a distance by invisible means." He laughed a little, deep in his chest. "The most powerful weapon ever devised."

"The classic definition of sorcery," Pakravan added. "The Imam is not so wrong, is he?"

Paul looked around him again, as if with new eyes. There was an eeriness about the place. It was all so bright and fresh—and haunted. Control of the mind from a distance. The final power. If the gates of hell had a lock, the crazy-looking contraption hanging from the ceiling might be the key.

"Jamshid, come here. Demonstrate for this man. On him."

"On me? Now wait just a minute—"

"He is very . . . how say Shazdeh . . . ver-ry afraid, no?"

"No! He is our American friend. The one who will save us from the Imam."

"Ah." A sadness seemed to pour from the boy's eyes and

into Paul's heart. Sadness cut by a cold blade. "I show the *jinn* of his fear."

"Show him love, Jamshid."

The boy lowered his eyes, took Paul's wrist in cold fingers. "Come, sir." As Paul went down into the theater, Hassan continued to speak, his voice rising to a certain definite urgency, as if Paul needed more information than there was time to impart.

"You will be experiencing an extra-low-frequency field tuned to the same harmonic as the human mind. ELF is normally generated in the brain and is the medium of all mental activity—thoughts, dreams, feelings. Until now it has been confined to the brain case except under the most unusual circumstances—"

"Turn on the Field, Shazdeh."

Who was in control here, Shazdeh Hassan or the boy? Hassan's voice grew more frantic. "When initiates in the past induced an alphoid brain wave with dancing or drugs or incantations, they could extend their own fields to include people around them—as long as they had a medium—"

"Turn the Field on!" The boy's voice was rough and loud. His face changed, grew slick, almost translucent, as if light were shining within. But it was not the fine light of martyrs and saints. Paul felt nausea undulating in his belly. Something seemed almost to fill Jamshid's face, as if another being were behind his skin, something infinitely more important and awful than a little boy.

"I must explain to him! He must not enter without understanding!"

"Field on!"

Hassan kept talking, a high, frantic drone. "There are certain places on the planet—places of power like Stonehenge or Dodona or Gizeh—where there are natural fields—"

Jamshid grabbed Paul's shoulders. "Look at me!" The tone admitted no dissension; Paul looked.

"Listen, Paul Winter," Hassan babbled, "they conjured

demons there—real demons, other-dimensional beings—
please wait, Jamshid, wait—''

The eyes were more gold than green, fierce, staring,
inhuman eyes. Their sight seemed as palpable as a fist,
bursting into his mind with devastating force.

The boy stood before him as calm and beautiful as an angel. Paul could actually feel him inside his own body,
breathing, thinking, feeling. It was an intimacy so close that
it was revolting. He twisted in a desperate effort to free himself from this real, physical presence.

''Mr. Winter, please understand; his mind is being projected into yours. His mind only! The rest is your own private nightmare.''

Paul's hands floated up before his face. It was exactly as
if they belonged to another person, and yet there was his
class ring, and the diamond Irene had given him. Control.
Jamshid was in control. Paul wanted desperately to cry out
for help, to signal Amir somehow, but this iron grip was a
thousand, a million times too strong for him.

Now there came a thought. It was not like other thoughts;
it had form and substance. It was pictures and smells and a
sharp, maddening shriek of a sound. The pictures were
long, blurry tendrils. Snakes. The thought was snakes, hundreds of them, swarming in the cavities of his brain.

Paul remembered the *bangungut* of the Laotian hill tribes,
the nightmare so horrible that it killed. Were these . . .
tendrils . . . the beginning of *bangungut?* Westerners were
supposed to be immune to killer dreams, but Paul knew dif-
ferently. To know that such things exist is all you need;
from the moment you find out about *bangungut* you live forever in danger of having one.

Somebody was screaming as if from afar, but Paul knew
it was he.

''Listen to him howl! He is a coward; he will not help
me!''

''Jamshid!''

Paul's blood was rushing now. He had the distinct impression that the snakes were slithering and searching among the organs of his body. His vision changed. He was looking not into a room but across a desolate gray plain—a place so infinitely dreary that to look upon it was to lose life's warmth, perhaps forever. The snakes were swarming across the plain, clumping and lumping together into three tall creatures . . . cat's eyes and teeth came jutting from twisted lips.

They moved their huge heads, their eyes lighting the gray air. They were going to see Paul, and when they did he was going to die.

"No!"

Their angular heads wobbled on thin necks; their eyes blazed bright with lust for the kill.

Evil.

The boy before him was dancing, calling up half-fantasized obscenities and longings, going through his subconscious like a rat in sewage.

And the demons came on.

They were hate fired pure. They longed only to spread ashen silence in human souls.

"I will scatter the bones of the living, I will cast their hearts into the deep."

Bitter mutterings . . . images of flesh blackening and dissolving, the earth and the very sky destroyed . . .

A cry without words left Paul's throat. The boy was changing his mind, turning away from evil. He began conjuring images of green fields and blessed girls sleeping amid the corn, of laughter and drifting blossoms, of the fresh voices of children.

A roar of angry laughter exploded from his mind, then fell to echoing peals and at last departing, fading titters.

Thanks be.

Paul was being guided out from under the antenna, the boy-thing hovering at his side.

"Help me, Amir."

They took him to a chair. Jamshid looked at him, touched

his face. Once again he was a child, glowing with the promise of boyhood.

"You fainted," Amir was saying. "You need air."

Paul was more completely exhausted than he had ever been. He felt as if he had just experienced some sort of unholy orgasm of an intensity so great that one more second would have killed.

Killed. He hung on Amir's arm. The boy came along as they left the facility, and kept glancing at Paul with the knowing eyes of a lover. It was sickening.

Paul had no doubt whatsoever that Jamshid had actually been inside his mind.

"We use a man-made extra-low-frequency field instead of a natural ELF source. It is much more reliable and, as you experienced, much stronger than anything appearing in nature."

Hassan was courting Paul now, smiling and twisting his hands in his urgency to placate. "Of course the boy's extraordinary talent helps. But you see the implications anyway—the way he moved your arms—you see, there is the possibility of control of others from a distance—"

"My God." Paul looked at Amir. "This is pure gold. The most powerful weapon in history. By far!"

"I told you."

It was still going to be a hard sell at the embassy. Mind-control machines would not be at the top of Harmon Wiser's salvage list.

They went up the long corridor. Paul found that he could literally smell Jamshid, a curious, unwashed odor . . . like some of those really raunchy whorehouses in places like Cairo. "Get rid of the kid, will you, Amir?"

Pakravan spoke softly to him. The boy's eyes became humid with sorrow, but he wandered away at last, casting long glances back. "He is afraid that you will abandon us," Hassan said.

"No way. Your work is incredibly valuable. No way will we abandon you."

17

From far down the corridor there came a burst of hurt, mocking laughter, as if the boy had heard the lie behind Paul's words.

As soon as they stepped out into the courtyard, something cold and wet touched Paul's face. For an instant the terror returned and he leaped back.

"Bats," Hassan explained. "The ELF field disrupts their sonar." They were falling to the gravel with soft, fluttering thuds. As he walked Paul could feel them beneath his feet.

He was grateful to see the Buick. Amir would have to drive despite his hair-raising Iranian habit of never going below eighty. Paul intended to prop his knees against the dash and think.

There were human sounds in the dark around the car, the shuffle of feet on gravel, the rustle of clothing. When Amir turned on the lights, Paul saw that Hassan was surrounded by his whole staff, standing together as a reminder of their numbers and their plight. They looked like a group of students and professors from MIT or Harvard, young for the most part, pipes and beards. Hollow expressions. They watched in silence as the car departed.

Riding through the night, watching idly as Amir negotiated the steep roads, Paul gradually calmed down. The memory of Jamshid's intrusion lingered like an intimate and not very pleasant odor of another body.

Paul remembered the demons. Had they come from hell, or from somewhere deep in his own mind? Or was that one and the same place?

Once he heard the guttering of tanks. Were the revolution's soldiers already on their way to Hassan's redoubt?

Paul, always lonely since Irene's death, grew more lonely still. He wished that somebody loved him enough to hold him. Knowledge of something as big as this was cold and fearsome. Where would it lead? With ELF governments could—oh, Jesus.

"You had quite an experience, Paul."

"That's putting it mildly. You should have warned me."

Pakravan laughed nervously. "I know that now. But please realize that I had never seen the thing in operation before. In this case knowing the theory is no substitute for seeing the actual results."

"I'll agree with that." Which got him to the problem of his report. When he arrived at his office the next morning he was still worrying about it. How do you commit a thing like that to paper without getting yourself posted to a desert island? Paul's had been an unusual career, but not a blameless one. He had not gathered the kind of credits it would take to survive making a fool of himself.

He would try the dispassionate approach. Be cool, factual, to the point. He labored three days over the wording. History went on around him.

When Bakhtiar fell, the embassy shuddered; dependents were sent home. Paul remembered Saigon, the foreboding that gripped the embassy, the confused flurry when the proud began to flee.

Yes, remember that in the hard Iranian March, steel-gray month before the limes and the pomegranates bloom.

Jamshid haunted him. The whole experience came to assume the quality of a religious insight. He began to see the edge of the future. The world wasn't going to be much like it had been, not with ELF.

Paul wrote a brilliant report. The boy and the device both had to go to the United States.

"Paul, Paul, Paul." Harmon Wiser was looking over his glasses into Paul's office. "The Amazing Randi would never buy this and I can't sell it to anybody else."

Paul felt sick inside. This was exactly the reaction he had feared. "Who the hell is the Amazing Randi?"

"Guy who debunks fraudulent psychics. It's his religion." Harmon came in, dropped his tidy frame into the chair across from Paul's desk. "I can tell that you care a lot. What can I say?"

"You've transmitted the memorandum, of course?"

"To whom? Psychological Services? Come on, Paul, you're too good a man to waste on this sort of nonsense."

"Transmit the memorandum, Harmon."

"What the hell do you have, a death wish? You'll end up out of the Agency!"

"It was my duty to write it. Yours is to circulate it to the concerned department heads—which in this case is everybody from DDO on down."

Harmon circulated the memorandum.

A week later he returned to Paul's office. He tossed a heavily initialed cover sheet onto the desk. "Read and weep. You are now a figure of fun."

"Is this guy slipping?" read a note from Omar Jones, the Associate Deputy Director of Operations. The rest of it was simply junk. But if Omar thought a man was slipping, that was important.

"He wants you to come home for a while."

"No. I'm going to take those people out."

"I see. How?"

"Trucks. I'll get Amir to spread some *baksheesh* around and truck the whole bunch up to Afghanistan."

"That leads me to more bad news, I'm afraid. Amir and all his people got rolled up last night. Amir is selling for his life."

"He'll never sell me."

"He already has. You're blown, Paul. You're going home. There's a place for you on the six-ten Swissair."

"This feels like a palace coup. Goddamn brusque."

Harmon gestured to the report. "The best field intelligence officer anybody ever encountered, and he ends up behind a desk for going cuckoo."

Paul was driven out to the airport in an embassy limo. It was hit by a little random saliva, but nobody knew who was inside. As matters turned out, that was just as well. Paul's name was published by the *Komiteh* within hours of his departure.

Huddled into the jammed plane, he felt numbed. A brilliant career had been compromised. But worse, Jamshid and the ELF device were *not* in American hands. Paul recognized that he was in the process of becoming a very lonely man. Lonelier, to be accurate about it.

He stared long at the purple night beyond the window of the plane. Jamshid's fingers seemed to seek upward from the land, brushing his heart with sorrow.

Paul wished that the Shah's Institute for Bioenergy Studies would be forgotten by everybody, not just America.

But ELF was the ultimate, the final weapon. It offered absolute and total control. Total terror.

Total power.

It was not going to be forgotten.

2

THE PRESENT

GENERAL-LIEUTENANT V. I. BELIK'S Chaika limousine moved swiftly down the traffic lane reserved for official vehicles in the center of Kutuzov Prospekt. It was five o'clock in the evening. He had left the Institute of Bioenergetics at Sverdlovsk as soon as the failure of his part of Black Magic had become certain.

Disappointment and fatigue made him feel chilly even though the summer evening was mild. In the privacy of the YAK-40 jet assigned him by the General Staff Transport Pool he had fought for calm. The trip to Moscow took four hours. They had been spent in an agony of suspense. Typically, the radiotelephone was out of order on the plane—encoding system not operational—and so he had been without communications even while the Americans might be in the process of discovering the Black Magic personnel on their soil.

Toward the end of the flight he had tried to shave, but the water was inoperative. His scraped cheeks burned. With rumpled uniform and bloodied jowls he was not going to cut a very impressive figure in what would certainly be a difficult meeting with KGB. Belik believed that soldiers should look like soldiers. Tall, sharply tailored by the best the General Officers' shop in the Voyentorg could offer, he worked hard to project an image of youth and ruthless competence.

Beyond the window of the car Moscow passed its heedless way. As the Chaika picked up speed in the long stretch of the Prospekt, Belik began to feel a familiar sensation in his chest, one he despised and hid from the world, even people as insignificant as drivers. He pulled the velvet curtain between the seats to hide himself, then tore impatiently at the catch on his briefcase. By the time he had the intricate English mechanism opened his chest was burning, his breath coming in painful gasps. Then the asthma inhaler was in his hand—and blessed relief.

The Asthma/Nefrin inhalers came from the military intelligence attaché in Washington. Belik had carefully arranged their status as state-security imports. It was vital that other officers not become aware of his weakness. Ruthless young officers did not wheeze.

Belik buried the inhaler in the briefcase and drew out his notes, two hastily scrawled pages and one COSMOS photograph of the American missile field. Red grease pencil marked the tiny dots where silo covers had been blown off. At least that one positive effective had occurred, proving that the system was basically operational.

Why the missiles had not been fired was the problem. Nothing like it had happened in the simulations. The contingency had been gamed, however, and that was what made Belik uneasy. In the "aborted firing" game the Americans had done an immediate ground search of the whole of South Dakota—and found the forward ELF control group in the Black Hills.

He stared out the window, miserable with the thought of what might be happening to the volatile men in South Dakota. They believed themselves to be members of the Muslim Brotherhood, trying to induce the United States and the USSR to destroy each other in a nuclear exchange and

23

free the world from superpower bondage. If captured, they would be unable to implicate the USSR.

KGB owned those men, just as it owned the sixty small ELF antennas that were to be set up in the United States as soon as the military phase of Black Magic had neutralized the American missile force and compelled the Pentagon to surrender.

Once set up, the antennas would blanket the United States with an ELF field that would place the population under absolute control. The beauty of it was that they would never know. America was about to fight and lose its final war, and do so in total ignorance. Except for those few killed in the surgically neat nuclear bombardment of the missile fields, the American people would remain unaware that they had been attacked. And ELF would create in them a kind of dream state of perfect order. Only one wish would be broadcast by the Field—the wish to work. And only one emotional state would be felt—joy in the work assigned.

Perfect communism. To keep ELF secret, the Soviet Union itself was not yet under the general influence of antennas. But the test areas—Sverdlovsk and the prison province of Kolyma—were officially paradises. Joy reigned in the steel mills and the crumbling depths of the mines.

Joy in work. Even if it led to an early death.

Belik used his inhaler again. He hated the happy mines where men sang themselves to death, and the mills where mangled accident victims were viewed with amused resignation.

ELF was a great power. Misuse of it was an incredible evil. The KGB's Pyotr Teplov had concocted the ugly part of the plan. Belik had intended only to neutralize the American missiles, to defeat the warmongering Pentagon on behalf of peace and the safety of the Motherland.

But then this horrible new project had been added . . . to make men into automatons. Pyotr Alexandrovich Teplov was KGB's ELF project director, and he had developed the monstrous idea. Belik knew that he was seeking absolute control of the project, even the military part. Teplov was right to do so; soldiers hated him and he hated soldiers. Ironic that the soldiers were on the side of decency. But they were Soviet soldiers, so of course!

It was the worst kind of conflict that Soviet politics could produce. Either Belik or Teplov was going to win it.

And the other, with all his supporters, was going to die.

The car moved swiftly on.

A cadre of elderly women struggled with brooms and buckets in Arbat Square. Belik looked at the old *babushki* with longing. His own childhood in Leningrad during the Nazi siege had been a blinding, loveless miscry. At age ten his consuming passion was to have his very own *babushka*, but the starved women of Leningrad had no time for him.

Mist swirled around the street lights. Moscow, always quick to acquire a somber air, seemed to frown at the rushing, nervous soldier. Belik would have liked just now to slip from his car and enter that mist, to seek the hidden city of warmth and joy he had always hoped would be there and disappear like a shadow among its stones.

The Field had risen from the ground beneath their feet at three A.M. At first all had gone well, but then Jamshid had begun to shake and gasp.

The moment Ismail had seen him curl up in the dust, his mouth frothing and spitting, his hands on his throat, he knew that ELF had failed. His first reaction was astonishment. In training this had not even been considered. Yet here it was: Jamshid was in agony on the ground and the missiles were not rising from their silos in the dark plain below. Ismail's second thought was that they must try again. Soon, though, for their time was very limited.

Ismail and Kajenouri carried the weeping Jamshid back to their cabin. He slept hours and hours, his breathing deep and slow.

Morning rose to noon, and afternoon became evening. Even so, no searching jet roared in the sky nor truck upon the land. As the light faded, unfamiliar American birds raised their voices in peaceful night song. After the failure Jamshid had wept furious tears, but the down of his cheeks was now dry. During his long sleep the placidity of youth had returned to his face.

Despite the disappointment, despite the danger, Jamshid could still capture sleep.

The Americans might come muddling up here at any time now that they knew something was amiss. Ismail prayed in silence for the skill necessary to preserve their mission from the wrath of the U.S. Air Force, then touched Jamshid's soft cheek. "Rise," he murmured, "for God has given us the day."

Jamshid stirred, turned his face away. Ismail recalled the sorrows of morning. In the predawn, when the air had been as soft as the touch of Mumtaz, in the cool, secret mist of the Black Hills . . . Jamshid, the child of the pearl and the rose, had known despair. "At least I killed them," he had said before he dropped off, and his voice had risen to a slicing edge of hate: "I broke one's neck and tore the throat of the other. They will never be able to reveal that I was within them."

Then Ismail had suffered Jamshid's presence in his own mind, that fierce young spirit, borne on the dying flickers of the ELF field . . .

There came a clatter from the chemical toilet. "The world is a witch," old Kajenouri snapped from within. Then he emerged, his soutane damp with blue chemicals, his face dark in its fierce mask of beard. He was not one for Western gadgets and did not at all understand why they dared not drop their spoor outdoors as God had clearly intended men should.

Kajenouri's bulky body dominated the small cabin. He was nearly six and a half feet tall, a wild Tajik from Afghanistan, Jamshid's guardian as Ismail was his guide in the strange land of America. He began to bang and clatter with their dishes and utensils. There was little food, however. The mission was supposed to have ended last night.

Supposed to have ended . . . and with it the two great heathen powers, America and Russia. "Let the bear savage the eagle," Shazdeh Hassan had said, "and the eagle blind the bear. Then all the beasts of the earth will once again be free."

"Rise," Kajenouri shouted, sweeping Jamshid's cover from his lithe frame. The boy muttered and snatched at the quilt.

"What's the use of getting up?"

"The use? No man should sleep in the hour of prayer! Look, the sun has long ago touched the horizon. What's more, you need food and it's my duty to feed you. I'm hungry myself so you must be too."

"There is little to eat," Ismail murmured. He did not want to remind Jamshid any more forcefully than necessary of the disaster.

"No *durgh-e-hashish,* Ismail?" Kajenouri was making a tired joke. Ismail sighed. Kajenouri could afford jokes; unless Jamshid was physically attacked, he had no duties except to prepare food. All the worrying belonged to Ismail.

"There is none, and no plain yogurt either—nothing but peanut butter as a matter of fact."

"You woke me for that?" Jamshid stretched luxuriously. "Yogurt water without hashish is like a prick without balls."

"Where'd you hear that one, young man? Is it a saying of Rumi?"

"A saying of Jamshid."

The light in the cabin grew suddenly less. "The last of the sun," Kajenouri rumbled as he went to his prayer rug. "Let us recite the great Sura now before our tardiness disappoints God."

They unrolled their rugs, facing them east and weighting them with stones. Ismail closed his heart around the prayer. He needed the intercession of Allah now; he asked for it

27

only rarely, not wishing to bring petty cares to God's door-step, but this was no petty care.

"O God of mercy and compassion," he said. "Praise is thine, O Lord of All Being. All-Merciful and All-Compassionate, Master of the Day of Wrath."

He thought of what this land with God's help would soon become—a sea of burning fire.

"Thee only we serve; to Thee alone we pray for deliverance. Guide us on the straight road, the path of Thy blessed ones, not of those against whom Thou art angry, nor those who have gone astray."

His mind went to the war they were trying to start between the two superpowers: "Help us, O Lord, to smite those who walk the paths of folly, to relieve the earth of their weight."

"Just now the sun left the tops of the trees," Kajenouri said with satisfaction. "We have prayed honorably."

Jamshid arose and rolled his rug. "Follow me," he said, and ducked through the door of the cabin. At night they allowed themselves no lights, and only after dark did they leave the concealing walls of the old hunter's cabin.

Jamshid went to the circle, with Ismail and Kajenouri not far behind. Ismail was concerned for his charge; the boy's constitution was delicate. In training the Brothers had said, "You have no name, no face, no feelings. Your life belongs to Jamshid." But the Brothers were not here with this trembling sixteen-year-old. Theirs was not the sacrifice of watching him suffer, or of dying with him.

From the circle the dark plain of South Dakota spread before them. Lights twinkled here and there, and ghostly clouds rushed through the moonlight. There was life in land and sky; sometimes Ismail felt as if the earth were a creature as definite as a woman, and he wondered at her sorrows.

"I will wait here until the Field rises again," Jamshid said. He was standing in the center of the circle, his thin shoulders slumped. Ismail went to him.

"It is understood that the Field will never come until after midnight."

An engine rumbled somewhere. From a great distance there came the sound of music. Off in the dark people were dancing.

"I will wait!"

Kajenouri went into the shadows to watch. His duty was to remain concealed, revealing himself only to a threat. Ismail stayed silent a long time, knowing that there was nothing to be gained by contradicting the volatile Jamshid.

"Do not grieve: He will not become lost to thee;
No, but the whole world will be lost to Him."

Jamshid's voice was low and bitter; his words were carried off on the rising moon-wind.

The music from the twinkling little town in the dark grew wilder and wilder, its throbbing rhythms corrupting the secret sounds of darkness. A deer snorted; in the sky some bird cried. The voices of crickets began. Ismail had to act and could delay telling Jamshid no longer. "I must go into the town," he said carefully.

"No! Stay with me."

"You have Kajenouri. I must make contact with the Brotherhood and tell them what happened last night, and get new instructions.

"You leave me to the dogs and the jackals."

"I must go, if we are to complete our mission."

Jamshid hugged himself, his body as frail as a thing of sticks. "Tell them that it was not me but the Field. There was static in it, and at the end it began to become very much weaker. I could not risk losing control of the men and letting them live to inform on my presence."

"Yes, Jamshid, what you did was right."

Jamshid grabbed Ismail's hands. "Tell them how much it hurt me; be sure and tell them that!"

Ismail withdrew as gently as he could. The boy was often

29

in these states, impossible to fathom, oceans removed from the normal concerns of adolescents. But that was to be expected. He had gone too often into other men's minds. Shazdeh Hassan had said that he had become a sort of parasite, needing to feel the passions of others to feed his own insatiable need for human contact. Touching him was like touching an old man. His skin felt as delicate as paper.

Shazdeh Hassan had not worried about Jamshid's suffering. "He is the heart of the ELF field. Without him it is only the emotions. He is the medium of control." The boy had been found on the streets of Islamabad, making his way by thievery and casual prostitution. He was a Sindhi child of the lowest caste, to the Urdu and Punjabi majority hardly more valuable than a dog.

Step by step Ismail withdrew from the silent, huddled boy. At last his form swam into the shadows and his dismal eyes were lost in the night.

Ismail hurried down the mountain. He was frantic to contact the Brotherhood. Not a moment must be lost, not a single instant. He tore his clothes in the thick pine forest that blanketed the mountain, but finally reached the road and his well-concealed car.

There were yet miles to go to a telephone in a place large enough to be safe, miles and hours when the success of this great work might depend on seconds. He drove alone and in silence, trying to find the hand of God in their doings. Was it there? It must be, if they had gotten this far.

Two Dzerzhinsky Square was never quiet, not even after five o'clock in the afternoon. The vast lobby echoed with voices, the subdued murmur of guards and the louder chatter of workers swabbing down the floors. At this time of the day the North American Division of Military Intelligence was running at its fastest pace; government offices would soon reopen in Washington. Also here was the Lubyanka Prison, occupying most of the basement floors, deep and huge, the clanging, dripping interior of Soviet experience. Belik had visited the Lubyanka more than once to observe electro-chemical interrogations, the howling reduction of the suspect.

He entered General-Colonel Sukovsky's outer office and found himself made to wait, undoubtedly for the supposed effect the suspense would have on him. He despised the old general-colonel, a time server whose only function was to be Belik's commanding officer. His warden.

Without Sukovsky to control him, Belik would report directly to the Defense Planning Council—in other words, he would be an all but free agent since the council's function was to approve, not manage it.

Free agents were rare in the system and it treated them well. Stalin had been one just before his rise to power, as had N.S. Khrushchev.

"You damn fool," Sukovsky rumbled as he burst through the door without the least warning, "you've created a hell of a problem."

Belik got to his feet. "I am aware of the situation."

Sukovsky smiled his nasty peasant's leer. "Are you? Colonel Teplov is going to be here shortly. I hope you're ready for him."

Belik replied with a curt nod. The general's hard black eyes raged. He was obviously hoping to see fear. Let the fat boar hope. Belik gave no outward sign of concern, but he wished for his inhaler.

"Do you realize how big an operation this is? Just to cut the orders takes—"

"With all respect, my General-Colonel, I designed Black Magic."

"The military part. Forgive me, but that is the least of it! Try and imagine the enormity of the thing—the scheduling problems alone . . . my God."

"Yes, since they are scheduling the enslavement of half the world. Perhaps in the end the whole of it. Naturally it's complicated. You would expect that, Comrade General!"

Sukovsky's eyes had grown narrow with fear. He glanced

at the dirty gray walls of his office. Merely to have heard such sedition accounted him as guilty as the speaker.

Belik laughed aloud. "I assure you that we are the only ones privy to this conversation, General Sukovsky. Military intelligence keeps your suite free of KGB bugs. At my request, my General."

"A likely story! You take every opportunity to hurt me. You're trying to destroy me, you blond bastard, and don't think I'm blind to it. I might be a dumb Slav *krestanye*, but I know when somebody's turning on the gas!" As he shouted he waved his arms. Spittle sprayed Belik's face.

"If you really fear Teplov, I pity you!"

"Valentin Ilyich, my boy. Of course I fear him! And even the shining youths should fear him! In Directorate V they called him—"

"I know. The Executioner. So he's ruthless. I'm at least as bad."

"You've never killed a man!"

"You know nothing! Am I to doubt your loyalty, my commander?"

Sukovsky was no fool. He understood his real position. Now he became the cringing lackey. He appealed to the bond of Leningrad.

"Two old siege engines, yes? Let's toss back a few before the *nachalstvo* bastard comes in."

Belik obediently drank with his superior officer. As both had been in Leningrad during the war, they shared the bond. When Belik was a fifty-pound child of twelve, Sukovsky had been a pudgy NKVD corporal. A real *urla.*

"Here's to the four years. May they never be forgotten!"

"To the four years."

"Slova bogu!"

Let Sukovsky *slova bogu* like the old man he was. Belik knew to toast the Party when the moment was right. "To communism!"

There came from the doorway a smart clatter of applause. Belik turned to the grinning, cadaverous face of Pyotr Teplov, red-eyed and weary. "Nothing like yet another dose of patriotism at six o'clock in the evening, eh?" He embraced Belik and they traded kisses. Teplov's were neat and quick. He was a man of formalities. Within he was colder than death; Belik had seen him interrogating Shazdeh Hassan.

It was Teplov who had finally broken the old *chernomazy* and made him spew out the design parameters and all-important tuning of the ELF antenna. Everybody in Black Magic owed Teplov. More than could be repaid, as a matter of fact.

The thought came in the night sometimes of how nice it would be if Teplov and Sukovsky would go flying together . . . and the engines just happened to fail. But that was quite beyond arrangement, of course.

"Ah, Valentin Ilyich, that cool, cool stare again. You're plotting against me!" Teplov laughed, high and quick.

It was the moment to act; Belik had to take control of the meeting. He did not respond to Teplov's statement, except by attempting to soften his expression. "Very well, let's get on with it. As I see matters, there are two problems tied together in one. What went wrong? There was either a technical failure on my end or a personnel problem on yours, Pyotr Alexandrovich."

"I train my fanatics well."

"And yet look at this." Belik drew the COSMOS photograph from his briefcase. "The silo doors are opened on all ten missiles of the flight. We must have gotten to within a few seconds of firing. Our indications are that the Field was functioning properly."

"My advance team has not yet been in contact with the Iranians."

This was critical. The on-site operatives were the weakest link in the Black Magic chain. "When we gamed this out, the team was captured by the Americans."

"Ah, yes, but your protocols assumed that the Winter report on ELF had been effective. They will take the position that it's nothing but another form of radio. Winter failed."

"But he's still alive?"

"At the moment. He will be contained before morning."

Teplov went to the window, tapped on the glass. Beyond his thin form Belik could see that the mist of evening had become slow rain. Moscow days . . .

"I know you haven't wanted to call attention to him by killing him, but the time for such concerns has passed. Pyotr, I suggest that you clean up your American house."

Sukovsky winked as if to say, "That's telling him." Old idiot, he understood nothing. If Black Magic fell apart, every career in this room would be ruined, no matter the details of blame.

Teplov, however, understood quite well. He continued tapping on the glass, rapping as if trying to attract some attention from the emptiness beyond. "I am taking emergency measures to ensure the stability of the operation. But I must warn you, Valentin Ilyich, there is a strong likelihood that matters will grow more critical. The longer the delay, the greater the danger."

"We're going to perform another operational test on the device as soon as possible. If we don't find a fault, we will be ready within forty-eight hours."

Teplov turned from the window. His eyes were burning. When he licked his lips there was a sound as of paper contacting paper. "That seems a very long time."

Belik found his tone deeply disturbing. The situation in America must be more unstable than he was admitting if two days was too long to expect it to hold together.

Teplov stood, hunched and tense, the window behind him dripping with summer rain.

3

FOR PAUL WINTER IT started again just when he had begun to hope it never would. It began as a small sound in the night—it might have been no more than a rat chewing—but it drew him awake instantly. The Sequoia Hotel was not the sort of place for rats. Furthermore, this sound did not have the frantic purpose of animal need; it was soft and deliberate, a human creation.

Anger was followed by frustration as he listened to the spike microphone being implanted in the wall behind his head. When the final softest taps subsided to silence, frustration slowly became fear.

He lay in a slick of sweat, hardly able to breath. Desperate now, he stared into the mottled darkness of the room, a dark invaded by the glow of street lights five stories below.

Softly, into the dark, he whispered a sound somewhere between a curse and a moan. Then he closed his eyes, ran his hands along his cool satin sheets. He had to do better than this; fear was not the desired emotion.

Perhaps it would help to come back to the reality of his own world. He sat up and looked around his room. Even in

35

the darkness it was beautiful, decorated to his own impeccable specifications in ivory and blue. The antique rosewood furniture gleamed. A natural silk jacket lay across a Louis XIV chair. He reminded himself that he was not only rich but a highly skilled technician of deceit. Hell, an artist. Fifteen years in the purgatory of Central Intelligence had fired him to the strength of a diamond. He might just defeat whoever was doing the drilling.

He laughed to himself; was that a professional opinion or the whistling of a lost soul?

The ratcheting changed pitch. Paul wanted to kick somebody. For the past couple of years he had actually been happy.

He could well imagine the man on the other side of the wall. He would be a quick sort of man, sharpened by lies until he hurt, a man who ran as easily as most men strolled. He might be KGB or he might be Soviet Military Intelligence, the GRU . . . or even the new Iranian service, SODO. Whichever acronym identified him, one thing was certain about the man on the other side of the wall. He was the leading edge of a wave; his was not an isolated intrusion. Which service, though? That was an important question.

Who had finally remembered Paul Winter's trip to the Zagros? Certainly it must be that; there was nothing else in his career that would draw this kind of attention.

Only that one incredible event stood out. Pakravan had died because of it; Hassan had died too. No doubt the boy was dead as well. He could not have taken refuge in some more common life, become a farmhand somewhere in the fertile plain of the Susiana or perhaps a soldier on the dun ramparts of Abadan.

Paul dreamed even now of that boy, of the death he had probably suffered . . . the frail little thing struggling at the bottom of a hole . . . the muffled curses beneath the dirt . . . the revolutionary guards standing around waiting for the cries to cease . . .

You never forgot a person like Jamshid—those frantic

eyes, that strange mind, the loneliness, and the terror. Of all the mysteries Paul had known, that child was the greatest, and the most tragic.

It was pointless to seek deliverance. He knew what he knew, and nothing but death could erase it. He sighed and at once wished he hadn't. Already every sound he made would be heard by others, every breath and every frightened writhing. The intimacy of it was a peculiar torture. He had won privacy by being thrown out of the career he loved. It was no even trade, but he had worked hard to discover the worthwhile compensations.

The spike microphone was aptly named; it penetrated a wall like a little living nail—and in this case also a man's mind. The knowledge of it was a needle to the core of reason.

Perhaps that was its real purpose—to needle him into breaking cover, to make him run to some place where he was less well known and could therefore be killed in greater anonymity.

Yes, that was why the drilling was a hair too loud. Somewhere some operational planner had read "Sleeps lightly" in some dusty file and thought it out, a plan that began with this noise in the gray night—and would end in a moment of incredible violence at the bottom of whatever miserable hole Paul might dig to hide himself. Yes . . . that was the way they wanted it to go. Real operations were designed like that. Places of seeming safety were made to hide blades that slit a man eyes to groin.

They would be testing their device now, even as the installer exited the Sequoia Hotel, padding quickly and quietly through the halls. Paul imagined his adversaries: they would be young, of course, and so intense about their work that they would seem bland. For all their health and cleanliness the young men would be uniformly corrupted by the disease that had driven Paul away from the intelligence community: they would be moral idiots, neutral to good and evil and therefore indifferent to the ethical bias of their doings.

Parked nearby there would be a van. Spotless in their white shirts, the young men would be sitting before their consoles in the back, their faces pale in the green glow of electronics.

Paul did not want to care about all this, wished it didn't matter. His hand went up, brushed along the cool plaster of the wall. His first move must be to determine the identity of his pursuers. The little spike, if he could see it, would reveal a great deal.

Footsteps sounded down the hall, came closer, paused at the door. Paul tensed—then realized that it must already be two A.M. Catherine was coming home from work.

They have caught me flagrant with love.

"It shall not burn, the candle of the heart, exposed to prison's hating air." Old man, young woman; ancient new story. His way was going to be made a thousand times harder by her involvement.

Had their relationship endangered her? Why wonder—he knew it had. They would want her life too, if only to keep the files orderly.

The lock clicked, the door swung open. She closed it softly behind her and put on the night latch. For a long moment she stared toward the bed. "You awake?"

"Yeah."

She came across to him, her young smoothness in the dim light hurting his heart with pleasure, her blondness ringing memories of his wife. "You OK?"

He thought of what might have happened to her on the sidewalk, in the elevator, in the hall. "I was thinking about you."

She smiled, tossed back her hair with a characteristic gesture. "Telepathy. I feel so energized! I was wonderful tonight, really good. I mean *really* good!"

He reached out, took her hand, kissed the soft tips of fingers. "I'm glad." His body began to attend her presence with enthusiasm.

"Paul, you should have seen it! I was really *on*, you know. I mean, they gave me a standing ovation."

He raised himself from the bed, dragging all the memories and destructions—and his new danger—with him into her arms. Her hand went to his nakedness, stroked gently. "I thought age slowed men down."

"Not possible with you."

She kissed him, reaching her heart of a face up to his, planting her lips with her usual good, honest lust. This honesty was the center of his delight—and amazement; he was, after all, twenty-four years her senior.

He had been unpardonably selfish in the matter of Catherine, telling her just enough of his past to make himself seem exotic, not enough to suggest the danger that the relationship might bring to her.

She was dropping her clothes to the floor, kicking off her boots. There was about her a faint, familiar odor of greasepaint and the baby oil she used to remove it. He kissed into it, touching his lips to her warm neck. He had longed helplessly to give this very kiss when he had first seen *Women and Strangers*, seen Catherine in the hard light of the stage and at the climax in the arms of Jennifer Hurst. It was a furious little play, centered on Paul's favorite themes of loyalty and honor and love, and in it Catherine expended genius nightly.

Of course it was sheer effrontery for an anonymous and fairly dull old man to pursue an actress—almost a star. He had sent oceans of flowers for nights and nights, and then presented himself to a laughing, blushing kid in a dressing room crammed full of dying gardenias and roses less than fresh. "I've got to get an *Encylopaedia Britannica* to press them in," she had said. "You're wonderfully crazy, old man."

He had stood before her in the agony of his own ridiculousness, aware that he was gaping, suspicious that he might be blushing too. "I need a moment of your time, ma'am," he had roared at her in a voice deepened by self-consciousness.

She had burst out laughing, and laughed herself into tears at him. But she had granted the moment, then two, then more. Moments had stretched to months, and at last to this shared accommodation in the luxurious secrecy of the Sequoia Hotel.

They stretched out in the bed together. Paul remembered the spike in the wall and thought of the bland young men hearing his coupling with his actress, how utterly unmoved they would be. In a world gone to immoralities the greatest in Paul's opinion was indifference. He kissed her hard and loved her with the best of heart and body. Let them be indifferent; he was not.

When she slept he crept from their bed, his mind returning to the urgency of their situation. The delay had wasted nothing; it was only prudent to give the others time to vacate the room next door. He dressed quietly, trying not to wake her. Let her have this last peaceful sleep. His brown Daks suit hugged his body. It was new, not tailored to hide the bulge of a weapon. He tucked a modified Smith & Wesson .32 into his morocco shoulder holster and left the jacket open.

If he was going to be doing a little breaking and entering in the august hallways of the Sequoia, he might as well look the part—elegant, a gentleman robber. This hotel was home to theater people during their shows. It was one of the city's remarkable secrets, six floors of extraordinary elegance in the middle of Hell's Kitchen, only a few steps from the Broadway theaters. On the outside it was barely clean, just another shabby remnant from the days of Packards and jacaranda plants.

He stepped out into the green silence of the hall. Here and there shoes had been left before doors. Tommy Barrow would be along to clean them soon. He had come from the old Twentieth Century Limited to the Sequoia and brought with him a high standard of service indeed. But it did not include looking the other way when somebody forced his way into a room where he didn't belong, even if that somebody was a guest. A quarter to three. Paul wished he knew when Tommy made his rounds.

The old practices returned quickly. He moved with precision and ease, calling on whatever was at hand for tools—in this case a Saks credit card with which he jimmied the lock.

His career had included a certain amount of this sort of work, especially in the early days. The room was neatly made up, empty of course, similar in layout to Paul's own. He did not turn on the lights, but crossed the wide, carpeted floor in the dark, fairly certain that he would not knock over the chairs or collide with the writing desk. He reached the wall that separated this room from his. Before him was a painting. In the dimness Paul could perceive the vague shape of a stage, figures half-lit upon it. No doubt a famous moment among performers.

Paul lifted the painting from its hook and placed it on the floor. Now came the confrontation: already the sound that had awakened him had come to seem a little like one of those sinister dreams that begin with the illusion of waking up.

He felt the plaster. Dry enough . . . but cooler in one particular spot, distinctly so. His heart gave a jump, began beating a furious tattoo, reminding him that he was not a kid. Not even in Vientiane in 1971, when he had searched the hotel room of Pyotr Teplov while the man was taking a shower, had he been this nervous.

He took out his nail parer and dug at the plaster. It was recent, a quick-drying compound. A gouge, another, white dust smearing his jacket—and there it was, as real as a nightmare, the little black head of the spike. He drew it out, and now he did risk a light. It looked like a new model, very much smaller than the ones he had known even a few years ago. It was black, tapering to a fine point. Inside was a subminiature transmitter that would be sending its peep of a signal to a relay somewhere in the room.

Paul did not bother to look for the relay; there was little chance of discovering such an implant. The spike microphone had been vulnerable only because its placement was limited to the one wall. Controlling his impulse to flush the spike down the toilet, Paul left the room and swiftly returned to his own. How quickly operational habits reasserted themselves. His cautionary pauses and quick movements were as precise a choreography as they had ever been.

He padded across the floor to the bathroom, and only in its sheer light—blue tile and anodized gold hardware—did he examine what was in his hand.

He was disappointed. There were no familiar characteristics that would identify the maker of the bug. In fact it was quite unusual; things had changed remarkably since his resignation. Its electronics must be microscopic. In 1979 the smallest such devices were the size of a finger. But for the fact that this was made of some sort of high-strength plastic it could pass for a common nail.

The fear, which had never been far from the surface, swept through him again. He became aware that the bathroom overlooked an airshaft. His image would be visible on the frosted glass of the window. A shudder passed through him. He turned out the light and stood in the darkness, listening. The tub dripped gently. Far, far away a siren moaned.

The device in his hand had not stopped broadcasting until Paul left the room where it had been implanted and took its weak transmitter out of range of whatever signal amplifier was hidden there. The risk that its owners would act as soon as he tampered with the spike had been worth the chance that their hardware would identify them.

An intelligent risk, but it hadn't worked out. He needed help now, professional and up-to-date. Although his scruples demanded he shun the philistine, he was nevertheless going to have to appeal to the mercy of Harmon Wiser.

What the devil did Harmon charge for his much-reported services—a thousand dollars a day, hadn't it said in the *Time* article? A thousand dollars a day to protect people like the Somoza family and Yamani, and—of course—the Pahlavis. And Paul Winter?

He stood a long time in the dark, looking at his shadowed face in the mirror. The boy and then the youth and then the young man had all in their turn escaped, each leaving the face a little more slack than before. He had been a handsome kid; he was far less now. Graying a good bit. Loosening up. And lately there was that hollowness, that haunted look. Was it Hemingway who had said he could see a certain darkness in the faces of men marked for death? Yes, somewhere in *A Moveable Feast*. Oh, God. Why is it that death, despite the fact that it is absolutely inevitable, seems like such a cheat?

Catherine stirred in their bed. He was drawn by the sound, went to her. His heart grew fierce with love and anger: we have a right to our peace. How dare they steal it from us.

He couldn't wake her with his call to Harmon and he had to make it now. Back in the hall he met Tommy Barrow. He smiled slightly; it was good to see another human face, one certain to be friendly. "Mr. Winter—good evening." Tommy's face was full of gentle questions, not too demanding. Discretion was the heart of the job.

"A little insomnia, Tommy. I think I'll get some air."

"I wouldn't leave the hotel at this hour, sir. But you go on down to the bar. They're still goin', I believe."

"Good idea." Paul stepped into the elevator and waited in its mahogany silence while it slowly descended to the lobby. The shorter the building, the slower the elevator. It seemed to be some kind of law.

This late the lobby was as if frozen. It was a study in classic understatement, rich Aubussons on the floor, a graceful chandelier hanging from the creamy oval of the ceiling. If the hotel did not make such an effort to hide itself, this room would be famous.

Paul went into the call box—a device easily as old as the hotel itself—and dialed a number he had long before memorized. It was answered on the first ring. "Hello," said a bland young voice. There was no sign of tiredness or confusion. Naturally not. Harmon's would have to be a twenty-four-hour business.

"My name is Paul Winter. I need to see Harmon as soon as possible."

"In reference to what?"

The tone, the question—just what Paul had feared. "It's a personal matter—"

"Security?"

"Yes."

"Please give me your name and the nature of your problem. We'll call you back."

"I told you my name was Winter. Paul Winter. Tell Harmon I've got to see him at once."

"Mr. Wiser is asleep."

"Then wake him up!"

"You'll have to tell me the nature of your problem, Mr. Winston."

"Winter! I'm about to get myself killed. Look, I'm an old colleague of your boss's."

"Mr. Wiser doesn't take calls before eight A.M."

Paul hung up. OK, perhaps it was understandable. In his new business Harmon probably kept harder hours than a burglar.

Tommy Barrow's advice had been intelligent, and Paul now took it. The *oubliette* was almost empty. Frances Harper was at the piano, singing softly, almost humming "Memories of You." This must be her last set of the evening. Not a week ago he and Catherine had been here together listening to this song, at an earlier and better hour. "Glenlivet neat, seltzer on the side, please, George."

"Yes, sir, Mr. Winter." The barman served the whiskey

properly, in a small goblet. The bouquet of good Scotch is too sharp for a snifter, too delicate for a regular bar glass.

Hating himself for reasserting old habits but knowing the necessity, Paul looked from couple to couple, not failing to notice the table waiter and the busboy. He fixed each face in his mind against the possibility that it would turn up again. This was the terrible thing about clandestine life, this was the prison of it—your right to trust others was withdrawn.

He realized that he should return to Catherine. He hadn't gotten used to the idea that it was now dangerous to leave her alone.

Sacrilege though it was, he tossed back the Scotch. The good and gentle life he had lived these past few years was over. Might as well settle from now on for the bar brand.

As he returned to the room, Paul deliberated about how—and what—to tell Catherine. She was so volatile, so intense, it was hard to know quite how to go about it. Opening the door, he consoled himself that he at least would have a few more hours to think until she woke up.

"What, may I ask, is going on?" she said the instant he closed the door behind him.

So much for time to think. "Darling—" his tone of voice communicated to her clearly. She turned on her bedside lamp. How beautiful, he wondered, could a woman be? She lay in the warm glow of the light, her face slightly flushed, her full lips parted in the touch of question, her jade-green eyes dewy with sleep. Around her head the halo of blond hair swirled like mist. The effect, combined with the knowledge of the spike microphone in his pocket, was at once wonderful and terrible. Hers was the saddest beauty of all— she was like a deer ignorant of the hunt.

"When I felt you weren't there I woke up."

It wasn't a question, but it wanted an answer. "Something's happened that you must know about."

"Yes?" Eyes widening, the ghost of concern. He drew close to her, sat on the bed beside her, took her hands in his. Hers were the most exquisite he had ever seen, more so even than his wife's had been. He considered them a privilege to hold, to take to his lips.

"Paul?"

"You know how I said that I was a consultant to the Army? I wasn't. Catherine, for fifteen years I was in the CIA."

This confession did not have the expected effect. She smiled, squeezed his hands. "I assumed it was something like that. Are you afraid I'll hate you for it? I don't at all, darling. I admire you." She leaned forward and kissed him on the cheek. "You must be a very brave man. I've hoped you would come to trust me enough to tell me."

To see the way she misunderstood hurt almost more than he could bear. Awash with an emotion somewhere between grief and despair, he clutched her to him. She was bed-warm and responsive; her arms came around him under his jacket. "I like silk shirts," she whispered, "the way they make your muscles feel."

"You don't understand, darling. This is a tragedy."

The words made her lean back, regard him with big eyes. Catherine knew the meaning of tragedy all too well. Her life had been damaged by the sudden death of her mother, and by her father's subsequent inability to deal with a daughter who was the image of his lost wife. For Catherine tragedy meant loss and loneliness, being turned away by those she loved. He hated to add to the pain he saw upwelling in her eyes. But add to it he must.

"There's something unresolved in my past. I know too much about an experimental weapon. Somebody has decided to contain a possible leak by getting rid of me."

"Getting rid?"

"Killing me, darling. And I think it's safest to assume that you're in danger too."

Again she surprised him. No fear shriveled her. She rose up in the bed, her eyes flashing. "Nobody's going to ruin things now. I won't let it happen, Paul Winter!"

He was proud of her, proud to be her lover.

"I'm a famous person, Paul. As soon as I get a big movie I'll become a star. The CIA can't just kill me—"

"Not them. They aren't involved." Of that much he was certain. CIA had no need to plant bugs. Working through the National Security Agency, they could turn his telephone into a bug without coming near the hotel. The phone company did not give similar cooperation to the KGB. "My concern is that the USSR has gotten hold of the weapon. That means we're up against the KGB. Assassination is their primary policy in matters like this. Me, because of what I know. You, because of your intimate association with me."

"The KGB? Paul, surely you're kidding. I mean, that's something out of a Charles Bronson flick. Does the KGB really exist?"

He had to smile a little, remembering his old adversaries, Kornikov and Teplov and their ilk. Hardworking, determined, canny. Ever so shabby, ever so dreary. Not much like Charles Bronson. "It certainly does." He drew the spike microphone out of his pocket. "Earlier tonight I heard someone placing this in the wall next door. It's a bugging device. The organization that placed it is going about this operation very carefully. They don't want to kill me openly and reveal the fact that I was important enough to require assassination. That would cause CIA to undertake an investigation of my past and almost certainly uncover exactly what the other side had killed me to hide."

"You found that little thing?"

"I think they may have wanted me to. They might be hoping that finding it will frighten me into hiding. If I'm out of sight, the kill will be that much cleaner."

"I guess that answers my next question. There's no point in running?"

"None. The better I hide, the harder it'll be for my friends to find out what happened to me."

She threw back the covers and went into the dressing room, fished in her purse, and brought out a packet of Benson & Hedges cigarettes. He watched her with some surprise. He had never seen her smoke. "Emergency," she said. "It helps me to think. Can't you get protection from the CIA?"

The humiliations that had led him out of the Agency returned to mind. He had fought and fought for recognition of ELF as a weapon of war, fought until Omar Jones had finally told him to take early retirement or be hit with a psychiatric discharge.

He could hardly believe it, at the end. He had actually failed. Paul Winter had failed. Simple as that. And then the nightmares came back, the demons with their yellow eyes, the snakes slithering in his brain . . .

The devil of it was that the victims of an ELF field could be controlled so completely that they wouldn't know anything was happening to them. A whole nation could be put in invisible chains. Paul had studied the principles thoroughly. He knew the potential of the device. It wasn't science fiction. Hell, it wasn't even very advanced physics. But it smacked of parapsychology, and that made it junk as far as the American scientific establishment was concerned.

"CIA won't help officially, but there might be a way. An old colleague of mine had formed a company of his own called Safeguard, Inc. His business is to protect people from sophisticated assassins. He's expensive, but he's good. The Saudi royal family and the Pahlavis are among his clients. You'll notice that they die only of natural causes despite the number of enemies they have."

She drew on her cigarette, exhaled smoke into the dim room. "Paul, will you answer me truthfully about something?"

Here it came. He got ready for the storm. "Certainly."

"Can you get me a gun? Legally?"

He almost laughed. He had forgotten how much bravado there was mixed up in being twenty-four years old. It was beginning to look as if there wasn't going to be a storm.

"I've got half a dozen pistols right here."

"I know that. I'd just like it to be legal."

"A celebrity can usually get a carry permit from the city. It takes weeks, but that's the kind of thing Harmon can fix up." He didn't bother to add that a pistol would be utterly useless against the kind of threat they faced. One couldn't protect oneself with a gun against artificially induced cardiac arrest or a sabotaged car. A gun, beautiful though it may be, a superb machine, could not stop a well-mounted KGB assassination.

Perhaps nothing could.

4

V. I. BELIK SLID into wakefulness the moment his dreams turned worker-heroic. The YAK-40 was in the steep bank that preceded landing at Sverdlovsk, and it had just entered the local ELF field. The devil with the feeling of enthusiasm that was washing over him; Belik hated life inside the damnable Field.

The pilots turned on the intercom. They were picking up a local station, singing along with the "Communists' Parade."

It was fine for the poor devils who didn't know what was happening to them. Very joyous. But to a man who knew—hell was eagerness, hell was this maddening feeling of good fellowship toward workers. Fuck them all.

From long experience flying in and out of Sverdlovsk and contending with the Field in place here, Belik knew that he could keep a little freedom by concentrating on his troubles.

Considering their number, that was not difficult. Teplov was terrified that he might lose Jamshid Rostram in South Dakota. He was essential to the mission. Without him the Americans couldn't be tricked into an accidental firing of their missiles, and without that accident the USSR couldn't retaliate and force the secret American surrender.

And without that surrender not even the ingenious Pyotr Teplov could construct the complex ELF network needed on American soil. It was too elaborate a project to carry out undetected.

So it all depended on Jamshid. Without him the weak Field being beamed from Belik's gigantic antenna at the Black Magic installation here could not be used to make a bird flutter. With him its small power was vastly amplified. Jamshid was extraordinarily skilled; he could exert absolute control over human minds in even a weak Field.

If he died, Black Magic as it was presently conceived died with him.

The devil with this ELF hellhole! He had been about to start singing along with the idiotic pilots.

He stared out the window as the plane descended into the military aerodrome. To the north sprawled the vast Bioenergetic Institute. Thank all the holies that it was beyond the limit of the Field. Only the workers in Sverdlovsk proper were affected.

Teplov would have loved to put Bioenergetics in the Field. In fact that had undoubtedly been his hope when he chose Sverdlovsk as a test city. But he couldn't, not without disturbing the incredibly delicate Field that Black Magic was projecting to America.

Belik looked toward the low buildings of the Institute as the plane banked again. There was nothing to identify the fact that this was the greatest facility on earth devoted to psychotronics. Extra-low frequency was only one of its many projects. The fifty-five thousand military and civilian scientists were responsible for everything from the energy-transference devices that would one day be able to project the power of explosions to points distant from the site of the blast to the ten-hertz deep-earth transmissions that were so successfully heating the volcanic magma beneath America's Pacific Northwest.

The pitch of the engines changed. "Comrade General-Lieutenant," the pilot cried happily into the intercom, "we will land in two minutes!"

Off to the right Ozero Shuvakish loomed up, a vast spread of marshes that had been a clear mountain lake until the Uralmash Heavy Machinery Plant was built on its banks. Now Shuvakish was orange and its fumes could burn a man's throat. The Uralmash Political Action Committee had recently voted to rename the damned thing "Glorious First of May Lake."

Belik fastened his seat belt a moment before touchdown. As the plane shot across the apron of the runway, his mood seemed to shatter. Good! At last! They had left the Sverdlovsk ELF field.

As usual the two pilots suffered an emotional dive. They went sullenly out of the airplane as soon as they stopped it at the terminal, pushing past their general as if he were a drunken recruit.

Belik could see his chief of staff, Colonel Florinsky, arriving in the staff car as he descended the plane's steps. The car was a cramped Volga Saloon. Only in Moscow did the complex system of *nomenklatura* privileges allow Belik the luxury of a Chaika.

As Belik approached, Florinsky jumped from the car, ever the highly polished officer. He did not need an ELF field to make him loyal to his general. "Comrade General-Lieutenant, welcome back to the Institute!"

"Thank you, Comrade Colonel."

Belik liked his men polished, as befitted Soviet officers. Too many of the soldiers attached to the Institute affected a Western casualness of demeanor. A soldier here might hold a doctoral degree, but he was still a soldier.

They got into the car. Belik settled into the maroon velvet seat as Florinsky closed the soundproof glass partition that separated them from Junior Lieutenant Nevitsky, Belik's Sverdlovsk driver.

Time was not wasted on pleasantries. "Report, please," Belik said.

"We are scheduled to begin the operational test the moment you arrive."

They would run through the whole procedure on a test stage, using as a local substitute for Jamshid Rostram the best Russian ever found for the job, Viktor Milodan.

"And Comrade Milodan?"

"He will be at the alphoid state within the hour. The alpha and beta waves were in sporadic convergence when I left. He was dancing."

Milodan had to dance his way into the alphoid brain-wave pattern needed to project the mind. Jamshid was always in that extraordinary state. Apparently he had been born that way.

To his own surprise, Belik found himself trembling. They were all so far from the boy, and he was so vulnerable. Belik was no atheist; he prayed daily for the success of Soviet endeavors. For Russia. And, at this difficult moment, for Jamshid.

Florinsky touched his sleeve, an almost hidden gesture. But Belik noticed it. There was much between them. On more than one occasion they had shared a bottle together.

"The trouble will lie with Teplov's *chernomazy* in America, Comrade General-Lieutenant."

Belik snorted. As they passed the enormous tower of the Subsurface Destabilization Program's ten-hertz transmitter, his breathing grew difficult. He knew that it was only a psychological effect, not a physical one. The transmissions were heating American magma, not V.I. Belik's brain.

When Mount St. Helens had exploded, General-Lieutenant Tuchin had been promoted to general-colonel. Worse, the swine now drove about in a foreign car, a Mercedes-Benz. This proved that he was favored even beyond his *nomenklatura* rights. He was becoming politically powerful enough to get exactly what pleased him.

Belik wished he could use his inhaler but would not show

his weakness even to Florinsky. Only his beloved Ludmilla Semilovna knew, and from her he hid nothing. In lieu of the inhaler he closed his eyes and attempted to relax, leaning far back into the seat. They were now leaving the main part of the Institute of Bioenergetics, proceeding down the nondescript dirt road that ended at Black Magic.

Stands of birch lined the road, their dark green leaves shaking in the afternoon sunlight. It was necessary to pass through a village. This one was well out of the Sverdlovsk ELF field, and the peasants here were unaffected by it. They didn't like soldiers. Florinsky drew the curtains on the windows and the driver increased their speed. Even so, a stone hit the bumper a good crack.

"Bastards are getting mean again."

"Beets went up."

"Good for them."

The birches beyond the village hid a battalion of crack KGB guard troops equipped with everything from night-vision capability to laser-aimed machine guns. Had this car not been identified by a special code issuing from its transponder, it would have been stopped, and that was only peacetime security. In wartime an unidentified vehicle would be fired on without warning.

This was only one small part of the security system Belik himself had designed. The facility was completely underground. Its only surface structures were the mine shaft that hid the entrance and the air intakes. To approach, one had to park the car in the woods and enter a tunnel. American spy satellites would detect very little.

All to trick America into launching ten missiles at the USSR. Then retaliation would be justified. And world opinion would be placated by the humane Soviet use of the small, super-accurate quarter-kiloton bombs that would destroy the Minuteman missiles and SAC bombers with no fallout and minimal loss of life.

America would be left intact and healthy, as open as an Odessa whore. Ready for Teplov to string his wires.

Belik remembered the time he had gone to Kolyma with Teplov, to observe the great achievement there. The great, the glorious . . . the prisoners working in thirty-below cold . . . singing until they froze to death . . . being brought in like logs, their faces stiff with smiles, their lips split to ribbons from grinning while frozen.

Kolyma gold. How proud Pyotr Alexandrovich Teplov had been.

The car came to a halt deep in the forest.

Out of the green shadows a KGB unit appeared, ten men. Florinsky took care of the presentation of papers, the Ministry of Defense travel documents in their leather portfolios, the military identification cards, the green internal passports.

The KGB major pulled open Belik's door and saluted smartly as he emerged. The mine shaft with its electric railway was a dark opening in the ground at the edge of the grove of trees. Into the damp earth they descended, down a spiral staircase wet with the sweat of the forest floor, around and around to the stuffy, ill-lit access tunnel. One of the rickety electric train cars stood waiting.

The things were czarist, or worse, early revolutionary designs. "Here we go," Florinsky muttered, taking hold of the tiller.

After a moment of deep and indecisive humming the car wobbled off into the earth, its undercarriage sparking as it swayed along beneath the glaring bulbs that lit the tunnel.

Five minutes of this got them to the administrative area, a chamber fifty feet below the surface where more identification checks took place. "Comrades," the KGB guard said, "remember to read the new posters."

Dutifully Belik and Florinsky looked around at the walls where the Internal Security Cadre had placed fresh bulletins. "CIA wants to know," was the caption beneath a crude drawing of a demon. "Sverdlovsk was Item Number One on the Soviet Russia Division's 1981 Budget."

Belik was annoyed that the chief of security had not given

him this information before he read it off a wall. Damned KGB types had no essential respect for the military. To them the chain of command was a mere inconvenience.

They passed on into the living quarters with its dismal rows of bunks and mess hall. The ceilings were low and the air was heavy with the smell of boiling turnips. There were men in this facility who saw the surface only once every sixty days, the men who used the bunks, engineers and technicians. Along with Milodan and the other scientists, Belik had an office and bedroom of his own and could come and go as he pleased. Officers also dined in a secret restaurant of which the common run of worker was unaware. Still, it was thoroughly unpleasant compared to home, and Belik spent as little time here as he could.

A yellowing banner hung over the rows of wooden tables in the mess hall: "The Communist party of the Soviet Union is the honor, truth, and justice of the twentieth century." Before each place was a worn table setting.

Despite—or perhaps because of—its dinginess, Belik found in himself the most poignant love for this Russian place. But it was not the sort of love that would make him want to eat here.

The next door was guarded by two KGB lieutenants with machine pistols. Otherwise it was unmarked. Florinsky again presented their green internal passports and military identification cards. Despite the fact that Lieutenant Gorodin and Lieutenant Nevesky both knew Belik and Florinsky well, they went through the full identification routine, including the acquisition of photographs from KGB HQ on the thermofax machine that stood against the wall. This was required for the "Special/Technical" clearances that Belik and Florinsky carried. Only the highest officials with their "First" clearances would be spared these procedures.

This door opened onto what appeared to be a large operating theater. It was by no means the most imposing room in the Black Magic complex, but it was ample, especially after the confined spaces that had come before.

Down a short aisle was a wide, empty stage—empty but for a bland schoolmaster of a man swaying about at its center. Milodan's face was beaded with sweat, his mouth was open, his eyes empty. The Dance of the Shamans was nearly over. Loudspeakers rattled with the grumble of drums. What an hour ago had been a mad whirl of a dance was by now only a rhythmic memory.

Milodan. He had once spent ten minutes inside Belik's mind, ten minutes of red hell for Belik. There was such a thing as intimacy beyond human endurance. The feeling of another personality, other thought patterns, excited, probing, calling up the deepest secrets, was more than a man could bear for very long.

"Let's get on with it," Belik said. This run-through was probably nothing more than a formality. The process had tested perfectly many times before.

Beyond the brightly lit windows of the control booth he could see the usual jam of equipment and personnel. He climbed the steep iron stairs into a confusion of activity. The place was choking to chaos with tangles of cable and tall racks of electronic equipment. Because it all ran so hot, the room was air-conditioned to a frigid temperature. Many of the personnel were in the habit of wearing scarves and coats over their lab smocks. "Gorkin is in the aiming room," somebody called when he saw Belik enter. Because of the confined space, Colonel Florinsky would remain downstairs until needed.

Belik went to the window that looked into the dust-free aiming room. Igor Gorkin, the Project Technical Director, stood over the row of technicians who were responsible for aiming the enormous ELF antenna housed below the test stage. The intercom wasn't working; Belik tapped on the glass until Gorkin turned around. He made an angry face behind his surgical mask and resumed his vigil.

"Is there some sort of aiming problem?" Belik asked anyone who was willing to answer. Nobody replied. Belik stifled his hurt and anger. He did not enjoy their hatred, although he understood it perfectly well. Officers were not required to be loved.

Right now he would have greatly enjoyed being hugged by his Ludmilla. It would be such a luxury to be with that beautiful partisan of V.I. Belik. To think that she was not five miles away, in their flat right now . . . and doing what? His heart hurt to consider her, Ludmilla of the soft voice, Ludmilla of the jewel-green eyes. Feeling himself the center of sullen, furtive glances, trapped in a little coffin of hatred amid the men and women who were supposed to be his colleagues, he wished mightily for one instant with her.

Gorkin burst out of the dust-free room and pulled the covers off his hair and face. "That's acceptable," he muttered, the slightest glance indicating that he was aware of Belik's presence. "Hey, you crowd of zombies, where the hell are we?"

"Point nine in the countdown. Ready to activate test field."

Gorkin brushed past Belik and picked up the tail of a sheet that was spewing out of an electroencephalograph. "That's good, good—point nine confirmed. Activate the Field."

Belik moved to the windows overlooking the test stage.

The small ELF antenna that hung above the test stage began to move, stopping when it was directly over Milodan's head.

"Test antenna aimed."

"Power the generators."

"Generators rotating. Speed. Antenna live."

Now the hard part, the part Belik really hated, began. So close to an active ELF antenna there were what the scientists called echo effects. Static from the Field affected the electrical environment of the observer's brains more than just emotionally. There was no effective shielding.

There would appear shadowy forms in the room, tall, angular creatures with cat's eyes, eyes that quested to meet your own glance. But you must not allow it to happen unless you were willing to risk your sanity.

The psychiatrists said that the demons were a pre-hallucination. To look into their eyes was to confirm the illusion, to make it real for oneself. The ones who had done that hadn't returned from the screaming madness that had resulted.

Experiments had been proposed to determine whether such illusion could be made to materialize. Psychic projection.

In any case, nobody but scientists would ever be this near an active antenna, and scientists could certainly cope with demons. As could soldiers.

"Is the trainer prepared?"

Belik looked at the TV monitor that was supposed to show the interior of their Minuteman Launch Control Capsule simulator. The picture was gyrating wildly. "Monitor's out," Gorkin said laconically.

"Has it been put on the repair schedule?"

Gorkin sniffed, returned to his work. "Give me audio from the trainer, please."

"Trainer ready," came a tinny voice. How Milodan's subjects in the trainer were able to endure what was done to them Belik could not understand. But endure they did, week after week letting Milodan enter their minds and take control of them, running them through the American launch sequence.

When they had been working with Jamshid at Kabul, he had often been required to kill the men in the trainers so that he could perfect his technique. As Muslims dedicated to the cause of freeing the world from superpower domination, these men had died eagerly despite the boy's early fumbling and compulsive brutality. In Kabul, Gorkin had been called "Dr. Hamman," and the project was run by a certain KGB officer of great loyalty, Amir Pakravan, who had stage-managed the Muslim Brotherhood from the beginning. Pakravan was now in South Dakota working as backup to Jamshid and his support team.

Belik's mind, strained from the effects of being near the Field, strove into the escape of memory. Those months in Kabul, when they had rebuilt Shazdeh Hassan's antenna in an abandoned drying barn, had been a kind of idyll . . . hope mingling daily with the mounting excitement of discovery. In the days before the invasion the Afghan capital was a thriving, colorful town, a good place to walk beneath the clear sun of the mountains . . . to love a woman and live in love, in mountain light as clear as truth itself.

These sullen old Urals were no match for Afghanistan. There were black stands of fir here, and grindings in the night, the deep suffering of the "creamed" mines that filled the area, and always the factories, Uralmash and Uralkimmash and all the lesser units, generating purple sunsets and stink.

"You're not here tonight, General."

The words brought Belik back to the present. "How so?"

"Staring at an inoperative monitor. Did matters go badly in Moscow?"

"Not for us, Igor. But Teplov had better tread carefully. He's concerned that he might lose the site team."

Gorkin did not answer. Out on the stage Milodan was now standing still. Ready. "I feel him," said one of the subjects from inside the Minuteman Control Capsule simulator.

"That's contact," a technician called out. "I'm getting traces from both subjects' brains." That would be the additional wave that appeared in the brain of an individual being entered by another, dubbed by Hassan the omega wave. It lay far down on the spectrum of intercranial activity, associated with the deepest levels of brain function. The first place one man's attention touched another's was in the seat of memory. An operator began by smelling his subject's earliest remembered smells, his mother's perfume, his dog's warm stench, the first scent of snow . . . From there, as

Milodan described it, one climbed the ladder of smells to the present.

Then you imagined your mind a fist, clutching the consciousness of your subject like a boy crushing a mouse in his hand. You *sat* in the center of him, the fat lord demon, and ran his body like a marionette.

"Field stable and holding."

Belik had been in that fist before. Remembering it now made him shudder. There was nothing a subject could hide from an operator, nothing a skilled operator could not make his subject do. He recalled how, in demonstrating to him what it was like, Milodan had as a jest activated him sexually. He put it out of his mind for the thousandth time. Some jest.

The two subjects were performing faultlessly, going through the Minuteman launch procedures as Milodan stood in the center of his stage with his hands to his temples, drooling, making sharp involuntary sounds.

The least slip of concentration and Milodan was lost. But he did not make any slips.

"They've gone down to launch."

"That's it then. Another flawless operational test."

"Just as I expected." Belik got up to leave. "The problem is in America." He started to make his way across the cluttered room.

"General Belik."

"Yes, Igor."

"There's something else."

Belik stopped. Here it came, the reason everybody was being so sullen.

"What's wrong, Igor?" The whole room dropped to silence. These men had a healthy fear of their general.

"We got the satellite telemetry two hours ago." Gorkin's face was impassive, another bad sign.

"And?"

"It indicates that there was a variance in Field intensity.

We think it was caused by some sort of ultra-low radio emission of natural origin, something in the earth's core."

Belik took a slow, careful breath. The anger that was rising in him must be controlled. How dare this man wait even one extra moment to give him such news. But the anger had to be managed; it too was a tool. Belik had long ago learned that it did little good to rage at Gorkin, who was impervious to fear. "Solution, Igor?"

"We're not sure."

Belik couldn't stand it. His next sentence was shouted—quite helplessly. "What do you mean?"

Gorkin's expression darkened. "The origin of the disturbance is not known. But there is something we can do to reduce its effect. We can recalibrate the antenna, cast an even narrower Field."

"Igor—how long?"

"There are seven hundred leaves on the antenna. The width of each must be reduced by exactly sixteen millimeters."

"Equipment—"

"We have six working microlasers for the eleven people who are able to use them."

"Igor, please let me know the amount of time this will take." Far from being Teplov's problem, the real trouble was here in this facility. Right here. His trouble.

"Right now the antenna casts a field forty percent larger than necessary to include both the operator in the Black Hills and his victims in the Launch Control Capsule in the plain below. We think that we can concentrate down to a twenty-percent overcast and still have a reasonably good chance of aiming properly. But it is a chance; it is not certain."

"Surely with all this aiming equipment—"

"An aiming error of one micromillimeter will throw the cast off by fifteen kilometers. General, we're going twelve thousand kilometers through the center of the earth with this thing. It would be a miracle of precision to come within a thousand meters of target. And usually, comrade, we are on target!"

"Yes."

"Give us five days."

"Five days," Belik repeated mechanically. Teplov had been frightened of a two-day delay. For the men in America five days might easily be five years.

Or forever.

5

EARLY MORNING WAS NOT to Catherine Harris a congenial time. The quiet of the streets seemed a kind of lie; the heavy old air left over from the night oppressed. As she and Paul made their way toward the Chrysler Building and the office of Harmon Wiser, Catherine felt the sadness of the hour and was drawn by association to thoughts of what she had begun to understand was a tragedy of love.

It had taken time for her to realize this. But now matters were quite clear. This man she had by misfortune come to love was not just the elegant, intensely gentle creature she knew, but something else, something closer to the lies of this hour than its seductions. And his association made him dangerous, exactly as if he carried plague. He had infected her and she was battling herself not to hate him for it.

Why hadn't she bothered to consider that a man who loved a collection of fine handguns must contain another man who used them? He had put on his morocco shoulder holster with all the grace of a priest at ceremonies. She had wanted to touch its deep brown glow, so luscious against the silk of his shirt. Then he had taken a dark blue pistol from an ivory-and-velvet case and slipped it into the holster with the same delicate, probing touch that in their rosy nights drove her mad with pleasure.

The idea of his violence was not actually ugly. It was charged by a different aesthetic. His beautiful male body—worn by age to a fine and wiry glow—acquired a certain dross, as if it contained more power than good. The hardness within him was not temporary and exciting—an achievement of her sensuality—but as permanent and impersonal as the steel of his gun. It was not the same to touch such a body. She was reminded of the Confederate saber her father had bought on a trip to New Orleans. The proprietor of the antique shop had assured them with quiet pride, "It has killed, you know." She didn't like it then, and her father's honoring it in their den seemed the act of an ass.

Their cab reached the corner of 42nd and Madison.

She had never entered the Chrysler Building before. Life was hectic; the tourist places were always there. She hadn't been to the top of the Empire State Building either, or to see the Statue of Liberty. As they crossed the lobby, Catherine looked around and above her, astonished at the exuberance of the marble and the richness of the wood. It was all so sleek and graceful, the lost dream of the Jazz Age, the elegance of a dissolved world. Seeing her craning her neck, Paul said, "This building is what New York always wanted to be about."

They went up to the thirty-third floor in a wonderful mahogany elevator that creaked like a boat but rose like the wind. The corridor was also marble and wood. Paul rang a bell beside a door marked simply "Law Offices."

Suddenly they were out of the cuddling elegance of the Jazz Age. The sleek, hypermodern waiting room made their danger seem very real. Perhaps it was the lifelessness of the gray carpeting, or perhaps it was the lonely gaiety of the Calder horse lost in an off-white sea of wall that did it, but Catherine found herself able to believe in death in this place.

A man even taller than Paul came out of a doorway.

"You're armed," he said, holding out his hand. These people must just assume that Paul Winter would have a gun.

Paul shook his head; the man folded his arms. Paul shouted "Harmon," his voice solid in the delicate silence. Catherine was swept by a startled chill. She swallowed her cry of surprise, but only just.

From behind the door there came rich laughter. Then a small, tan man appeared, too perfect in his Palm Beach suit, his eyes darting in the crinkles of what he probably thought people would take for a smile. Catherine knew acting.

"Paul Winter. I thought you'd become a monk or something. Now you appear at my door with no less than Catherine Harris. I hope that I can be of many different kinds of service." He devoted his full attention to Catherine. "Welcome, your highness." He kissed her on the edge of her lips. She was annoyed by the slick touch of his mouth against her cheek. Just as Paul had suggested, he was one to avoid.

"I've got to talk," Paul said. "Immediately."

"That's obvious or you wouldn't have called at three A.M. and appeared at eight." Wiser turned and went down the hallway. "You'll be impressed by my setup, Paul. Very professional."

"But no Charter to worry about, no snooping congressmen."

"I'm a businessman. I'm within my rights."

Paul glanced at Catherine. He had explained to her what he had against this place, that it was really part of the CIA, set up to function outside the legal restrictions imposed on its parent. Wiser noticed the glance of comradeship. Catherine wondered if Paul could tell how Harmon Wiser felt about him. People cloak their loathing of the righteous in respect.

The office they entered seemed at first more pleasant than the rest of the place. It was centered by a huge rosewood desk. The wood was beautiful, but the size of the desk made it ugly. Against one wall were closet doors fronted by combination locks. They faced another wall on which were hung two cool, flat abstract paintings, probably as valuable as they were ugly. A plaster figure, hunched and painted as dark a blue as Paul's pistol, stood in the corner. Catherine recognized it as a work of George Segal.

Beyond the statue spread a festive view of Manhattan, buildings soaring into the morning sun, flung tatters of cloud, gold light on a multitude of windows, a jet crossing the sky.

Perhaps because Catherine knew that this was a place where death was talked, she found the overall effect to be fearsome.

Wiser went behind the desk and dropped into the chair.

"Beats the old Tehran station, doesn't it? I hope it meets with your approval."

"Harmon, I don't want to get into the morality of what you're doing. I've got money and a problem. Let's talk business."

"You remain the most sanctimonious of souls. I wasn't talking morality, I was talking aesthetics."

Paul hunched, clenched his fists as if preparing for a blow.

"Ever ask him where *he* got his money, sweetheart?"

Paul raised his head, looked with pleading eyes at Wiser. "I need help," he said. "The girl too. She's contaminated—"

"I know that! Just your style, too. All moral about the good old Charter but pretty quick with the self-justification when you find something you want—like a bedmate."

"I said I was here to do business. We need protection. I think Directorate V is on my case."

"I can't protect you from Teplov. He'll get you somehow or another."

"Maybe." He pulled what he had explained to Catherine was a spike microphone from his pocket. "If you can tell me who uses this type—"

"Good Lord, man, put that thing on the desk. Gently!

That's a high-pressure microaerosol of cyanide. Radio-controlled.''

Catherine heard the word *cyanide*, felt a rush of fear. Paul withdrew his hand from the little gray object as if it were hot. Wiser picked up the phone. ''Send Baxter in here with a box capable of safely holding one of these new microaerosols, like the ones we bought from Pakravan.''

''Pakravan? I thought he was dead!''

Wiser addressed Catherine. ''This thing was supposed to have killed you both. The only reason you're alive is that your boyfriend was and obviously remains one of the best clandestines in the business. It was a miracle he found it even if he's been pastured too long to know what it is.''

''Pakravan—you said—''

''He's alive and well and living here and there. Surfaced six weeks ago brokering merchandise and info for the First Chief Directorate.''

''Pakravan would never go KGB.''

''KGB, CIA, SODO—the pond is too dirty to tell who's under which lily pad. His present affiliation is the most profitable for him at the moment.''

That silenced Paul. Catherine could see that he had honored this Pakravan. Honored him, and just now been disappointed by him.

''I guess the guilt I felt over his capture was misplaced.''

''Premature. He's on many lists. The DDO's been asking me questions about him. I think we're going to give him the fight or switch option soon.''

''You say you bought some of these from him. Are they his calling cards?''

''I'd love to be able to say yes. He uses them, certainly, and he sells them for ten thousand dollars apiece. But they're made by Teplov's elves. Directorate V matériel. Used in vital 'must not miss' assassination efforts.'' He laughed. ''God, I wish I could be the one to tell old Pyotr that his boys *did* miss. He's going to be so upset.''

As Catherine listened to this monstrous conversation,

ashes seemed to sift down over her world, compelling it to the uniform shade of death. Wiser, who had never entirely lifted his attention from her, appeared to perceive her horror more clearly than Paul. As suddenly as a bird might move, he reached across the desk and snatched her hand, put it to his breast. "Youth," he murmured, "the liberal season." Catherine pulled back her hand. She felt acute discomfort at the man's cool, humid touch. "That's a paraphrase of Cicero," Wiser continued. "You'll find him listed after 'Cicada' in the encyclopedia, in case the name is unfamiliar."

"Why 'the liberal season'?" she asked, testing the acid of the conversation.

"You're a liberal woman." He drew his small self up from behind his gigantic desk and crossed to the locked closets. "Agency in the closet," he said, rolling back the door to reveal a small computer.

"You've even got a terminal," Paul said. "That's Harmon. Always up front about it."

"I'm not on the payroll. This little beauty is officially located in the Federal Building downtown. An extension cord, however, has been lent to me. A long one." He leaned over the terminal and began typing. "I think it's time your friend got initiated."

In seconds a printer was rattling a response to Wiser's query. He soon returned with a sheet of paper. "You ask why 'the liberal season,' dear." He handed Catherine the paper.

They knew her intimately but falsely. So very falsely. Her relationship with Jenny was reported as "a lesbian marriage," when in fact it was nothing more than a friendship, and scrupulously chaste. Jenny loved her and Jenny was a lesbian, but Catherine was not. She had dignified Jenny's longing by her kindness. There was beauty in their comradeship of a kind that men would not allow themselves to understand.

"This is full of filthy lies!"

"All true, my dear. They researched you when you took up with their former employee. A hazardous occupation, playing house with a spy."

She felt defiled. Paul grabbed the paper and tore it to bits. "Why put her through this? It's pointless."

"It's motivating. If she were to change beds again I could probably get her a reprieve. As it is she'll die by your side."

"You think in clichés! Actress equals whore, right? Well, I'm not a whore and I didn't sleep my way to Broadway, and neither did most of my sisters, you creep!"

Wiser looked desperately at Paul, then back to Catherine. She was surprised to see the depth of hurt in his eyes. He took her shoulders and raised his lips to her ear. He was on tiptoe. "Catherine, dear," he breathed, "trust me. Play along with the conversation and I might be able to salvage you."

She looked down into the little face. Behind the hurt and the concern she could see eager lust. "I won't play along! I love this man. And he loves me. Right, Paul?"

He stared as if frozen. The pain in his eyes was almost unbearable to her.

"I can protect you, Catherine. But not him. Paul is a dead man."

In answer to them both Catherine drew her arm around Paul's waist. She felt him breathe out relief and was touched that the thought of losing her had frightened him.

"That's a shame," Wiser said. "You screwed Jerry Tobin for *The Fox in the Garden* and you won't even consider me for your life."

"Jerry was my lover!"

"My dear boy, since I can't coerce her to accepting protection, perhaps you can. Tell her it's the only way she's got a chance to live."

"Don't bother, Paul! I don't sleep around."

"I can't," he muttered. He held her more tightly.

"Maybe when you understand the dimensions of the problem you'll both get more reasonable. Here, Paul, look at this." He handed him a newsletter called "The National Intelligence Daily." Paul glanced at Wiser, took the paper.

"You know, of course, that I was never cleared to see this."

"In this case I think 'need to know' supersedes the lack of clearance." His manner had changed, become grave and almost kind. "I wish to God I could help you, old buddy. But I just don't have the facilities. The Pahlavis, yes, I can build a cage for them that'll keep out the revolution's geeks. But I can't stop Pyotr."

Catherine thought that she wouldn't be able to endure much more of this. Compared to the world these men lived in, the entertainment jungle was a gentle country garden. She wished she could just disappear. Funny thing for an actress to want.

The words in the NID hit Paul like a hot wind. He felt his face flush and the hairs rise along the back of his neck. He kept reading and rereading the ten lines of the story. Terror in a Minuteman Launch Capsule.

A vivid image of Jamshid came to mind. Again he saw those gold eyes and heard that laughter. Jamshid was hate burned pure, hate refined. He could as easily work for one side as the other. It was destruction that interested him.

Paul remembered the snakes rushing through the folds of his brain, the demons, the magic voices.

Control. Enough to make missile crewmen kill themselves with their own bare hands. Enough to—

Make them fire their weapons? Certainly.

They fire a few missiles. The USSR justifiably retaliates by destroying Minuteman. Then we're helpless. But what does it matter? How could they control the anarchy of the U.S.A.?

He saw how. ELF had given them the means.

He felt cold, cloying fear come up from the depths of him and lodge in his mind. "ELF—"

Wiser gave him a mischievous look, then burst into

laughter. "I was waiting for you to say that. We've learned a little about ELF since you got shot down for trying to peddle it. Believe me, it got sillier later. The Navy's even having trouble trying to use it as a radio."

"If you don't believe it was ELF, why bother to show me this NID? This happens and a few hours later they get on the case of the one man in Western intelligence who believes in ELF. It's not a coincidence, Harmon." Even as he spoke, the outlines of an incredible mission were forming in Paul's mind. A mission so vital, so important, that it would require every resource he could find, every suggestion of courage, every bit of skill.

"Officially the position of CIA is that Sverdlovsk is the biggest boondoggle in the history of warfare. Give you an example you probably don't know about. For years the Sovs have been beaming absolutely pointless ten-hertz transmissions into the Pacific Northwest. When Mount St. Helens exploded, the project commander got a medal. ELF is another Sverdlovsk special, and CIA thinks it's just as nutty. The Kremlin's senile, Paul. Quack-ridden."

"You know what I'm going to do about this NID, don't you, Harmon?" Of course he did. Harmon had showed him this for a reason.

"You're the best, Paul. If anybody can protect a flank, it's you. Go out to South Dakota and see if there's anything the Air Force hasn't found."

Paul smoothed his lapels. He was self-conscious about the bulge of his pistol. He had enjoyed retiring the suits that had been tailored to conceal guns. Now he wished that he had them back from storage. The bulge in this beautiful garment was like the first lump of some ugly disease, spreading, unstoppable and terminal.

"I'll go. Is there any further evidence?"

"Pakravan might be out there."

The good friend. "He knows ELF."

"Exactly."

The swine had known how Paul would respond. He was

being used again. Harmon had always known how to get him to risk his neck.

"Can I get backup?"

"Not my department. Anyway, a man with your skills doesn't need backup. Surviving one of those microaerosols is must unusual."

"Gee, that's nice. Makes a guy feel so special. Tell me, Harmon, before I die—"

"Please. Before you go. I'll miss hell out of you if you die, you crazy old man."

"Thanks, dear. Tell me about any other little secrets I might be up against. New goodies."

Wiser picked up his phone. "Send Baxter in again. Tell him to bring the updated Clandestine Devices Report and some samples." He regarded Catherine. "How may they kill thee? Let me count the ways."

"A bad joke," she said in too loud a voice. It almost made Paul wince to hear. Her ignorant courage was embarrassing to him in the same way that a child's tone-deafness is to a music teacher.

The devices expert appeared with a large metal case, gingerly placed it on the desk, and opened it. Inside were several other boxes. "Just the lethal stuff," Harmon muttered.

"You've seen the spike, so I'll show you the other most recent goodies. KGB is getting very good at cardiovascular poisons. Stuff that collapses the vascular system and stops the heart. The reason they like them is that some of them are lethal in very small quantities, and their symptoms mimic heart attack so well." Baxter drew what appeared to be a Walther PPK out of the case. "This little toy delivers fléchettes of a concentrated derivative of asp toxin. The fléchettes are so small that they leave nary a trace on the body and cause little physical sensation. Death occurs in three to six seconds. Range is about fifty yards in the hands of an expert. The weapon is silent."

In the old days conversations like this had fascinated Paul. Death then was a kind of cultural event, an intricate show. Paul was still fascinated, but more, he felt, in the way that a mouse is fascinated by a copperhead. "Fifty yards maximum range?" His voice sounded admirably professional. Not an extra semitone, not a quaver.

"They would attempt to get closer. Thirty yards is a hell of a lot better. Thick clothing can sometimes stop the fléchettes at the longer ranges."

"Too bad it's summer." He was glad he was sitting down. These little tools were diabolical. Gone were the days of the gun camera and the spring-loaded spike in the umbrella. KGB was no longer in the funny-weapons business.

Baxter withdrew a small gray canister. "This is another really good one. An aerosol that can be sprayed onto the floor of a bathtub or shower stall. When it combines with water it forms a very lethal gas derived from prussic acid."

"Remind me to bathe only in public places."

"I'm fascinated that your sense of humor is intact. Just looking at this stuff makes me queasy, and I've been living with it for years."

Harmon didn't need to know how Paul really felt now—not really afraid so much as sad, as if he had been separated even more deeply than before from common humanity. As for the woman beside him—her surging vibrance made him feel ashamed. Must it always be the fate of the beast to love beauty?

"Let's see," Baxter continued, "here are the new firebombs. KGB likes arson. The charming thing about these nasties is their size." He laid six of them out across the palm of his hand. "One of these is easily capable of doing a large room in a matter of seconds. A favorite method is to mail one to the victim and then detonate it by remote control after he takes in the delivery. Since they leave no residue, the cause is usually ruled unknown, prob. accidental."

"I'd rather be gassed than burned," Paul said, trying to cling to the lightness, if only for Catherine's sake.

Baxter closed his black steel case. "You know about microaerosols already. Just remember that they can deliver many different kinds of substance. They can do worse than kill.''

"KGB's also very involved with electrostimulation of the brain," Harmon said. "They can achieve more or less absolute control. If they want you to laugh, you laugh. Or cry. Or talk. Torture by push button.''

"I want poppers," Paul said. He glanced at Catherine's blank look. "Suicide pills. Also called painkillers.'' At once he regretted the words. She went pallid. The idea of carrying death around in her mouth was something she didn't need to deal with just now. But later . . . yes. It would be best; cyanide was one of the greatest comforts to the wanderers in the labyrinth.

"I was just getting ready to offer.'' Baxter took a small box from his pocket. "Molar caps. Hard to see. But remember you have to take three good chews or you get nothing. Three good, hard chews." He took two shapeless blobs of what appeared to be white clay from the box. "Three good chews. Just stick 'em in the cheek like a plug of tobacco.''

"If we swallow?''

"No danger. That's another type of popper. These'll go right through your digestive system without harm. No more accidents.''

It had been a long time since Paul had seen a popper. The ones they had used in Nam were blue gunmetal and they broke your teeth, he had been told, when you bit them.

Holding the strange plastic clay in his hand, Paul felt ashamed of himself, of them all. He had never realized before confronting Catherine with it how vulgar was their convention of violence. "It's just an option,'' he murmured.

She backed away, her hands before her. "I'll never put that in my mouth. Never!'' Her eyes were frantic. As she moved, she brushed against the sculpture. Harmon scurried to prevent it from toppling. She whirled to the movement. *"He's* the poison, Paul!''

The look Harmon shot Paul mixed sympathy and contempt, creating in him another moment of deep sorrow and deeper fear—especially in view of what he must do now that he had read the NID. Paul could not hide from duty. His death was vital to the other side for a very good reason, and his life was therefore precious. He had to go into the eye of the storm. There could be no turning away, no protecting the innocent.

Somewhere in South Dakota he was going to find ELF and Jamshid Rostram. His fate awaited him there; he understood that with utter clarity.

"Catherine." He opened his arms. She watched him warily, made no move to go to him. "Come home with me?"

That reached her. She strode to the door of the room. Then she paused. "Give me the poison." Her voice had become clear and strong, but she was shaking. Her face was sheened with sweat, her eyes glittering wetly. "Like this?" She stuffed it back into her cheek. A slight bulge showed. As gently as he could Paul pressed it to invisibility.

"Like that."

To Catherine the mass of poison seemed huge and had a penetrating, metallic taste. She watched Paul moving warily closer to her. He was like a guilty child seeking to be spanked for the expiation it would bring. But this was not childhood. There would be no spanking, and the punishment would never end. His guilt would punish him until he died—which, judging from the terrifying conversation she had just witnessed, would be quite soon.

She had rarely thought of death; she was not a morbid person. But with the poison throbbing in her jaw her mind turned with intense interest to the actual fact of ceasing to exist, becoming a corpse. Her experience of death was very limited. Had she ever actually seen a dead body? No. They hadn't let her see Granddad Harris but from the doorway of the bedroom, a still form in the sheets.

Her mind raced into its mortal past, seeking some clue, some solace, finding only what is always found, the vastness and the silence. They all moved slowly about in their unconscious dance of death, little Harmon Wiser, the dark messenger they called Baxter, Paul too, against the wide view of clouds and spires. She understood why Wiser had that statue in his office. George Segal had somehow shaped the secret of death into it, and death must interest men like Harmon and Paul very much. Death the clandestine.

"Catherine, I think we could both use a drink."

"Yes." She went with him, moving like a robot beside a robot. In the elevator he planted himself before her. His lips moved, but there were no words. His hands, as careful as a surgeon's, again touched her cheeks. She reached up, covered his fingers with hers.

"I'm going to take it out, Paul."

"If they torture you—"

"I'll suffer! But I won't live with this in my mouth. I won't!"

She removed the poison.

"I've seen torture, Catherine."

"This is the right thing."

He gave her a strange, sad look. "How about the Algonquin? It's quiet and the windows are covered." That was his only response. How typical of Paul to hide so much.

Even the idea of crossing the street unnerved her. Getting a cab, going to a hotel, seemed impossibly dangerous.

"Trust me. I'll keep us safe."

She suffered the irony of death's creature claiming he could protect her from death. "I'll try to trust you. I will try."

He felt her lithe steps beside him. She had begun to move wonderfully—like a panther. Catherine had a great store of courage, and it wasn't just her youth. There was something uncommonly brave about her. Or perhaps he was just wishing that. He found a cab. They got in and Paul leaned back, closed his eyes for a moment. He turned his mind to the clandestine rituals. The old fires within were being relit, the demons dancing once again. Paul's body was even beginning to feel different—more taut, more *there*. He had once been known for his agility. But now?

He had the cab stop at an office building a block from the Algonquin.

"Just stay close to me," he said as he selected an appropriately crowded elevator, waiting until the doors were closing to get on. He punched the third floor and the twentieth. They got out on the third, a dingy hallway, frosted-glass doors. "Transat Shipping," "Reliant Co.," other gray names.

"Come on." He led her down the fire escape and back into the lobby, out the rear of the building and across the street to the hotel.

The lobby of the Algonquin was as always, the tiny round tables with their bells, the slightly seedy couches and chairs, the plants, and at the rear the dreary red wallpaper of the Rose Room. At ten o'clock in the morning there wasn't too much activity. A few of the lobby tables were occupied by people with morning coffee. The Rose Room was empty of diners; the waiters were spreading clean white tablecloths for lunch. Paul led the way into the Blue Bar—dark oak, ancient tables, dim and profoundly congenial.

"I feel better now that we're here," Catherine said. "Despite the route we took."

He had remembered that the Blue Bar had been her first place of refuge. Like generations of New Yorkers before her, she found the calm, pleasantly indifferent atmosphere of this place deeply satisfying. You heard tourists ask upon seeing the Algonquin, "Is this all there is to it?"

"Remember our first evening?" It had been spent here.

She didn't answer. He accepted that. He couldn't blame her. "Jimmy, bring me a vodka martini," she said, amending her usual Lillet. The barman brought it with Paul's Scotch. Their drinks before them, Catherine smiled in a strange way. The expression made him think of a panther again, but one that was trapped.

As they were coming into the hotel something awful had

occurred to him. It had been obvious since two o'clock this morning, but it hadn't risen to the surface until now. The clandestine method of thought is too difficult to stay long with a man after his need for it ceases. And it does not return quickly. He watched her drink, feeling like a spider waiting for the right moment to move down the web to the captured prey. Poor Catherine.

"You can't go on, you know." He wanted to sink into the floor forever as he said the words. Instead he sat and watched as her face passed through the predictable phases: confusion, realization, desperation.

Rage.

"I can't quit the show. I *am* the show—"

"Catherine, you haven't got a chance out on a stage. You saw the kind of weapons they use."

"I can't quit! That's my life, Paul Winter. You take me off that stage, you kill me!"

"Catherine—" He was painfully aware that her voice was filling the room. Other eyes were glancing, faces turning . . . Catherine Harris . . . How in the name of God could he protect a public person from the likes of Directorate V?

"You had no right to get me tangled up in this!"

"I—"

"You've as good as killed me." Her voice was harsh, but now it sank to a hollow moan. "I was finally getting started. And you're taking it away from me."

She lowered her eyes, hunched her shoulders, but took the drink to her lips with unexpectedly steady hands. There was that strength again, the same inner power that was propelling her to the top of her furiously competitive profession.

"You can survive this, Catherine. And there'll be other shows."

"I'm going to tell the press. Shepherd, Wilson, the Channel Five News, for God's sake. I'll call Freddy Seligmann this minute."

"Don't get your PR people involved. You drop an item in some column and you will be dead within an hour."

"The publicity—"

"They don't give a goddamn."

"What the hell am I supposed to do, then?"

"You could have gone into a cage. Harmon was offering you one."

"Him and me! I buy my life by becoming his whore. You people are so corrupt you don't know how corrupt you are."

"It isn't that simple. Remember that a place like his is probably bugged by KGB. He may even be involved in a double-blind routine, working for us while working for them while working for us. He'd have to obscure his motives to justify protecting you."

"You're such a fool. Don't you understand that he wanted me? Really, truly, in the real world. He wanted to steal me."

Paul knew that. "Harmon always has more than one motive. It's his weakness."

Her face was flushed with anger, her eyes were sharp, her lips a tight line. She looked wonderful in her fury.

"I love you so," he blurted. It came from so deep within that he hadn't even known he was going to say it. The words made him feel fierce. "If I have to die for you, I will." He knew in his heart that this was true. He chose to ignore the desire to crumple up, to lower his head.

She took his right hand. "I'll give you a ring," she said. "You still have a mark there, you know."

"I moved Irene's ring when she died."

Catherine kissed his fingers.

"Stay away from the theater tonight."

"No, and don't let's go on about it."

"Darling, please. Just until I get this straightened out."

"Paul—"

He hurt terribly inside, but he loved. He loved with passion meant only for extreme youth. In his sorrow and his fear his heart was nevertheless soaring up. "Never linger," he said laconically. "It's rule one in this business."

She laughed softly. "Your choreography fascinates me, Paul. You are a very hidden man."

They crossed the lobby and the Rose Room and went through the kitchen to 45th Street. A few waiters turned to watch them, but that was all.

The morning was opening toward noon. For a few moments Paul's drink was going to give him a sense of well-being. He wouldn't feel like the hobbled creature he was—hobbled by this glorious, stubborn woman. Old men's hearts are supposed to be filled with the past, especially dangerous old men. He felt obscurely happy. The years seemed to be pouring off his back. Years indeed. These days fifty was far from old.

As they walked he talked. He told her of ELF and his experience in the Zagros. More, he told her of what he thought must have happened to Shazdeh Hassan and his device, and where that device must now be: in the Black Hills of South Dakota.

The story of Jamshid he left for later—until he could understand how to tell it without saying crazy things about demons.

He explained the mission he had to undertake against the ELF device.

"You and Don Quixote."

He laughed. "That's apt. The thing even looks a little like a windmill."

"You're a romantic. A youth."

"I'm forty-eight."

"And I'm twenty-four, but I'm old enough to be your mother. Paul Winter against the Soviet Union and its magic machines. Whatever happens, Paul, it won't involve you killing the windmill."

He flared inside. Don Quixote's windmill was after all only a dream of danger. The Don's madness was the threat.

"You're puzzling the matter out, aren't you? 'Is ELF a

windmill or not?' you're asking yourself. Believe me, kid, it is."

"Then I should just forget about it?"

"You might try applying your brilliant spy stuff to saving the life of the woman who loves you, stupid fool that she is."

"The first order of business is to restrict their opportunities. We do that by sticking close to the Sequoia."

"Do we?"

The street was filled with fire equipment. A wisp of smoke was coming from a gaping hole that had been a fifth-floor window. Their window. So return to the Sequoia was not to be an option. Yes, that was good thinking on the part of their pursuers. If the bird wouldn't flush, burn the bush.

Catherine's hand found his.

6

As the report from the New York *residentura* jittered out of the teletype in Pyotr Teplov's office, he devoured it line by line, hovering over the machine, glaring at the words that were appearing on the paper.

"Damn."

This was failure in its pure form, the kind that was useful to one's enemies.

He rubbed his face, which was dusted with unshaved beard. He felt as if he were being vised between two great paws, the military on one hand and his own superiors on the other. He was what was once called "a convinced Communist," and in an age when real Communists were looked upon with suspicion in Russia he spent his time maneuvering and lying, keeping the truth of himself secret from the world. To keep his secret he had even avoided the temptation of marriage and its inevitable whispers.

But he knew a truth, which others denied or pretended was a lie. The truth was this: between the rise of Lenin in 1917 and the death of Stalin in 1953 there had been human freedom for the first and only time on earth. During that glorious period true Communists had been free. To think such thoughts in the "revised bourgeois" society of modern Russia was to risk the psychiatric hospitals.

He looked again at the cable from America. Winter was not yet dead. He cursed. The past six months had drained him. He had organized his humanitarian project step by step, forcing concessions from one *apparatchik* after another, working with the experts to discover the most efficient way of blanketing the U.S. with ELF fields, getting the equipment manufactured, and finally putting it on the twelve freighters that now waited just outside American territorial waters.

"Mikhail—bring me tea!" There was a shout of response from the outer office. Teplov's orderly began to clatter about the samovar. In a moment he came hurrying in with a glass of the delicious, incredibly scarce and contraband Chinese tea that Teplov favored. It was illegal, but Teplov liked China and things Chinese. They reminded him of the wonderful Maoist past, and of Stalin, yes. "All loyal, honest, active, and staunch Communists must unite to oppose liberalism." Mao, dead discredited genius.

Mao and Stalin. Glory days. And now a true Communist dared not even whisper their names. Teplov, standing amid his maps and bar charts and schedules, closed his eyes and allowed a brief dream of Father Stalin. He wanted just to say that name aloud once. Stalin. He mouthed it in silence. Stalin.

Sometimes Teplov would awaken at night, startled by what had seemed a vast crowd calling to him. Workers, calling for help. Calling for ELF. It would free them from socially induced "will." Communism is the will of the Communist. That is the essential dialectic.

Walking the clean, safe streets of Sverdlovsk, one knew that it was true. ELF was a great gift of Soviet science.

On the wall hung a plan of the Empire State Building. Where once they had thought to moor Nazi zeppelins an ELF antenna was to be erected. And on the Sears Tower in

Chicago and the Southland Life Building in Dallas, and in other cities—Houston, Los Angeles, Detroit, St. Louis, Boston.

He was bringing paradise to America.

And afterward to Russia—as soon as the Politburo was persuaded by the American example.

How ironic that the fortress of capitalism was going to become the first true workers' paradise.

"Colonel, sir?"

A voice. From where?

"Colonel, sir, please, sir."

Oh. I've fallen down. "Yes, Mikhail."

His orderly helped him to his feet. Angrily he brushed the tears that had soaked his face. Mikhail brought out a cloth, did a better job. Then he embraced and kissed his colonel.

Nothing needed to be said. Teplov considered himself even more sensitive to betrayal than Stalin had been. He knew what lay behind Mikhail's bourgeois affection for him.

When Mikhail was near, Teplov kept the cable he had gotten carefully folded.

The moment he withdrew, Teplov padded across his worn Armenian rug and picked up the center of his three telephones. The sorrows that had been upon him had passed now. As always they had left him renewed, filled him with fresh courage. The hopeful call of the American proletariat, yearning for communism. A tonic to their savior.

"Director's office," he said into the instrument, thinking of how brutal the Director could be, as ruthless as any bourgeois.

Raya Marakovna answered, her voice toneless.

"This is Teplov."

A moment of silence, then a response. "He has five minutes, Colonel." So sullen, so knowing. Teplov hated Marakovna, her deceptively sweet face, her Western perfume, her sneering laughter. The Director let her know too many secrets. He decadently indulged pretty faces without regard for actual usefulness. When Marakovna was in his office, his hands were always fluttering close, longing to touch her gleaming white skin. Teplov himself had not time for dalliance, not until the war was won.

Marakovna was too powerful. Teplov would have taken the greatest pleasure in sending her downstairs to Lubyanka.

He strode through the long corridor that separated his office from that of the Director. Despite the summer morning the deep interior of Two Dzerzhinsky Square was chill. Teplov reached the massive door of Andropov's suite and pushed it open across the thick carpet of the reception room. At the center of the room Marakovna sat, tiny and pretty, behind a pretty French antique desk. On her telephone table were six instruments. She shared all the Director's lines except the *Kremlevka,* which connected him to the Chairman.

Chafing as always at the implied indignity of it, Teplov handed her his internal passport and KGB identification papers. He could not do this without annoyance. Were he a general, none of it would be required. And how could a department head not be a general? To graft a powerful man to a lowly rank might make Andropov feel more secure, but it reduced Teplov's efficiency to a serious degree. Less important, but still infuriating, was the fact that others of lower usefulness to the state got better privileges. Marakovna had her own Chaika, for example, while Teplov drew old Ladas at random from the mid-staff motor pool.

"Enter," Marakovna said, handing back his documents without looking up at him.

For the moment the Director's office was empty. He would be in his private rooms adjoining. Teplov went to the tall windows that overlooked Marx Prospekt. Sunlight glowed on the red brick wall of Kitai-Gorod. A cadre of young Octobrists walked in file. Workers as slow as great gray beetles erected a new street crossing sign. Clouds drifted in a blue sky. Teplov wished now, as often, that he could fly away and never return. A cosmonaut to nowhere.

Behind the Director's desk was the famous portrait of

Dzerzhinsky, chief of the Cheka, looking over all that passed with the noble face of the Revolution. Noble, and lost in the revisionist muck of today.

The *Kremlevka* began to buzz. That brought the Director bursting out of his suite as Teplov's presence could not. He crossed the room with the combination of grace and slightly exaggerated care that had come to characterize his old age. In June he had turned sixty-seven. The birthday was celebrated only by the family, Teplov, and the five other chief deputies.

"He's with me now, comrade," the Director said heavily. "All is well," he added in a more cheerful tone. Then he laughed. "You know our Pyotr Alexandrovich!" He replaced the receiver. "Don't say you have bad news."

"A small delay."

"The devil with you."

"I've gone to the secondary plan. There is no cause for alarm."

"Winter is not dead?"

"The secondary plan—"

"Answer the question, Colonel!"

"He somehow managed to neutralize a DDK-forty aerosol—"

The Director clapped his hands together once, making a report like that of a small pistol. Teplov decided not to mention that Winter had gone to Harmon Wiser. Better Wiser was destroyed before the Director was told about that particular meeting.

"When will Winter be dead?"

"A few hours. We've burned him out of his hotel room to get him running. We'll have many more opportunities now."

The Director tossed his head. His face was leached of color. "I sense that this operation is in danger."

"We've had a setback—"

"Danger, I said! Look at the overall picture. Winter has discovered us. Therefore he will soon go to CIA."

"He's a proud man. He'd sooner seek other help, if he seeks any at all."

"Don't play about, man. I know perfectly well that he went to Harmon Wiser. And how do you think I know? Belik has your operation penetrated. Yes, look astonished. Belik! And he tells Sukovsky, who tells the Chairman, who is sitting in his dacha right now in a puddle of hot piss worrying about *your* loyalty!"

Teplov watched dust motes chasing one another through a shaft of sunlight. His loyalty! As if that revanchist knew anything about it!

Beneath him the chair, the floor, the very earth twisted and writhed. His body seemed actually to be shrinking. Then his mind came to his defense. Under sufficient pressure it had always been this way, the sudden flash of knowing, the absolute clarity. "I propose this," he heard himself say in a strong, confident tone. "Harmon Wiser will meet with an accident. I can get it accomplished within the hour."

"The New York *residentura* will protest. He's valuable to them."

"Nothing is more valuable than Black Magic."

"You will have to convince Panin of that."

"He will obey me. I will also take steps to capture Winter. I will hostage his mistress. Before we finish him we must ascertain exactly what he told Wiser. This will all be done."

As will something else. Belik was going to destroy him if it was not. Just this morning he had received a report from Ludmilla Semilovna, who stated that Belik was agitated about "some political matter he said he could not discuss." The political matter was undoubtedly the removal of Pyotr Teplov—and with him KGB—from participation in Black Magic. Belik hated the very idea of the ELF field being used in support of the true aims of the workers. He wouldn't even enter the Sverdlovsk Paradise, Ludmilla Semilovna had informed. In other words, he cherished bourgeois ideals of freedom. Western notions, like most other "Soviet officers."

"Sir, you say that General Belik has penetrated my own staff?"

"Most certainly."

"Then he must be trying to destroy KGB's influence over Black Magic. That is anti-Soviet agitation, in my opinion. The man has Bonapartist tendencies of the most dangerous sort. Let me deal with him."

The Director looked away. He made a tent of his fingers, then peered across it at Teplov. What did that face say? From long experience Teplov knew that it was unwise to try to read the Director's carefully controlled expressions.

"You play chess so well. If you did not I would long ago have lost all confidence in you. Be very clear, Pyotr Alexandrovitch. That man is the darling of the Politburo and the General Staff. If a soldier ever becomes Chairman, the soldier elected will be V. I. Belik. Do not discuss this subject further."

"Please—another word."

"No! Silence!"

"If he were dead I would be at the head of all phases of Black Magic. KGB would control it completely."

"Insubordination, I would remind you, is a serious offense. If you speak one more word on this subject, I will put a note in your file."

"Should I be arrested, I think you can count on Belik to fill the hole with one of his own people. It is really you he is attacking when he attacks me. You, Comrade Director."

"The subject is closed. Doing as you suggest is quite beyond our power, even if we wished it." There was in the Director's tone an edge of wistfulness. He of course understood the danger that Belik represented to KGB.

Understood, but had not the power to act. Officially. An audacious possibility occurred to Teplov. He decided to test the Director's true motives. "In any case," he said carefully, "I believe that I should move my HQ to Sverdlovsk. I can still direct the American operations from there, and it would put us in closer contact with the general. If he should meet with an accident—''

The Director nodded, but said nothing. That was more than enough, if Teplov still had the measure of his commandant. Teplov took his leave and returned to his own office feeling more hopeful than he had in days. At once he consulted the teletype for developments, but all it contained was a routine communications check from Pakravan in Rapid City.

''Mikhail, please arrange a place for me on the Sverdlovsk shuttle. I will be stopping at the Bioenergetics Institute for the next week to ten days.''

For a long time after he had cut the further orders for the New York *residentura,* Teplov sat in his comfortable old desk chair wondering who exactly was going to survive all this. The size and delicacy of his operations made him more than usually nervous. New York. Rapid City. Now Sverdlovsk.

If it all worked, the reviled Executioner, the man who was too dirty to become a general, would have the extraordinary pleasure of overtaking all the generals. In the name of the workers, too, and their Communist expectations.

And if it did not work? Well, then, the end of a troubled life.

Beyond Belik's parlor window rose wild soft hills, their mantle of pines touched by the last light. Night was spreading out to the east over hill and tree alike, bringing holy quiet to the great Russian land. Belik's flat was far from the rushing sprawl of Sverdlovsk itself, in an old czarist inn on the road to Berezovskiy. Here one could be near Russia's beauty and forget the rest.

He watched the gathering shadows while Ludmilla played her flute. She was serene; he was sour with fear.

Why was the Executioner coming here? Surely their meeting in Moscow had been sufficient to cover all possible points needing cooperation. GRU's information was scanty. "Expect Red Wind 0800 tomorrow" was all the cable had said. That was the bloody creature's code name, Red Wind. Was Teplov aware of the problem with the ELF antenna and rising like a shark to the scent of a wound?

He had watched Teplov coolly drill a hole in the skull of the shrieking Shazdeh Hassan and insert a long golden needle. When that needle was connected to an electric outlet, Hassan literally exploded with agony. A few minutes of such torment reduced the man to frantic cooperation.

For eleven days previously Belik had interrogated him without success.

Red Wind. All he had said when Hassan was dead was "It is a worse sensation than fire, I've been told." He was so polite, so soft-spoken was Red Wind. Now, just as Sukovsky had suggested, he was moving in on Black Magic.

"Do I seem formidable to you, Ludmilla Semilovna?"

She took a breath. "Very formidable." She went on playing her flute. "A Lark Sings in the Blackberry Bush." Very, very beautiful.

"You don't really think so." On the table between them was an arrangement of summer flowers, daisies from the roadside and the little orange flowers the peasants called cat's eye. They had an intense fragrance that Belik forever associated with Ural summers, the easy hours in the sloping forests, the taste of Ludmilla's kisses in a bower of green.

He touched the cat's eye as she played on, the sweet, complex music complementary to the woman herself. "Order more roses," he said.

"Very well."

Teplov, Teplov, Teplov—the word was like a nail being driven into the softness of the moment. Arrest. Torture. Death. Red Wind. The thin face of Teplov appeared in his mind's eye, the wan face, the expression more blank than that of a snake.

More blank even than the joyful faces of the workers in

Sverdlovsk Paradise. Not even the Americans deserved Teplov and his satanic ideas. In their wildness and exuberance the Americans were actually somewhat wonderful. Removing the insane threat of the Pentagon's warheads was one thing, but those wonderful people did not need to be . . . what was the right word? Automatized.

"Ludmilla Semilovna, please, I must talk to you." Normally he shared his secrets with no one, but this he could not keep. He raised his voice to be heard over the melody. I think I'm going to have some political trouble."

At last she stopped playing. "You, Valentin Ilyich? You deserve an Order; how could they bother you?"

"You know of Pyotr Teplov?"

"I don't think so."

"He's coming down here. He's the former chief of Directorate V. Now in charge of the American end of the Black Magic project." It all sounded so innocent, speaking it aloud. But that was deceptive. He went on. "I think he is coming to take over my end of things as well. They suspect that we soldiers don't care for the kind of ELF paradise they plan—not even for America. They are looking for a pretext to purge me."

"What pretext, Valentin Ilyich? You're the most loyal patriot I've ever encountered."

"Pretexts are manufactured as needed."

She came into his arms; she offered herself for kissing. His lips contacted hers and she made a throaty sound of pleasure. Her hands worked speedily, skillfully, unbuttoning his trousers, slipping within. The electrifying coolness of her touch never failed to inspire him. Instantly he was a thousand times ready. She drew back and laughed a little. "You see? Love is the cure for your worry."

In that she could not have been more right.

"Ludmilla Semilovna, has Belik a gun?"

"Of course, comrade. His service pistol."

"You will shoot him in the brain while he sleeps. You

will then place the gun in his hand and telephone the KGB patrol station. The officer who comes will rule it a suicide.''

"Very well, comrade. When is this operation to be carried out?"

"You will get a telephone call from me. I will say two words, 'Wrong number.' I will then ring off. That night, do it."

Ludmilla nodded. Teplov left quickly. Ludmilla listened to General Belik snoring in the bedroom. She went to the window and looked a long while at the moonlight on the distant mountains. The tears that touched her cheeks she wiped away.

She played her flute softly, old songs, deep Russian songs full of the spirit of the people—her people. She played songs of love and loss, noble laments. Through the night she continued, patiently reconciling her duty with her troubled heart.

Despite the fact that Belik arrived at his office an hour before Teplov was due, the KGB officer was already there. Belik knew it the moment he walked into his reception room. His staff moved hastily away from the whispered convocation they were having around the electric samovar.

"Yevgeni," he said to the receptionist, "a glass of tea, please. I'll take it here." The junior lieutenant brought the glass. Belik took a seat in the cramped reception room. The metal chair was unstable, tilting precariously to the right. He had paused out here to build up his courage among his loyal entourage.

"Well, comrades," he said, "what is the famous Teplov like?"

"He is wearing a Russian suit," Major Florinsky said.

"Only to confuse us. In Moscow he dresses like any other *nachalstvo*, I can assure you. How long has he been here?"

"He let himself in before I even opened the office," the junior lieutenant said nervously. Teplov was obviously confident of his authorizations.

Belik realized that this should not surprise him. Teplov was here to take over this operation. He would be expected to reconnoiter the territory before joining battle in it. Belik drank down what was left of his tea and went into his private lavatory. There he took four large breaths on his inhaler, straightened his tunic, and constructed an expression of self-assurance. He hoped that there would be no tremor in his voice.

When he reappeared, his staff came to attention. Nobody could fail to recognize the importance of this occasion. Belik saluted and went through the door to his private office and Teplov. Normally this place was his refuge. GRU swept it of bugs weekly, which made it feel exceptionally safe. V. I. Belik's fortress. It was a pleasant room, mahogany desk backed by windows, portraits of Lenin on one wall and of the defense minister on another. In the corner between the two portraits were a pair of plastic chairs, a lamp, and a small table. Opposite was the case containing Belik's books, his classics, his textbooks, even his precious collection of Dorothy L. Sayers novels and his *samizdat* Solzhenitsyn.

The view from this window was bucolic, green hills rising to distant mountains. Belik did his important thinking before that view. The space before the window was the most private place in a very private room.

Teplov stood there with his back to the office. On Belik's desk lay his opened briefcase. He neither spoke nor turned around.

"Colonel Teplov?"

He seemed to be studying the horizon; still he did not turn around. Belik knew that the performance was intended to intimidate—which it must not. He brought an image of Ludmilla's admiring face to his mind to give him strength.

"Colonel, you are standing in a spot of historic importance to the socialist peoples. Looking out that very window I conceived Black Magic."

"The military portion. The rest is mine, General."

"Well, of course, but—"

"Too bad you can't work in an ELF field out here. It must be painful to have Sverdlovsk Paradise so close. I could hardly bear to leave the aerodrome. It will be such a blessing when we can all live in Fields!"

His *apparatchik* suit—yards of blue serge, wrinkled back, shiny elbows—made him look the minor official, and his pomaded hair marked him as a man of proletarian tastes. He reeked of cheap cologne.

It was ridiculous, surely, to fear such a man.

Perhaps, but also wise. This, after all, was the very man Belik had been attempting to slice to political bits.

Belik put his own briefcase down on top of Teplov's. "I suppose you're here to coordinate further with me."

"I am here to work. As soon as my own quarters are prepared I will move to them. In the meantime we will have to share this space."

"You intend to remain in Sverdlovsk?"

"As long as necessary."

Belik went around the desk and started gazing out the window. He and Teplov were shoulder to shoulder. "See that birch forest just beyond the Institute grounds? Black Magic is there, hidden from American satellites." Belik liked looking toward the vast installation beneath the forest, thinking of all the effort that his group had buried in the rich Russian soil.

"I wish to visit the antenna as soon as possible, General."

That was blunt, but adroitly done. There was no easy way around it. Belik decided to parry. "Have you got a General Clearance?"

"Yes."

"Too bad. You need a Special/Technical to get in. That has to be granted by the General Staff Intelligence Operations Group."

"I also have a First."

So much for parrying. In the whole Soviet system there were not a hundred First clearances. No doubt the only thing off limits to this particular colonel was the Chairman's toilet, and perhaps not even that. Belik reached around behind him and pressed the intercom. "Tell Major Florinsky that the colonel and I are going out to the installation."

During the first ten minutes in the car nothing was said. Belik was glad; conversational exchanges with Teplov were obviously full of peril. As the car rumbled along the unpaved road between the Institute and the hamlet of Pyshma where the birch forest began, Belik tried to ascertain the full reason Teplov was here. How dangerous was he now, at this moment?

He must suspect the problem with the antenna. Certainly he would like it if such a thing were true, in case his own end of the operation collapsed. "Belik wasn't ready," he could say. "He sent us in too soon." Yes, getting what the bureaucracy called "coverage" must be the immediate intention.

In the hideous suit and worse homburg Teplov looked like some grim apparition from the Soviet past—which in a sense he was. He belonged to Andropov and the other old ones; he was their instrument.

The car slowed for the wooden bridge across the Shuvakish. The marshy little river drifted sluggishly beneath the boards. On the far bank some naked peasant boys capered and shouted, their laughter sounding like bell notes in the warm air. Why amid such scenes of peace must men do evil deeds?

"Beautiful country, isn't it, Colonel?"

"Lazy country. Those boys should be doing some useful work."

Belik said nothing. The workers called people like Teplov "Moscow dreamers." Outside Sverdlovsk Paradise the Urals district was like the rest of Russia. It functioned hardly at all. Komsomol, Young Pioneers—nothing like that remained intact. These kids were on their own and quite happy about it from the look of them.

The car roared through Pyshma, raising dust among the

wooden houses. A stone hit the door on Teplov's side with a thud. Belik saw a flowered dress flash between two houses. Other than that there was no sign of the inhabitants. He made a note that Pyshma was due another show of force.

"Didn't somebody just throw a stone?"

"The tires must have knocked it up. The people hereabouts love the army. If they were to throw anything it would be a flower."

Teplov lapsed again into silence.

They began the last kilometer of the journey, through the birch forest. Belik wished that he could use his inhaler. He concentrated on breathing as easily as possible and concocting some way to keep Teplov from learning the truth.

On the underground railway he realized that there was no way to do it. Gorkin's men were working full-time recalibrating the antenna. The place would be roaring.

There was only one thing to do with Teplov, and Belik was not certain that he could bear it. He had his fantasies of killing his opponents, but in practice it was hard to imagine. To be cruel one must be either indifferent or fanatical. Belik looked again at his adversary. The essential seedy *apparatchik*. Perfect. On the backs of such men Russia was built as certainly as on the backs of her workers and her soldiers.

But he was being foolish again, to think of Teplov as a mere state functionary. Remember, please, Valentin Ilyich, he is in costume. This man is as dangerous as a wolfhound, and far more wanton than any animal. And he is at war with you.

Very well. In war soldiers kill or get killed. It is nothing more than that.

No, it is more. Much more. Rattling along the tunnel to his beloved ELF installation, under the tremendous pressure that Teplov's presence generated, Belik regretted even more deeply what he had unleashed by championing ELF. He had created a monster, and its head was Pyotr Teplov.

The military aspect was now a minor factor. America Paradise was what had possessed the imagination of the Politburo. It must have been heavenly for the Chairman when he was mobbed by the workers of Sverdlovsk. Did he dream of being mobbed by the workers of Detroit and Flint? Of course. An unpopular leader must crave such love, never mind how falsely it had been won.

The train rattled along the tunnel.

At the moment of Black Magic's success its leader would be the most popular man in Soviet history. He looked at Teplov, sitting there so staunch and crazy.

If I became Chairman, and that man died . . . there would be no America Paradise, and no Russia Paradise either.

On the other hand, if he takes over all of Black Magic, he will be able to do exactly as he pleases.

He is not here for any innocent coordinating task. He is here to make a coup.

One of us has to die. For the sake of humanity, let it be him.

7

HARMON WISER WATCHED THE man across his desk as he might watch a lethal animal. Omar Jones spoke quietly, as if it was necessary for him to compel attention. He was high Agency, assistant to the Deputy Director of Operations. His smooth boy's face was genially lined by laughter; one eye had been put out and he wore a patch. His brown hair was thinning, but the good eye was as quick as ever. Harmon did not know how Omar had lost his eye—there were as many stories about that as there were people to tell them. Omar never spoke of it.

"I swear I don't see why Winter doesn't come to us if he's in as much trouble as you say." The brow over the sighted eye rose. "We're still good people at the Agency; we protect our own."

"You sound hurt. You ought to be glad."

"Why so?"

"It's less expensive this way."

"Ouch. Surely you didn't invite me here just to say a thing like that."

"I want you to give Paul some help."

"Will he take it from me? After all, I fired him."

"Do it without his knowledge."

"Oh, now Harmon, that kind of thing hardly ever works."

"Just signal the *residentura* that you're concerned."

"That'll only make them act more quickly."

"It'll scare them off." Harmon was surprised that Omar was being so difficult. Obviously CIA concern with Winter's welfare would make KGB hesitate.

"They want him too badly."

"So far their approaches have been relatively subtle." Harmon gestured toward the spike aerosol, which was lying on the desk between the two men. "They didn't want us to know about it."

"That's routine when they assassinate our people on American soil. Otherwise the State Department grumbles and farts. But why Winter? He wasn't into much. He never even played cards with them as far as we know."

"Maybe there's something to the secret weapon."

"Hogwash. ELF is a naval communications system. Nothing more."

"The Pentagon's Psychotronic Task Force puts out some pretty astonishing data about Sverdlovsk."

"The more psychotronic mumbo jumbo the Russians waste their time on, the better off we are."

"That's an opinion, Omar. Only an opinion."

It occurred to Harmon that Paul Winter might know something that was embarrassing to Omar himself. If ELF was real, then a very unfortunate mistake had been made by the man who bartered Shazdeh Hassan to KGB.

Harmon himself had played a certain role in that particular affair. KGB had paid a lot of money for what at the time had seemed a sack of ashes. He looked long at Omar Jones. The good eye regarded him as steadily. A suggestion of a smile came into the face.

"I think you're getting the picture, old man. You win

some and you lose some. They were ahead of us on that one.''

"You're saying it's not hogwash after all? It's serious?''

Omar crossed his legs, leaned back in his chair, and folded his arms.

"Are we in an endgame with them?''

The slight smile faded slowly. "There's a great deal I can't discuss. Let's say that Sverdlovsk isn't a complete washout for them.''

"If you know as much as that implies, why ignore Winter?''

"There are several projects going forward at their Institute of Bioenergetics. ELF hasn't been one of our top tracking priorities, but as soon as I get back to Langley I intend to issue a revision of the study protocols on Sverdlovsk that will put some emphasis on the subject. And I intend to suggest a new approach to the investigation of the events at Ellsworth. Perhaps external influence of the crewmen is a possibility.''

"So Paul won't have died in vain.''

The face dissolved into a frown. "You were always such a dramatist. Maybe he won't die at all. One Winter is worth six of their geeks.''

"He's frightened because of the woman. The guy's having a very rough time. He loves her and he's probably killed her.''

"That should be motivating.''

"He isn't at his best scared. I know the man.''

"I can't help it if Paul uses bad judgment.''

"Is that what it says in his file?''

"Hell no, it says worse. Funny farm. You oughta know. Bury him alive—wasn't that your phrase?''

"I'm going to try to help him even if you don't.''

"All the dirt will come out if you do that. Your part in it, too, Harmon. It's all in the B file. Selling Hassan to KGB . . . worse than selling Einstein to Hitler.''

"I can stand the disclosures. I sell disinfo to KGB all the time. It'll look like routine."

"For you, maybe. I might have a directorship riding on this. Not to mention my freedom. I could go to jail, quite frankly."

"Who'll nail you? Nobody's clean enough."

The smile again. "That's a fact. But I'll be nailed. You could blow me and a lot of other people to pieces playing sweetheart with Paul."

"This is getting too heavy, Omar. I think we ought to put a stop to it before we end up choosing our weapons." He wanted to get Omar Jones out of his office. This conversation had made his decision to support Paul, and he was eager to get started. The lifetime of a man in Winter's position could usually be measured in hours. Wiser set up supersensitive operations like this from an apartment on 53rd Street where he was known as Hank Gresham, a fabrics wholesaler. The place was a hive of electronic equipment. From there he could enter the telephone system via a sensitive magnetic induction device that made bugging all but impossible. This equipment was in a floating room which was itself impervious to cavesdropping. Harmon wanted to get to it—now.

He looked at his watch. "It's six. We'd best say goodbye. Go down with me?"

"Very acceptable to me. I can get the eight o'clock shuttle."

It pleased Harmon that Omar Jones was willing to be seen on the street with him. Of course it would lead the other side to speculate that CIA was interested in Paul, at least a little.

As they left the office Harmon reflected that Winter meant a lot more to him than he had allowed himself to feel. He had always claimed to be as cynical about Paul's invincible decency and as awed by his skill in the field as everybody else was. But it wasn't quite that way. There was something fine about Winter, something that his fellow hu-

man beings ought to protect—and if that was letting senti-
ment get in the way of professionalism, so be it.

He remembered how ruthlessly he had tried to take the
woman from Paul. Hell, she was stunning. Paul loved her
. . . as in most other things his taste in women was superb.
The greed of Harmon's attempt never occurred to Paul. The
man was maddening that way. As often as not he simply
didn't know when people were being bad.

Like the setup in Tehran. KGB had wanted Hassan and
his device very badly. Once Paul was out of the way the sale
went forward smoothly. And why not? Who knew the
harm—then?

"I owe the man," he said in an undertone as they stood
waiting for the elevator.

"Who doesn't? I kicked the bastard around in Laos something awful."

Harmon had heard about that particular horror. It hadn't
been expected that Winter would survive his mission to
Laos at all. But he had—for eighteen months of what must
have been absolute agony. Winter's reports were famous—
laconic radioed messages every twenty-four hours. Troop
positions and movements, orders of battle, valuable stuff.
And never a complaint.

He had walked into the embassy one morning during the
fall of Saigon and requested airlift for himself and twenty-
five hundred Hmong tribesmen he had guided across North
Vietnamese territory all the way from Laos.

How he had accomplished this was still not known.

Nobody ever told him that his beloved General Dong was
a Malay-Chinese opium runner and his Laotians a simple
gang of smugglers. It certainly never occurred to Paul. He
just didn't think that way. Probably couldn't.

The arrival of the elevator interrupted Harmon's recollec-
tions. "I think there's room for two more," he said as they
pushed in. Harmon had chosen this floor for his office carefully. It was high and he liked that, but more important the

elevator was express from here to the lobby. He hated elevators and preferred his trips to be fast.

They were moving smoothly along when Harmon smelled a heart-stopping odor of overheated wiring. Simultaneously there were voices raised at the back of the car. "Something's getting hot!" The crowd rustled and squirmed in the small space. People were still maintaining their fronts. "It's real hot now!" The passengers against the back wall of the car began to press forward. From the rear of the car there came a loud crackling sound. The odor of melting plastic mixed with the sharp scent of burning wood.

"Get us out!" Omar looked at Harmon, his one eye steady and calm. Blue smoke began to billow around them. The jammed car was swaying now as it dropped. People were pushing and shoving, trying to avoid touching the smoking walls.

Harmon Wiser was not the first to scream, but he did it when the flickering blue flames came up around his shoes. People started stomping and dancing. Somebody jammed on the emergency call and the alarm bell began ringing, the sound adding to the agony of enclosure. Hands hammered on the door. Bodies slammed into him. His feet felt as if the skin were being sanded off. One man's screams rose to shrieks. He burst up out of the seething crowd, his pants blazing, leaped on backs and necks and shoulders, and then fell among them. Others caught fire. Harmon could see that Omar's mouth was open but could not hear his shouts. His patch was gone, his raw eye horrible to see. The eyeball wasn't gone; the lid had been cut off.

Something hit Harmon's head so hard he saw flashes. Then bright yellow light filled the smoke. The screams rose to a desperate fever of agony. Harmon wanted madly to get out, to get away from the fire and the burning people. It couldn't happen like this, not now, surely he—oh. *He* was burning. Burning, yes, that's what hurt, it was like hot water going down his back. It made him leap forward; there was no way not to try to run from it. A woman, scorched black, her head blazing furiously, fell from above amid a shower of sparks, and every spark was a brand hissing into his own crackling flesh.

My God, I—blind pain, the dim realization that the floor was cracking, opening, the car dropping its cargo of humanity into the basement as indifferently as an unloading hopper.

Silence follows tragedy. In New York it is broken by sirens and the yammer of police radio units. That soon happened, but the dead never knew.

8

THE ROOM WAS DARK and small and reminded Paul of a prison cell. Down the hall a radio played gospel music, the energetic rhythms contrasting oddly in Paul's ear with the message of loss. Catherine lay on the bed with her legs spread apart, her hair fanning out around her face. It was brutally hot, and since the windows overlooked a light well, no air moved. The overhead fan buzzed loudly, the blades hardly turning. From beyond the door there came the sound of slow footsteps, one of the Hotel Excelsior's aged passengers on his way to a confrontation with the bathroom at the end of the hall.

"Will you please quit cleaning that gun!"

He snatched his hands away as if the pistol had gone off. She was right; he had been cleaning it for hours. "I'm sorry."

She had been as still as a summer-dulled swan. Now she raised herself up and sat on the edge of the bed. Her body glowed in the shadowy room, impossibly beautiful. The vision of her like that filled him with desire.

"You're sorry," she said in a harsh voice. "Truer words, Paul—"

Her tone hurt; it was a blow. "Don't, Catherine." Despite everything he did not feel he had lost the right to her love, not quite.

She rose from the bed and paced to the window, her lithe nakedness an assault on her surroundings. Without her this place would just have been drab. Her presence made it sad. "It's seven," he said. "Would you like something to eat?"

"Yeah. But not room service. Fried rats I can do without."

"I'll go out."

"Go get some Greek food at Molfetas. I'd like a little souvlaki."

It was what she ate in the theater. He had seen the cartons from Molfetas on her dressing table. He leaned down and kissed her hair, inhaling its soft aroma. For the briefest instant she pressed herself back against him. They stood together in the hot dark, two as alone as one.

"I have a plan," he whispered. How histrionic he sounded. And what a lie was hidden in his words. They implied some salvation when in truth they meant even greater danger.

Her only response to his statement was to move away from him. He wondered if she knew their true position, that they had become victims in the deepest sense: instead of trying to escape their enemy, they were going to have to plunge into the depth of his redoubt and expend their lives on a gesture.

He drew on his jacket. His suit was now wrinkled. In a matter of hours his elegance, the smoothness of silk against skin, the rare scent of his sandalwood cologne, the sleek tailoring, had all been swept away by the heat and the desperate escape to this hole. The shabby old man was plain to see.

"I'm going," he said. "I'll tell you the plan when I get back."

"Fine. And Paul, one more thing."

"Yes?"

"While you're gone, please find some way to stop feeling

sorry for yourself. I'd like it if I could have some confidence in you.''

"Yes.''

He would once have risked his life for her supper, but such an act was out of the question now. No matter what he thought of himself, his life had become important to others, millions of them—the whole country, in fact. Downstairs in the filthy, urine-smelling lobby of the hotel he went into the phone booth and called the Sequoia.

"Mr. Winter, we've been terribly concerned! Where are you?''

"Excelsior.''

There was shocked silence on the other end of the line.

"It was all we could find on short notice.''

"Let me put Mr. Blankenship on the line. He's been frantic to talk to you, Mr. Winter.'' There was a click, the buzz of a telephone, and the manager of the Sequoia answered. "Mr. Winter! I cannot say how sorry we all are. The authorities tell us it started in the wires.'' His voice droned on . . . nobody hurt . . . but your clothing . . . effects . . . "Well, of course we'll replace it all. Just a list for the insurance . . . anything will do!'' And finally: "When are you coming home?''

"This evening. Please send somebody out to get Catherine some food at Molfetas and a bottle of Beaujolais. Serve it here. We'll come home afterward.''

"Yes, sir. We know exactly what she wants. Just leave it to us.''

"Thanks, Blankenship.''

Paul hung up. Two causes were served: one, Catherine would get her meal; two, the ones who had undoubtedly listened to that call would make plans to do their act of mercy while he and Catherine were in transit between hotels.

But there would be no such transit. Paul had chosen the Excelsior because it had a unique feature: an abandoned underground shopping arcade that opened into the 34th Street subway station. From there a pedestrian tunnel led uptown to the 42nd Street station. A two-stop trip on the Flushing line took you to Grand Central. Other pedestrian tunnels went north from the station, ending up at 47th and Madison Avenue. From there a quick walk to the British Empire Building at Rockefeller Center enabled one to enter the belowground maze there and get to the Sixth Avenue line. A two-stop ride let you off at 34th Street a few hundred feet from where you had started twenty minutes before.

Unless they knew the city very well, his pursuers would be lost by that maneuver.

The Excelsior looked a poor choice. Its main lobby and kitchens both opened onto 34th Street. There was no access to the adjoining buildings. It was taller than its neighbors, making the roof a trap.

The KGB *residentura* was a highly professional organization, but they were used to a life aboveground. The temptation of diplomatic license plates was great; they moved through the city in their DPL-identified Chevys and Fords, Russia's private police force in America, parking where they pleased and doing as they wished.

The subways were full of nonwhites, and the Soviets found them scary. *Chernomazy* they called them, niggers. Soviet officers did not mix with the people of the subways, but Paul did. He returned to the room to be with Catherine; he had been gone six minutes. His limit was ten. Above all he did not want to give KGB a chance to abduct her. That would be the end of the game, checkmate for him.

His instructions to her had been simple. Do not open the door for anybody, not even for me. If they don't have a key, they won't have time enough to get in before I come back.

If they do have one, they'll have to get past the night latch and—if Catherine could do what she claimed she could—a fusillade from the gun Paul had left her.

He put his key in the door, paused, and gave the three soft raps he had promised. Then he pushed open the door, expecting it to hang on the night latch. "You left the latch off," he said as he entered. "We've both got to start remembering how important those details are."

She wasn't there.

"Catherine!"

Quiet. No sense in shouting. He fought for presence of mind, tried to think.

What woe.

His flesh crawled; he felt filthy for what he had done to her. He would trade himself for her. That was his only choice. He turned to the door, mentally reviewing how to go about this. The *residentura* was in the Empire State Building. He would go there.

No. The raw truth was that there could not be a trade. He had no choice but to continue the mission.

His grief at this realization made him stagger. Sweat poured from his body. The hypnotic whirring of the fan seemed to mock him.

Catherine had taken out her popper; she was going to die in agony for her scruples. Die in agony.

He literally battled himself not to scream. Grief has an end, but this was not mere grief. There would be no end to this; it was sorrow made flesh, the heart beating guilt, the black, corroding snow of conscience stifling all happy thoughts. She was dying, and he was to blame.

There came a knock at the door. "Yes," he said, "please come in." Even now he had taken the weak way. He had stood here feeling guilty when he should have been running like a creature possessed, taking his escape route, going west to the confrontation in South Dakota.

But no, he had remained here a moment too long. It would almost be a relief to feel the pain of their tortures, to be dismantled and destroyed. They would torture, of course, to discover what he had said to Harmon.

It was Tommy Barrow with food.

"I see you've acquired a taste for Molfetas's cooking from Miss Harris," he said as he stepped into the room. Paul stared at him as he might at a dream image. "I just got two of everything. She didn't have a chance to eat hers before the show started." He glanced around the room. "Well, we'll have you out of this mess in no time, Mr. Winter. Mr. Winter? Good Lord!"

Paul took the hall at a run, hammered on the elevator button, and then burst onto the fire escape. "Before the show started," his mind roared in time to his breath as he clambered down the rickety iron steps. The poor little idiot is at the theater. At the theater! He leaped down the final story to the street, staggered, and began to run. Across the street a man started pacing him, the silhouette moving fast against lighted store windows. A gray Chevy pulled up at the corner. "Taxi!"

Paul jumped into a Checker that was just getting ready to draw away from the light. A man and a woman were in the back. "Out," the man said in the too-clear tones of the habitually arrogant. These people couldn't be offered money; they were obviously rich. The driver turned around.

"What the fuck? Get outa my cab, I got a fare."

"Matter of life or death."

"Come on," the young man said. "We're going to be late as it is." From the girl, on whose side Paul was crouching, there came a wild tinkle of laughter. She was terrified.

"I must get to the Music Box Theatre or my wife will die. She forgot her medication."

"Goddamn it. Driver, let him off at the Music Box. We'll walk to the Belasco from there."

"I'll pay." Paul opened one of the jumpseats, folded himself into it. "Please forgive me. I'm terribly sorry about this." Inwardly he could not help but be proud of her courage. He should have been furious with her but he could not manage it. Anger was slow to come to Paul, especially toward one he loved so much.

The cab stopped for a light at 42nd and Sixth and Paul slipped out into traffic, opening the door only a little, crawling under the vehicle, avoiding the hot muffler as best he could, then running at a crouch to the curb. As the light changed and the cars began to move, he rose to his feet and disappeared into Bryant Park. Lovers had once owned this place. No more; addicts cuddled on the benches and bums strolled the walks.

Then Paul was through the park. He descended into the tunnel that led to the Seventh Avenue IRT at Times Square. He moved fast in the tunnel, his feet echoing on the floor. A few people were ahead of him and a few entered behind him. There was no way to tell whether he was eluding his tail or not, but then there was never any way to tell.

He got in the last car of a local, ran ahead two cars, and held a door with his foot. Once, twice the motorman slammed the doors on him. Then in annoyance he opened them for a further instant. Paul jumped back onto the platform and left the station at once.

He had been moving fast and he was not in the best shape. His chest had begun to ache and his body was chilled by sweat and fear. He went quickly through the streets toward Duffy Square, crossed against traffic at the convergence of Seventh Avenue and Broadway, and arrived before the Music Box just as the last of the night's patrons was filing in.

"Anything left?" he asked at the ticket window.

"Standing room."

That was unfortunate. Paul had hoped that the house was sold out. No such luck; if they were coming here, they were going to get in. For that matter they might already be in. In any case Paul couldn't risk giving even this man too much to remember of him. It was better that they have to guess at his presence in the Music Box. Without a further word he left the lobby and went into the alley. He was known backstage. Bill Dodson would let him in.

"Come to see the show, Mr. Winter?"

"Yeah."

"I think Cathy's seats are being used by the house." He looked pleased. "They got sold."

"Good news is bad news. I'll wait for her in her room."

He went past Dodson into the dimmer reaches of the theater. It was a three-set play and the area around the stage was cluttered with an orderly chaos of props. Immediately behind the stage—dressed as a living room, circa 1936—was a garden, dark now, to be moonlit for act two. The prop men would roll the massive rotating stage around to put the garden in front at the end of the act. They would then re-dress the living room to be a bedroom for act three. Backstage might look chaotic, but everything—chairs, desk, bedstead—was in an exactly planned location, waiting to be placed on the stage that was now in use.

Paul arrived at the stage-left opening. Immediately before him was the chair where Catherine would sit when she had her extraordinary act-one confrontation with Jenny. From twelve inches behind her head Paul intended to try to talk her off the stage.

He could almost feel the tension of the house as Catherine began to move through the set, the silence broken by her occasional half-stifled sobs. At any moment she might keel over, the finger of truth plunging into the illusion of the theater. "Actress Catherine Harris collapsed and died on the stage of the Music Box Theatre last night. A heart attack—"

The doorbell rang. Catherine looked stage right, where Jenny stood behind a door. Catherine went to the door with a little cry of relief, snatched it open. "Daddy! Oh, it's you." She stood frozen as Jenny entered the set. As best he could Paul watched the house. In a few seconds more Catherine would be in the chair. The audience was rapt, but beyond the first few rows it was too dark to see much. Every visible face was attentive to the play.

Jenny and Catherine stood ten feet apart. "I don't want you to stay here."

"I loved him too, Amy."

Catherine moved to stage center. She glanced toward the chair. "Did Dad show you what he left?"

"Amy, what does it matter? He's dead and we've got to continue. Even me." She strode toward Catherine, who

113

drifted closer to stage left. Beyond her shoulder Paul could see the house, those anonymous faces, expressions so richly alive. He had never actually looked at an audience from this vantage point before. They looked so very *aware,* so much a part of what was happening on stage.

"Janet, I can't bear you right now. I can't!" She pressed her fists to her eyes, then slumped, as Paul had seen her do a dozen times, and stared toward the chair. With a defeated little shrug she threw herself into it. "I always do what you want, don't I?"

Jenny smiled, walked forward. Paul had stepped up to the chair and Jenny must certainly see him. No inappropriate expression crossed her face though. "Don't scream," Paul whispered on Jenny's line. Catherine's head jerked slightly. "It's me, Paul."

Catherine delivered her own line. "Why won't you leave me alone! Why must you stalk me like this, Janet?"

"You've got to get off of that stage, darling. Please, get sick, do anything, but get off."

Again Catherine delivered her line. "Don't you understand what a life really is? How delicate? How easily broken? You always have to get under the surface." Her voice grew thick with anger and disgust. "You had to tell him! To *tell* him!"

"Catherine, at least stay in motion on the stage! They'll kill you any second in that chair."

"He had gone an immense distance. Farther than you could bear to let him go, Janet."

"Catherine, I beg of you. At least move!"

Jenny Hurst was glaring directly at Paul, using her stage expression of anger to communicate with him. He didn't blame her; by all standards what he was doing was an absolute outrage. Catherine had never been discussed between them, but Paul had always assumed that Jenny was a sort of rival—for Catherine's loyalty if not her passion. Jenny took a much more direct view. She was consumed with jealousy.

Paul looked past her face and yet again into the audience.

114

Standing room was invisible, as were the back rows of the orchestra. The assassin would naturally be at the back of the theater; there was no problem of range, not even with that dart gun Harmon had demonstrated. The place was claustrophobic. Seeing that Catherine was going to ignore him, Paul retreated a little into the wing.

The first act drew to a close. At last the curtain dropped. Working lights went up and the stagehands began turning the sets. Jenny Hurst swarmed toward Paul, her eyes like small chips of glass. In her way Jenny was a beautiful woman, but not when she was this mad. Behind her Catherine came hurrying along.

"What the hell are you doing here, you stupid fool?"

"Jenny, there's been a family emergency. Catherine has to come with me. Put Nell in for the rest of the show."

"No, Paul."

"Catherine, you can't go back out on that stage. It's suicide!"

"What's he saying, Cath? Has sex made him senile or what?"

He could not restrain himself; he grabbed Catherine by the shoulders. "Somebody get Dodson," Jenny yelled.

"Catherine, you're so young—you don't know, you don't understand—"

"Curtain in five minutes."

"Oh, shit, Cath, we've got to change." The security man appeared. "Dodson, Mr. Winter is drunk or crazy. Please deal with him. Come on, Cath."

"Catherine—"

"Mr. Winter—"

"Relax, Dodson. I'm as sober as death. Unfortunately."

"Perhaps it would be best if you went out front, Mr. Winter."

"No, I'll stay out of Jenny's way. What she doesn't see won't make her crazy."

Dodson allowed the edges of a smile. "If she asks me, I'll tell her you passed out."

"That she'll believe." Paul looked toward the door to the dressing rooms, tried to remember if there was a direct exit to the alley. There was, down the hall past Dodson's station—and it had been unguarded for two minutes.

Paul burst into Catherine's dressing room to find Jenny hanging over her like a great vulture. He was too surprised not to reveal his disgust in his expression.

"Get out," Jenny hissed.

"I'll turn my back but I'm not leaving. Catherine is in danger."

"Paul, stop it! If those people wanted to kill me I'd be dead! If they even exist."

"If they *exist!* You must have taken leave of your senses. You saw our hotel room."

"Tommy Barrow said that it was the wiring. Not Russian agents. Wires!"

Jenny put on her bra and panties and stalked through the connecting door into her own dressing room. Catherine stretched, cupped her breasts in her hands. "I really wish you hadn't done that, Paul. It was very embarrassing."

"For the dyke. You probably enjoyed it."

She shook her head. Paul was forcefully reminded by the resignation and understanding in the movement that Catherine was a more frightened person than she was allowing herself to seem.

"Catherine, I'm sorry. I did what I did out there for your own good. I see now that I can't stop your finishing the show. It was stupid of me to try. But I'm going to stay backstage for the rest of the evening. If I can help you, I will."

She was getting her clothes on. He went close to her. "You're incredibly beautiful. I think you're driving me crazy."

She laughed. "I think so!"

For act two he stationed himself stage left again. This was a semi-box set, partially enclosed, but there were entrances in both wings. Paul tried to remember which one Jenny used so that he could avoid her.

"Curtain in one minute."

There was a murmur in the shadows, the sound of lips touching lips, a girlish laugh. Jenny and Catherine appeared a few feet from Paul. Catherine reached out and brushed his face with her hand. Intent on her entrance, Jenny had not seen him.

"Places, please, ladies."

The last of the stagehands departed the set. A path of glowing tape guided Jenny and Catherine to their opening positions.

"Curtain going up!" There was a whir of machinery as the curtain rose. The sea of faces appeared. In the rapidly dropping house lights Paul caught not even a glimpse of trouble. Before him the stage was suffused with an eerily realistic glow of moonlight. There were as always gasps from the audience; it was a superb set.

Paul realized that if he continued this way he was going to be standing here doing nothing when Catherine sank to the floor. Action was demanded. He had to find the inner resources of courage and imagination that would lead him to the right plan. No, it was easier than that. The plan was obvious; he just needed the guts to execute it.

"The issue is never love," Catherine said on the stage. "The issue is possession." Thus began her monologue, the center of the play. At the moment she started to speak, Paul became aware that he was not alone.

The figure was more still than any watching stagehand would be. That was what had concealed him and what now revealed him. How long he had been there Paul could not tell. Possibly from the beginning of the act, possibly for the entire evening. Attempting to seem indifferent, Paul began to move around to the other side of the stage. His own life was at this moment in even greater danger than Catherine's.

A few feet away stagehands were working to re-dress the offstage set from living room to bedroom. It was a choreography of mayhem, almost silent, being carried out under dim lights. Paul moved to the rear of the set, trying to appear to focus on the work.

He stopped when he saw another of the figures in the far wings. So there were two. No doubt even more in the halls, in the alley, in the street.

Paul was frantic now. He had no backup to call on, no little radio to pull out of his pocket and whisper into. On the stage Catherine's voice rose with passion and intensity, the words ringing through the silenced hall. "You infected him with death. It was your own special brand, but it was just as real in the end as all the others. I will never submit to you!"

Paul looked around the stage house, then up into the framing of the set. Above the arms that formed the entrances to the stage itself was the head block of the counterweight system that flew the garden backdrop. Paul could climb onto the counterweight and from there reach the head block. It was a frighteningly dangerous alternative, but he felt sure that it was the only one. They would never allow him to get to the electrical switchboard and black out the house. He heaved himself up. The scenery shook, and Jenny glared into the dark entryway.

Paul did not care. He was in a strange state, a kind of trance of martyrdom. Duty or not, he was almost hungry to die for Catherine. His eagerness frightened him. Over the years he had become rather sure that death is the end of self. "The awful rowing toward God," a poet had called it. He longed and feared to give his life for hers.

His weight on the system was causing the backdrop to move slightly. In the dark the audience probably wouldn't notice, but Jenny was getting furious.

If she had yet more reserves of fury she would in a few moments be using them also.

Paul grasped the head block and swung to the ceiling beam, causing the whole set to shudder. Jenny's voice quavered just a little. Catherine, getting ready to make her exit, seemed not to notice.

In seconds she would be off the stage and into their hands.

Paul had always hated heights and dared not look down now for fear of losing the tendril of madness that was enabling him to do this. He drew a breath and with the loudest bellow he could generate dropped to stage center.

It was twenty-odd feet. The air rushed up around him. He tried hard to land and roll. Then he lay still. As the audience erupted with shouts and the house lights went up, Paul methodically checked his legs and ankles. Nothing broken.

"It's him!" Jenny shouted when there was enough light to see. "Him!"

"Help me," he screamed. "Help me!" The audience answered with more shouts. Catherine rushed to him, threw herself down beside him.

"Oh, God, they—" She cut herself off when she realized that he was alive.

"Honey, get me to a hospital," he rasped. "Please— they—" He closed his eyes. Now she jumped to her feet, stared out at the audience.

"Is there a doctor out there," she shouted. "Somebody call a doctor!"

Dodson and a crowd of set decorators and stagehands rushed out. "Bring it down," somebody yelled, and the stage was cut off from the milling audience. In a moment the stage manager rushed past, ordering, "Hold the a.b.; I'm going out front." It was hard to enter and leave the proscenium with the heavy fire curtain in place. "Ladies and gentlemen," he said in an admirably calm voice, "please accept our apologies. Due to the nature of this accident we will not be able to continue the performance. You may obtain refunds at the box office as you leave the theater."

It took ten minutes for the Emergency Medical Service to appear. "You hurt anywhere?" one of the paramedics asked as they unfolded their stretcher.

"My leg—right leg."

"OK. Let's move him, Eddie."

Paul shouted as they lifted him onto the stretcher even though he was not in pain. Clasping Catherine's hand the whole way to make sure she remained close by, he let them carry him out to the ambulance. She was still in costume, a yellow flower-printed dress circa the thirties. Jenny Hurst had disappeared, no doubt to go back to her dressing room and throw shoes until she could sink something sharp into Paul's neck.

In the ambulance Paul kept his eyes closed. They moved through Midtown with siren screaming and lights blazing, but their progress even so was not rapid. Paul let Catherine stroke his face. Under her touch he found deep reserves of compassion within him. He was not angry at her for the danger she had caused. On the contrary, he found that he loved her courage and dedication.

When at length they arrived at Bellevue, it was time for the ambulance crew to be astonished. "It's a miracle," Paul said as they opened the doors. He trotted down the steps to the ground.

"Paul!" She embraced him, too relieved to join the general outrage.

"I must have been stunned," he said into furious faces. "I'm fine now." He turned to Catherine. "Let's go, kid." They left through the hospital's main entrance. Bellevue is a crowded place, and they were not molested there.

He wouldn't have minded their becoming invisible, but instead he had to hope that their pursuers had been unbalanced enough at the theater to lose track of them temporarily.

They got a cab on First Avenue and checked in at the UN Plaza Hotel. Inside they were surrounded by high gloss and luxury not quite so overstated that it was unendurable, but opulent enough to satisfy the third-world political wealth that patronized the place. To Paul the hotel's main advantage was that it happened to be close to where they were.

Their room overlooked the United Nations Building and the East River. Catherine went to the window, stood watching an oil barge being nosed upstream by tugs. Paul put his arm around her. "When I was in the ELF field with Jamshid

Rostram, I lost all control of myself. I became like—like another man's hand."

She seemed about to whisper something, then fell quiet again.

Paul had harmed her tonight. He wanted somehow to justify himself. "If the Soviet Union neutralizes our missiles with this thing, they will have won World War Three."

"Paul, I don't care about wars! Life goes on as long as we're not all blown up."

"What kind of life? What if they set up ELF generators in every city?"

"Science fiction."

"There is no science fiction anymore."

She laughed bitterly. "I love boats," she said, nodding toward the distant water. Her tone stabbed Paul deeply and he took her into his arms. He led her to the bed. "No, Paul. Absolutely not. Not the—" He kissed her lips. "Not the right damned moment!"

"I'm sorry."

"Paul, it's going to take time. You've got to understand that I hate what you did to me out on that stage. I hate what you did, and I'm trying very hard not to hate you as well. But it's going to take time. So tonight just leave me alone. Don't apologize and don't appeal. Just let me work out my feelings in my own way."

Her tone and expression were harder than he had known they could be.

She dropped her dress to the floor and strode into the bathroom. "I'm going to take a shower and go to bed. I suggest you do the same."

He stood at the window, listening to the water run. He was crying and he knew it and he damned himself for it. Didn't it matter to her that he had saved her life tonight?

He wanted a drink, dared not order one. He couldn't even recall the name he had used at check-in anyway. Frank something or other, wasn't it? Yeah, Frank Kennard. Where had that one come from? Some friend, probably, from a thousand years ago.

"God help me, I'm scared to death." He paced back and forth across the room. " 'Your shadow at morning striding behind you/Or your shadow at evening rising to meet you;/I will show you fear in a handful of dust.' "

A handful of dust.

He lunged over and turned on the TV. The idea of watching Johnny Carson had come like a handhold on an icy cliff. But it wasn't Carson, it was the news.

He sat staring at the screen, stunned. He knew without even hearing the name that Harmon Wiser was dead, that the fire had been meant for him. To KGB the deaths of the other forty people would have been of little concern.

Death by water, the welcomed death. Death by fire, the death most dreaded. Fear in a handful of ash.

Paul went to the door, looked out. Nobody. He had to get a paper from the lobby; the TV wasn't going to list names. Despite his near certainty he had to *know*.

As Paul hurried down the hallway to the elevators, he did not see the quiet figures in the far shadows. By the time the elevator was halfway to the lobby the door to the room had been snapped open.

Catherine did not even have a chance to scream.

9

JAMSHID LAY SO STILL in the sun that birds alighted beside him to peck at grass seeds. It had been two days since the ELF field had last risen out of the ground. He tried to keep believing that it would come again. The summer sun seemed to shine through his body, to warm the grass beneath it. He could imagine that he wasn't here at all as far as the world was concerned. He could imagine himself less than a shadow.

Only in the Field was he truly alive. In the blue freedom of another's mind he became solid and real. Sometimes he sipped their remembered pleasures or stole their dreams. If he chose he could judge them with the insight of a god and could punish with all the severity he thought fitting. With great severity. It felt like having a mouse in your hands, feeling it try to dig out as your palms came closer and closer, feeling it struggle, its muscles swarming with effort, and the crushing of the bones, the small cries, the body tossed aside, then the hunting of another. A way to spend the hours between the visits from the street.

Tehran . . . city of mourning and begging . . . so many

cars, so much money . . . cassette tape decks and Jordache jeans and Porsches and salmon sandwiches and Shah so bright in the sun. Shah so bright.

Jamshid narrowed his eyes and turned them to the pain of the sun. Then he opened them wide and looked until he wanted to scream. His body thrilled with the pleasure of suffering. This was real; this could be felt.

A sparrow wandered near his right hand. No, don't even let your heart beat in anticipation. Close your mind to the mind of the bird, yes, think on the errors of the breeze in the pines . . . think . . . nothing . . .

Caught! *Chee chee chee,* you darting-eyed darling. He felt the hot little thing in his palm, looked at it through sundazzled eyes. It was different from the birds of home, more delicate and intricate. Exactly the difference of America.

The creature stopped struggling. They often did that. Birds were less stupid than mice. When they lost hope they gave up. To rekindle its fervor Jamshid transferred his grasp to a single claw. It soon came back to life, striving with its wings for the heavens, for the blue freedom.

Blue freedom.

He let it go, watched it flutter into the blue freedom. "O Father, the sky is thine."

He wanted to be in the Field so badly that it made his head thunder and his skin crawl at the touch of the grass.

He raised his left hand and tasted the salt wetness of his skin, his sweat. The shadow of his hand before his face was like the shadow of a cloud, and like a cloud it was a portent of the great trial he sensed was coming. He got up from the meadow and looked out over the huge bright sweep of summer land, the smiling land of America.

Someone has discovered me. Someone is coming through the paths of that land, up the valleys and across the fields, coming like a shadow to do battle with me.

"I am thy battlement, O Satan, I am the edge of thy ax."

The fools of Allah praise me. They do not know the heart

of the magician. They would tremble to see the one he serves. "And down will come the houses of the just, and the Unseen One will rejoice."

He spat into the air.

Soon my guardians must give up their lives for me. Kajenouri, yes, he will throw himself into the dust for his beloved.

But what of Ismail?

He adores the sweetness of the world. Life to him is a delicate confection. But the one that comes, who comes like the shadow, who travels swiftly across the silent land—he is powerful. I will need both my guardians.

Kajenouri will die on the hill, far from home. But Ismail must lay down his life at my side.

I must do a thing to him. Ismail must come to love me more than he loves himself.

By American standards Rapid City was just another town—and to Ismail that made it all the more wondrous. He had known a lie of America before he actually came here. Seeing the bustling shops, the thriving children, the happy, laughing women, he could not believe anything but that Allah smiled most warmly upon this land. The addictions, the vices, the poverty of home were a terrible curse indeed compared to this.

Had the curse really been laid, as the Brotherhood taught, by these gay, innocent souls? Ismail could hardly believe it, but when he saw the fat American men in their pickup trucks with rifles slung in the rear windows, he thought perhaps it was so after all.

Just at this moment a group of American boys of Jamshid's age passed by on bicycles, their faces full of laughter, their voices clear and free. When American boys spoke one heard joy; when Jamshid spoke one heard many things. He had been so driven by hunger that he had whored in the streets at the age of eleven.

The light changed and Ismail stepped on the gas pedal,

forcing himself to do it gently. This sedate American traffic could madden a driver used to Tehran.

He watched two women coming down the sidewalk with shopping bags in their hands. They were laughing and talking. One wore shorts and a bit of cloth covering her breasts. The other was in blue jeans. Both smoked in public, as some women at home had done before the revolution. They were so beautiful, these women, and they appeared as available as fruits hanging from a tree. But there was something missing from them, a glaring, overwhelming error. They had no mystery of person. They were like the westernized Iranians in this respect, wearing their hearts on their faces.

Ismail remembered how people had scorned the Shah for revealing his true feelings in his face like a westerner. He came then to seem weak. Persians could endure a harsh ruler if he was noble. A weak bully they could not stand. And the eerie way Western ideas spread from the palace had frightened many of the people. It was horrible to see Iranians trade their subtlety and depth for jeans and phonograph albums. To be really Western it was necessary to open oneself to others as a man should open himself only to God.

Toward the end the Shah had emptied himself into his face. Khomeini by comparison—dense with secrets, God hidden in his heart—towered over the pallid, grinning Shah.

As mystery is not understood in the West, so the revolution was not understood. The revolution was a return to mystery, a renewal of man's long approach to Ahad, the one, the word of Allah. It was not fundamentally political, but in the West only the politics were noticed.

Ismail turned the corner again, now looking for a parking place on 6th Street. The meeting point with Pakravan was the Alex Johnson Hotel. He parked the car, put a dime in the meter, and began to cross the street. Music was being broadcast along the sidewalk by the American State Bank at the corner of 7th and Main. Ismail found this music both too simple and too captivating. The drubbing rhythms, the repeated melodies, seemed to reach a part of the soul that should not be touched by the hand of man—and rock music to teach the language of hell. At least this was not rock music playing in the street.

After the bright sunlight outside, the interior of the Alex Johnson was deliciously cool and quiet. It was far less luxurious than the Intercontinental or the Arya in Tehran had been before the revolution, but it had an atmosphere of comfort and friendliness not present at home. He crossed the lobby with its beamed ceiling and great country fireplace and went into the Landmark Restaurant. It wasn't crowded at one o'clock in the afternoon and Pakravan was easy to see, the only foreign face in the place.

"Sit down," he said. The waitress appeared immediately. "We're going to the salad bar."

"Anything to drink?"

"Iced tea for both of us."

Ismail said nothing. Icing tea was the custom here, so he would take it cold no matter what it might do to his stomach. Anything to avoid unwanted attention. They went to get their salad. "The pickles and the preserved vegetables are quite edible," Pakravan said. "I've been living on them these past few days." Ismail looked down at the profusion of green things. The lettuce was thick and dark-leaved, the preserved American corn fat, the radishes huge and moist —it was a wonder, this salad bar. The Americans were good farmers.

"Now," Pakravan said when they had their food, "why have you done something so dangerous as coming here?"

"The boy is going mad."

Parkavan took some of his food. "Ah. He is addicted to the Field."

"Something like that. Each night since the failure he has waited. He doesn't eat. He makes heathen prayers. I think that he is praying to Zoroaster."

"Allah will forgive him."

"You know the heart of Allah?"

"Our work is great, our spirits are weak. Allah will for-

give us all. Jamshid for his fear, you for your cowardice."
Pakravan's expression was hard, lips compressed. Ismail
could have struck that haughty face.

"I know the risk I have taken coming here. But I have
done it for the boy. Tell me for Jamshid's sake when the
Field will rise once more. And tell me above all why he
failed as he did. Was it his fault or was it the Field's? He
needs to know, for his sanity."

"You have your orders, Ismail Fekrat. Go back and follow them."

"Sit there waiting, you mean. I cannot! My first requirement is to preserve the life and good health of the boy. If I
must break the order to remain at all costs on station to do it,
then I must. The one supersedes the other."

"You have a legalistic mind. You will do as I say. I cannot answer your questions. But if you must for the sake of
the mission, lie to Jamshid. Tell him the Field was at fault."

"What about timing? When will it come again?"

"I do not know." He laughed around a mouthful of pick-
led melon. "Perhaps you will die up there—of old age."

Ismail ate some of the corn. It was very sweet and very
good. Afterward he put a small tomato in his mouth. This
had not the flavor of the ones grown at home, but it passed
down easily enough. Certainly this food was better than the
provisions at the cabin, the foul peanut butter and the tinned
things.

"I've got to buy more supplies. We need food."

"You want money from me, then. How much?"

Dare he ask for a few hundred dollars? If he wished he
could escape with that much. If. "I don't know—about three
hundred." He controlled his expression carefully. "We
don't want to come down more often than we must." Inwardly he was astonished with himself. Until this moment
he had not even been aware that he could dare to consider
leaving.

The old world, the one he was trying to defend, was not

as good as this one, the world of fat corn and happiness in the streets. He wanted to live in America, not to destroy it.

"Three hundred indeed. You don't fool me for a moment, Ismail Fekrat. I will take you out to the supermarket myself and buy you what you need. But money you do not need, not beyond the twenty-five I gave you when you arrived here."

Ismail had not thought himself so obvious. But Pakravan, after all, had been a SAVAK before his conversion. Those bastards knew people, knew them too well. Evidently the swine had not forgotten his early training.

"Let us go, then, I want to get back to the station before dark."

Pakravan reached across the table and clapped him on the shoulder. "Eat, soldier. Do you good." Ismail accepted the invitation willingly.

Pakravan came with him in the Ford.

When they reached Baken Park Shopping Center, Ismail wished that Pakravan were not so astute. He found that he very much wanted his chance to escape. The supermarket they entered was far more magnificent than any food shop he had ever seen at home. Not even in the Tehran bazaar was there such a profusion of superb produce. And there was air conditioning, as in all interior places in this city. Rapid City, Ismail concluded, must be one of the richest communities in the United States. No doubt they made much money from the missile installation, or the government provided special amenities to keep the troops content. Ismail wished that he could know whether Rapid City was unique or typical. If it was typical there could be no question about it: God did not hate this land.

He had seen little of the United States except Rapid City. They had trained in Afghanistan until the Soviet invasion and then moved to Kurdistan. Much had been taught them, including the English language, the American laws that would enable them to leave police custody if they were detained as illegal aliens, and all the details they needed to know to mount their operation. But they had been told little of the reality of life in America.

They had been flown from Iran to Switzerland and from there to Mexico. A long trip beneath the floor of a specially altered truck took the three of them from Mexico into Texas. There Captain Pakravan met them, and they flew at night to Rapid City in a small airplane.

He hurried along behind Pakravan as he selected tinned meats and vegetables and other supplies. Soon the cart was full. Pakravan paid and they returned to the Ford. "I'll ride with you to the point."

"You will? How will you return to town?"

"Oh, Ismail, my innocent one. I'm going to take this car back with me. No more trips to town for you—or away from it."

This told Ismail the answer to his question about America. It was all like this, all just as his grandfather had said. It was not the dark abode that the Brotherhood claimed it was. No, the dark abode was home.

He drove silently up the Sturgis Highway, through the sultry August afternoon. He remembered Iran in August, sweltering and indolent, everybody moving as little as possible. Then, toward the close of day, the family would move to the *bonigah* and sit eating pomegranates on the island between the crystal flow of the waters. Grandfather would recite the old poems. "Out of the ocean like a cloud go and wander—for without wandering you cannot become a pearl."

Out of the ocean . . . the car drummed on the hot road. Pakravan had turned on the radio, which made a crazy chatter in English too fast for Ismail to follow. Knowing what he now knew, Ismail experienced the most ineffable sensation of loneliness and loss. He was going to bring this land low. "It will be reduced to a sea of glass," their instructor had said. "Not a stone on a stone. And Russia, also, will be no more."

In the distance tall clouds stood like sentinels. The horizon was jagged, the Black Hills dark even in the brightest sunlight. What wondrous happiness the Persians might have found in land like this.

The First Sura obtained a new and powerful meaning for Ismail despite the fact that he had recited it every day of his life. "Praise be Allah the merciful . . . the Master of the Day of Doom . . ." Most of the people around him were living in their last hours. He; also. There was no provision to save their lives.

"Allah," he said aloud, causing Pakravan to stir in his seat. The name of God seemed as sweet as the kiss of ripe fruit. His whole heart and mind, the very stuff of his being, became prayer. The old Ford purred along, his ark in the wilderness. A pickup truck roared past honking; he was now driving conspicuously slow. On the fender of the truck was a sticker; "Love it or Leave It." In the rear window was the inevitable rack of rifles. Ismail sped up also, trying to keep to the customs of the road.

"I thought you wanted to delay."

"No. I want to hurry."

"You want to quit. You're being seduced by restaurants and groceries. It's too bad you fellows weren't given a little tour before being brought out here. You think America is all as beautiful as this. I ought to show you Bedford-Stuyvesant in New York or some of the other slums, or the Indian reservations south of here. You'd soon discover the correctness of what you are doing."

"You're mistaken about me." He knew that Pakravan would kill him instantly if he thought that he was a serious danger to the mission.

"I know the seductions of America. I spent years working with CIA. Sacrificing my honor for the greater glory of Islam."

"That's one way of explaining yourself."

Pakravan hissed through his teeth. Some said that he had been driven into the Brotherhood because he couldn't find a place for himself in the revolution—except against a wall.

Even he, perhaps, did not realize that the Muslim Brotherhood was the purity of the revolution, its hidden engine.

"I know the evil of the Americans. I know how they think. That is why I am here with you. And why I will take your car away. You cannot be expected to resist temptations you do not understand."

Ismail made the turn onto the winding dirt track that led to the place where they hid the car. Soon he stopped. Pakravan took out the keys. "Go back to your Brothers. Do your duty."

On his way up the mountain Ismail wept openly. He felt each tear as it rolled down his cheek, felt them in pride. They were treasured messages from his heart. "Those who struggle in Our cause, surely We shall guide them in Our ways; and God is with the doers of good." That was the only prayer he would speak on his doubts. The Christian will pray and listen for an answer. To the Muslim this is abomination; the prayer and its answer are one and the same.

As he clambered up the rough path, his rucksack dangling behind him, there came suddenly a roar from the sky. He looked up in time to see the fuselage of an F-4 flash past the tops of the pines.

What was this? There were no F-4s based at Ellsworth. That was a tactical aircraft. The nearest TAC squadrons were in North Dakota. What if this was a reconnaissance mission ordered down by SAC? Would Air National Guard helicopters come sailing up the passes soon?

Ismail reached the crest of the ridge that overlooked the road. Far below he could see the highway and on it the Ford crawling slowly back toward Rapid City. Beyond the road the plains spread out, miles of summer-yellow grass beneath a grandeur of clouds.

Their clearing was high in the hills, at the top of a long draw that spread into the valley in which the target Minuteman Launch Control Capsule was located. From this vantage point they had an eastward view of twenty kilometers.

Ismail made his way along Buck Mountain until he was well above their camp. He could see the little hunter's cabin nestled against a stand of pine. Twenty yards away was the earthen circle, the carefully measured locus of the ELF field. When it rose, the Field had their Circle as one limit and the distant LCC as the other.

To his surprise Ismail saw Jamshid lying out in the open. That was forbidden during the day. An errant part of his mind whispered, I hope they saw us. I hope that the F-4 will send troops.

When he arrived at the camp Jamshid was squatting, his hands resting on his knees. His eyes were half closed; he was deep in contemplation.

An arrow of longing pierced Ismail's heart. Angrily he stifled the emotion. Jamshid was filled with an enviable peace squatting there among the wild flowers. Around him swarmed a cloud of bees.

Ismail did not do as he intended and shout at Jamshid to get under cover. Instead he spoke softly, out of respect for the sacredness of the boy's being. "Jamshid, you're going to get a sting."

" 'Every bee that enters the hive speaks a thousand and one blessings over Muhammad.' "

"The *diktir* of Yunus will not protect you from real bees."

"So far you are wrong. What message do you bring?"

A great deal hung on Ismail's next words. He could perhaps destroy Jamshid. Even as he opened his mouth he wasn't certain of what he was going to say. "No new message. We continue as before."

He had been truthful; he had been kind. He loved Allah more than America, it seemed. "Come help me put away this food."

"You disturb my prayers for little reason, Brother."

"If that is true, forgive me. But you must realize that you can be seen from the air out here. There have been planes about."

"Those F-4s? That was a training mission. They were armed with air-to-air missiles."

"Come in anyway. The sun is too hot." He touched Jamshid's shoulder to encourage him. The bees buzzed and darted, adding their own tension to the moment.

"Move so quickly again, Ismail, and our little friends will not forgive you."

"I am responsible for you. Please come in."

"May Allah be with you, O Ismail."

"And with you, my Brother."

Jamshid reached up and took Ismail's hands. "The old man is preparing a meal." He drew himself to his full height before Ismail. He was still a boy, not yet sprouted up. "The shadows are growing longer. Will this be the night?"

Ismail could not answer. They walked together into the cabin. As soon as they entered, Ismail smelled the familiar and awful odor of tomato soup and peanut-butter sandwiches.

"Throw it out," Ismail said. "I've brought new supplies."

"Put them aside. We may need it all in the end. Nothing must be wasted."

To answer Ismail unpacked the rucksack. He had seen many packages go into it, many treasures. "I offer no hashish, Kajenouri, but I have brought something almost as pleasing." He had said nothing when he saw the captain drop the box of dates into the shopping basket, but he had understood that Amir Pakravan was not an unkind man.

"Well, this is a wonder," said Kajenouri. "These cannot wait to be eaten."

Jamshid's hand flashed out, snapped the cellophane, and took one of the fruits. Chewing, he commented that it was not quite a real date, but it reminded you of one.

"By all the *jinn* I wish for some hashish," Kajenouri wailed. "God provided it to fill the sorrows of men."

His big frame shook; his black beard bobbed. Ismail had seen him in training; he was a magnificent fighter. In his eyes were the two expressions of the killer: indifference and love. Men like Kajenouri were as rare as they were dangerous, men who could destroy what they loved. It was one of his missions to kill Jamshid if capture threatened.

"Kajenouri," Ismail asked, "did you see the jets?"

"I do not go out."

"How long was Jamshid in the open?"

"I watched over him from the window. His shadow traversed one quarter."

Even now the Americans might be searching their files for his face. If Jamshid was by some mischance recorded there—

"Jamshid, did the planes pass once or many times?"

The boy regarded him through a long moment of silence. "Which answer will please you most, my Brother?"

It was a disturbing response. Ismail must not forget that Jamshid had been many times inside his mind. "My mission is to protect you, Jamshid."

"You worry needlessly. The airplanes were kilometers away."

Ismail took some peanut butter and forced it into his mouth. It was the consistency of tar and it smelled like mule piss. It had the flavor of strong vinegar. "Oh, for a hot, salted turnip!"

"Be glad we have food," Jamshid said. "In my neighborhood mothers would sometimes squeeze their breasts until nothing but blood came out. We used to barter for the right to sift the garbage from American bases. First sifting was so much, second sifting less, and so forth. We boys got the last sifting for a kiss." He laughed, the sound growing rapidly into a deep, rattling cough. It was the more awful because of the youth of his body and the freshness of his face. "This stuff is good enough for me."

"That's the correct spirit," Kajenouri added. "But I still wish for my hashish."

By the time they finished it was again time to recite the First Sura. On a normal day, which began at dawn, this

135

would be the fourth recitation. But it was also proper to count the hours from the time of awakening. Since they were always up all night on the Circle, their days usually began in the afternoon. This was the second recitation.

During prayer Ismail noticed that Jamshid was watching him very carefully, casting long glances. Afterward Kajenouri announced that they would sleep until evening. It was the usual thing; during training they had gotten used to broken sleep, four hours from seven to eleven A.M. and four hours from four until eight P.M. That left them the night for their work and the day to watch for intruders.

"God give thee the strength of ten," Jamshid said to Kajenouri. He did so each time they rested; it was his prayer for his protector. They settled onto their pallets. Soon all was quiet except for the soft rattle of prayer beads. Even that ended at length. Kajenouri began to snore. Ismail lay watching the sunlight creep across the floor. Something cool brushed against his cheek. Startled, he turned his head. Jamshid was very close, his face soft with unexpected kindness. "I feel your confusion, Ismail." It was the comment of a father.

"I am afraid that the jets were searching for us."

The boy looked disbelieving. "We rest in the lap of Allah. He will protect us."

"Don't talk so loud; you'll wake the old man."

Jamshid laughed. "He whom I have made sleep?" He leaned across Ismail and thrust his face into Kajenouri's. "Wake up!"

"Are you mad?" Ismail hissed.

But Kajenouri did not stir. "He will not awaken unless I wish it." There was assurance in Jamshid's voice. Next Jamshid sprang up and gave Kajenouri a kick. Still the old man slept on, his angular face fierce even in peace.

Outside some animal coughed. Ismail listened, half expecting the Americans. But this was different; he had the strange impression that some very large presence had drawn close to the cabin. He got up to investigate.

Instantly Jamshid was before him. His face had grown hard; it was clear that he intended to prevent Ismail from seeing whatever was outside. Ismail was confused, surprised—then a deer blew and bounded away across the clearing.

"I have some business with you, my confused friend," Jamshid said. He was standing three feet in front of Ismail. Now he came closer and boldly began unbuttoning Ismail's shirt. "You do not understand yourself," he said as his quick hands undid the buttons. "You don't really want to leave me. You love me." His hands slipped around Ismail's naked waist.

"What are you doing?"

"Wait a little. Then you'll know." He drew Ismail's shirt off and tossed it to the floor. Then he unzipped his pants. Ismail was more than a little revolted and stepped back. Then he looked down in amazement at his own obvious desire. He felt trapped, revealed. "I have seen the conflict in your heart, Ismail. You must be made to know that you love me."

Jamshid came close, rolled Ismail's trousers to the floor. The coolness of the air against his skin thrilled Ismail, and he was ashamed. It was not seemly to be naked before another man, but it gave unexpected pleasure.

"When I watched you leave I wondered if you would ever come back."

Ismail reached down and drew his pants back up. "I am here, Jamshid."

The boy cocked his head, raised an eyebrow. His movements had been reminding Ismail of something, and now he understood exactly what it was. The way Jamshid moved was like a pet monkey's way, a sort of parody. The boy's lips parted; he fluttered his eyelids.

"Jamshid—abomination!"

"Admit the truth!" Jamshid thrust his hand out and grasped Ismail's privates through his jeans. There was a shock of pleasure so great that Ismail sank to his knees. As supple as a girl, Jamshid moved with him. He slipped Ismail's trousers away from his midriff. "Now, let me see . . . abomination indeed!"

Before this moment Ismail had not been aware that he could experience such feelings for another male, for Jamshid. "I will not have you longing for America, Ismail. I need you. I am far from home and I cannot endure without you."

Pleasure and loathing swirled together in Ismail's heart, but he did not move away from the cool fingers, the golden eyes, the calm and angelic face.

"Allah, please, give me strength—"

Never in his life had Ismail felt anything like this before, not with a woman, not alone.

"Allah, please, Allah, give—"

Jamshid's hand lashed out and Ismail saw a flash, felt the sting of the blow. "Leave God alone. I'm sick of the way you whine to Allah!"

"Sacrilege!"

Jamshid laughed loudly, throwing his head back, his boy's voice echoing sharply in the stillness. The old man slept on.

In his private self Ismail despaired. But he did not, could not, move. Jamshid was right, he did belong to him. As he thought this a warmth spread through his loins and into his whole being. The cool, rough fingers tickled his flesh. Ismail's protests withered in the white heat of delight. He was Jamshid's slave, had always been . . . in the darkness under his mind.

"So you know now whom you love," Jamshid whispered.

Ismail looked at the calm face. It was true. Jamshid had exposed truth. Ismail had known women—the sudden, fierce coupling in the secret night, then the long lonely journey through the streets, trying somehow to reconcile the demands of the flesh with the commandments of God.

Ismail finally was able to pull Jamshid's hand away. Jamshid did not resist this time. He let Ismail lean against him, took him in his arms. For a long time they stayed like that, in the slow decline of the hour.

"You're growing drowsy," the boy said at last. "Go to sleep now."

"Not yet."

"Yes, now."

He went heavily to his pallet and was glad to lie down. Jamshid came and covered him, then went to his own pallet. Gazing at him through drowsy eyes, Ismail wondered how he could ever have thought to betray this holy being.

A dream marched upon him. In it he died and his soul poured from his body like the yolk from a broken egg. He fell through earth and past all the stars and landed in a deep wood, a jungle of warty plants with fat leaves and slick stems. There came swiftly a huge green worm, its black mouth gaping. Ismail ran and ran but the worm came on. It sucked him into its belly and he began to be crushed, a relentless agony. As his eyes were bulging from his head and his lungs bursting for lack of air, he heard a great voice: "As man slaughters the lamb, I slaughter the man."

His own screaming awoke him.

The cabin was in deep shadow. Hours had passed. His throat ached; in his mouth there was a base foulness of a taste.

Jamshid, naked also now, brought him a cup of water from the pump in the kitchen. "You haven't been poisoned," he said lightly. "Just forget about it."

Ismail had a terrible thought. "Jamshid, what did you do to me?"

"Forget about it!"

Outside the window a light flickered. Kajenouri was striking a match. "No lights," Ismail cried. "Remember orders!"

Jamshid patted him on the shoulder.

"Shut up in there," Kajenouri muttered. "You'll scare the owls away. I like their voices."

"Merciful God, protect me."

"Ismail, be at peace with yourself. You understand nothing. I am not just a child named Jamshid; I am other things as well. Among them your master. Serve me and you serve God. There is a great battle coming, Ismail, and I cannot win it without your absolute and total loyalty."

"We fight for Allah."

"*I* fight for God. You fight for me."

Ismail felt the truth of it. His heart swelled with a dark blossom of love. The image of the worm returned, its body hissing through the shadows of the grass.

"That's right, Ismail, remember your dream. It was a true dream." Jamshid went to the door of the cabin. "Dress yourself in your soutane," he said. "Night is here and we must go to the Circle."

Ismail was filled with a new feeling. It was the fiercest loyalty, the most intense terror, he had ever known. His heart told him a great secret about Jamshid, a secret that made him tremble. "Sorcerers are not the same as other men," his grandfather once had said. "Part of their magic is to appear like us."

As he left the cabin he saw Jamshid striding toward the Circle in the hairs of light that still remained. Kajenouri shagged along also, the sorcerer's faithful beast. Ismail fell in place behind.

10

THE MISSION OF A Communist is compassionate; it is also cruel, for revolution is always painful. Pyotr Teplov sometimes felt that he was the only powerful Russian who understood this. The others had been dreaming about the overthrow of the United States for so long that they had ceased to understand it as a revolutionary event. For them it was nothing more than rhetoric.

Because it was so profoundly revolutionary, the person who controlled it was going to become the center of the world. If that man was not a Communist, it would be a world-historic tragedy.

This was why Pyotr Teplov had come to Sverdlovsk, and why he had a revolutionary obligation to take full command of Black Magic.

There were frowning forces awake in this place. Teplov had commandeered Belik's office at the Black Magic Installation. Let Belik stay back at the Institute. This was the place of power. The ventilation system might sputter and the concrete walls sweat, but it made little difference to Teplov. He would endure whatever was necessary to achieve America Paradise.

He would also remove any obstacle, and no matter Andropov's bourgeois cowardice.

He tested the image of Belik in his mind: he was tall and fair, coal-blue eyes beneath a thatch of blond hair. His hands were graceful and aristocratic; his face was a concert of pleasing angles. He did not convey a Russian impression. One might have seen such a man toward the end of the war riding in a battered Mercedes staff car, the lean body swathed in leather, the face fierce with breaking Teutonic pride.

Belik was a half-bred descendant of Volga Germans. His mother had been a blond beast of a woman, his father a sturdy little Russian. And what had she done when the thunder of her spellbound race had sounded on the horizon? She had run to them, that's what. The husband had disappeared into the war. Belik was left, a ten-year-old expendable trapped in the siege of Leningrad.

Not, however, expended. He looked so marvelous, so created for power. He was the beautiful German blended with the indomitable Russian. He had his mother's Aryan features and his father's stolid heart.

He was aggression fused to cunning; Germanic romanticism and Russian cleverness.

Executing this incipient superman had become more than an obsession with Teplov; it was the highest passion. So concerned was he with this necessity that he had to be careful not to ignore the rest of his responsibilities.

Until the Belik business was finished, Teplov could not place his full attention on the urgent matter of preserving the American operation. At first he had planned to wait until the very final moment to destroy the general, but he had seen the peril of that in Moscow. Andropov had said it himself: if any soldier became Chairman, that soldier would be Belik. Those words had decided Teplov. For the good of communism, this profoundly revisionist man must be destroyed.

And he had arranged it. He had only to make a simple phone call.

Then why didn't he? Every time he picked up the instrument he hesitated.

Why? Was he unconsciously aware of some subtle danger? He thought on this, leaning far back in his chair and staring at the rough beams that supported the ceiling. Perhaps Ludmilla Semilovna was more attached to her general than she seemed. Although she was a dispassionate officer, Belik was by her own reports a most appealing man. He might be harsh to his command, but he was gentle and kind to Ludmilla, a charming lover.

Teplov picked up his telephone once again. But not to call Captain Semilovna. "Have my car ready. I'm coming out."

He rose from behind the small plywood desk. Then he stood quite still. This place stank of raw concrete, a bunker odor like that of the Lubyanka. Bunker, hole, prison . . . whatever you wanted to call it, it was a situation even more than a place, a prison situation.

The teletype clattered again. Teplov snatched up the flimsy and read of the killing of Harmon Wiser. At last a definite victory. Progress.

He jammed his hat down on his head and left for the general's flat. Ludmilla Semilovna, you are going to convince me of your loyalty, or you are going to meet your end.

Teplov was to Belik like a parasite lodging in the heart of its victim. All he had needed was the least sign of trouble out here and he had appeared. There was a man of deep plots. He had lost no time in moving to the installation, even taking Belik's own office there. It was an invitation to duel, almost as if Teplov wanted to force a confrontation before Black Magic was attempted again and all positions were frozen by the outcome.

Or wanted to force Belik to do something foolish. He certainly intended to make a move. But it would not be a foolish one.

"Colonel Florinsky," he called, "come here, please."

The colonel tipped a nice salute. "Yes, Comrade General?"

"At ease, Colonel."

This had to be done very carefully.

He clapped the colonel on the shoulder and guided him to the chairs in the corner. Seated here the two men habitually dropped a little of the military formality that both normally preferred to maintain.

Belik was about to take Florinsky on the major journey of his career, into as deep a test as the system could present a man. But the seduction had to be done very carefully, a Plisetskaya *pas de deux.*

"Colonel, let's break out the vodka. We have some good news."

"The recalibration is complete?"

The dutiful soldier, as always. "Personal news . . . about you."

Florinsky busied himself at the vodka and glasses. Belik understood why. It was poor form to display eagerness to hear of promotion.

"I have nothing official, but I have heard a very strong rumor that the officer who will command the Joint Weapons Standardization Program we intend to undertake with the U.S. after Black Magic is none other than yourself. I gave you the highest recommendation, of course."

Florinsky began to smolder with stifled glee. He was proud enough to believe the lie, a sufficient egotist to imagine that the army would have to dig down to him to find an officer worthy of that much-wanted position.

They toasted.

"Of course, this is all dependent upon Black Magic's remaining a military command."

"This is in doubt?"

Belik pretended amazement. "But of course! Why do you think Teplov has come here?"

"He's only a colonel."

"A deception. After Andropov he is the most powerful man in KGB."

"I wasn't aware of that."

"But it's quite true, rest assured. They are attempting a coup against the General Staff. Teplov is here to arrange my death and then present himself as the most qualified man to fill the void."

"There'd have to be an arrest. A trial. And you might be exonerated—an excellent chance of it."

"Teplov was for nine years head of Directorate V. He is an assassin by training. That's why Andropov put him in Black Magic. Teplov deals in accidents, and KGB wants us officers to have some. Each time I get in my car or close my eyes to go to sleep I could be preparing to die. You must understand, Colonel Florinsky, that Teplov is here to kill me. Without a trial."

Florinsky grew wary. Like everybody else in the country, he loathed dangerous knowledge.

"Colonel, you must remove the threat of Teplov."

"But I have no authorization. He's a high official—"

"If I die, so will you. It's inevitable. You and the rest of the military staff of Black Magic. KGB will not be satisfied until their control is absolute."

"But there are no orders, no papers."

"I will draw up orders if you feel a need for them."

"Why, yes, certainly, there must be orders—"

Ah, that was it, the opening Belik had been seeking. "There will be orders. But you must act at once."

"Act? How? I'm not trained in this sort of thing. I'm an administrative officer."

"Teplov has been issued transport. His car is a dark blue Lada; you might have issued the authorization yourself."

"Yes, I know the car."

"It has a code transponder. Turn that off and the KGB's own troops will shoot him to pieces when he tries to reenter the installation."

"Again, there are procedural difficulties. First, he never

leaves the installation. Second, at our present alert level the orders of the day specify only that nonauthorized vehicles shall be stopped and the occupants arrested. For him it would be a minor inconvenience."

"I am going to raise the alert level of the installation to a war warning. You will rewrite the orders of the day according to regulations. Nonauthorized vehicles will be assumed to be hostiles and fired upon. As far as his never leaving the installation goes, I've been told that he is not there now. You'll find his car parked at my flat."

"At your flat, sir?"

"He's spying, no doubt by trying to bully my Ludmilla. Now get going; get the orders cut so that I can sign them."

Ludmilla Semilovna answered the door. "Colonel, won't you come in? I was just sitting down to lunch."

"Thank you, Captain Semilovna." He took off his hat and gave it to her. She took it in soft, white hands and placed it on the closet shelf. Ludmilla Semilovna was glorious, quite certainly one of the most beautiful women in Russia. Teplov was moved to take her hand and kiss it. She smiled then and turned gaily into the flat. "I hope you enjoy fruit and cheese."

How well the General Staff cared for itself. Teplov hadn't seen an apple in a year, much less a sweet blood orange like the ones on the dining table. The Internal Economic Report had very clearly stated that the citrus crop had failed. For the generals, apparently, this was not so. As if that was not enough, Ludmilla Semilovna proceeded to bring out a plate of exotic West European cheeses such as Teplov had quite simply never seen in Russia, not even in the house of Yuri Andropov.

In her light blue dress, serving him fruit and cheese, Ludmilla Semilovna seemed to Teplov more perfect even than a memory of beauty.

Soon he was in a kind of rapture of unexpected pleasures. He loved cheese and this was like something made for gods, this that she called Leicester. The oranges and the apples were rich with flavor, and her face lit by a sort of kindliness, the eyes as brown as vellum, the lips moist and perfectly colored, the night-black hair rich against the cream of her skin.

The table across which they ate was decorated with roses, the flowers framing her face. "Valentin demands them," she said with a wave of her hand. "So they get flown from Rumania."

"This is standard?"

"For all general-lieutenants? Hardly. But the General Staff does literally anything Valentin wants. He's their darling, he and that idiotic General Tuchin. Almost more so, that one. He has a Mercedes bigger than Brezhnev's, and the dacha of the Kistinov family out toward Berezovskiy. Well outside the ELF field, of course, like all the rest of the military." She laughed bitterly.

"They fear true communism, even when they can see it at work in Sverdlovsk Paradise."

"I spend as much time there as I can."

"I know that, Comrade Captain."

"While you're here, by the way, would you like to smoke some American cigarettes and drink some fine German pilsner? We have such things in huge quantities, believe me."

"You sound put out."

"When the workers don't have beets!"

The words burst out of her. Still, it wasn't a decisive indication of loyalty. Teplov continued to test her.

"They have beets at the moment, at least in Moscow."

"The *kholkozniks* out here live well enough. But the workers at the factories—it's a crime. We Party members owe them a great debt for their determination. There are men at Uralmash who haven't had meat in a year. And as for beets—the only way to get them is *na levo.*"

Her voice assaulted his ears. It had an unmistakable tone of honest outrage about it. Andropov had once said, "Give me Communists at mid-level, pragmatists at the top." He had meant by that men without morality. Too bad Semilovna would have to be expended. Her sort was an ideal antidote to the decadence now infecting the Politburo. When he got power he would search Russia for hundreds of Semilovnas.

When he had walked in the door Teplov had intended to test Semilovna further with a romantic seduction.

He saw now that such a technique would infuriate this comrade. But seduced she must be. If she refused the right kind of request, it would mean that she was secretly loyal to Belik. In that case he would shoot her on the spot.

"Ludmilla Semilovna, I agree with all that you have said about the plight of the workers. That is one reason we're removing the military commander. Soldiers are loyal only to the military, not to the workers. A sad truth. So you see that you have been entrusted with a most critical mission."

"I am proud of the trust of the Directorate!"

"Yes, but quite frankly, Captain, I am concerned. You have been living with this man for nearly two years. He makes love to you nightly—"

"With a fury."

"I can imagine. And you are certain that you're capable of shooting him through the head?"

She colored. "I am not sentimental, comrade. Lovemaking is a professional requirement."

"Then you would make love with anybody?"

"If it was required, certainly."

"I want that proved. You must convince me that you are not sentimental about it."

Quite suddenly the earnest, pinched expression was replaced by one of amusement. "So you dream about Ludmilla Semilovna, too. Very well, Colonel, it would be my pleasure to make your dream a reality."

"Ludmilla Semilovna, this is entirely professional—"

She emitted a burst of warm peasant's laughter, completely at odds with her looks. From such a face one would have expected an arch glare.

"You cannot imagine how many men want to make love to me. Most of them are bourgeois rubbish. But with you it would be a privilege."

Overcome by joy and delight, he rushed around the table and seized her hands in his. "Ludmilla Semilovna!"

She got up, lifted her face. "And anyway, your approach was so audacious! To rest your proposition on my loyalty to the state, you wretched, clever man!"

"This is not a 'proposition,' as you call it. We are required by duty, both of us!"

"Very well, comrade. Duty calls us to the general's bed. Or shall we go to my daybed instead? Yes, I think so. It's cozier there."

She strolled into a delightfully sun-drenched room. Potted plants lined the walls, and beyond the open windows flowering vines climbed. Against one wall there was an antique couchette covered in pink silk. Beautiful. "I think that the daybed is your preference, also. You are a little afraid of General Belik, after all."

"The soldier who frightens me has not been born."

"Ah. Well, I like the daybed then."

"It appears both comfortable and sturdy."

She dropped her clothes off and twirled about before him, her body perfect in the dapples of sunlight. Her breasts were round, her buttocks flat. She looked the sculptor's ideal of youthful beauty. Then she gave him a fierce kiss, plunging her tongue between his teeth.

There was something in her eyes now that he did not quite understand. She unsnapped his belt. "You wear hideous clothes, Pyotr. You'll be better off naked, don't you think?" She cuddled up to him pecked out small kisses on his lips and cheeks, all the while working with his buttons. His trousers dropped to the floor, his shirt slipped away. He stood beside the daybed and accepted her scrutiny. She smiled, touched him privately. "I approve. You shall gain entry."

It turned out to be an oddly cheerless experience. And why? Certainly she was responsive, gasping and sweating, even scratching his back a little as he pounded through the five minutes it took him. But there was a choreography to it all. She had been trained to a certain technique, and she followed the book.

Teplov felt satisfied, at any rate, that Semilovna had retained sufficient professional detachment to do her duty.

The trees of the birch forest flashed past as he returned to the installation.

He wondered if her willingness to make love with him proved anything beyond professional skill. No, unfortunately, it did not. Lovemaking was obviously of minor consequence to her. And so it should be: that was how she had been trained. Those girls were taught that their bodies were weapons of the class struggle. To compel somebody to do something unimportant to them was no test, so he ought to be no more sure of her than he had been before. But somehow he was. He would not hesitate again to make his call.

His thoughts were broken by a sudden decrease in the speed of the car. Was the wretched thing failing? "What's wrong?"

"I think they're setting up a roadblock, sir."

Roadblock? Oh, God. Instantly he saw it all. Belik was a subtle devil. "Stop! At once!" The driver jammed on the brakes. Teplov leaped out of the car, dashed to the side of the road. The driver was still staring at him in astonishment when the bullets ripped through the vehicle.

Murder by regulations. And nobody would be able to tell whether the transponder had been tampered with after the beating the car was taking. The driver dissolved into red haze. Teplov lay very still in the ditch by the roadside, his papers in his outstretched hand. Soon there was the sound of a vehicle on the road, then the screech of brakes and the clatter of soldiers jumping to the ground.

KGB guards, thanks be. Without making a move, Teplov bellowed out his name and rank. An unseen hand snatched up the papers.

"Your car wasn't transmitting," a voice snapped. "We've just gotten—"

"A war warning from the military commander?"

"That's right, but how did you know?"

"There aren't any other conditions under which you'd be shooting before you carried out an investigation."

"Stand up."

Teplov obeyed. He knew that he had just survived quite a clever assassination attempt, compliments of General Belik. What better way to kill a KGB official than this? KGB itself would have been responsible for the death.

The Security Service captain drove him to the tunnel entrance in his BRDM armored car. Upon returning to his office, Teplov's first impulse was to report this whole incident to Andropov.

Then he saw the cable traffic from America. There would be time for talking to Andropov later. This required immediate attention. Winter's woman was in the *residentura*'s hands at last.

When Florinsky burst in with the bad news, Belik's first impulse was to try to flee the country. Then he realized that, even if it were possible, it would be the act that destroyed him. No, better always to withdraw a little than to retreat a lot.

"We must explain ourselves to Colonel Teplov," Florinsky wailed, "somehow convince him—"

"Ignore the matter."

"But, sir!"

"If there are any inquiries, say that it's an internal KGB affair. They maintain the transponders. It was their troops who were so stupid as to attack that familiar Lada."

"Sir, I beg to differ with you. By far the safest course is to convince Teplov that we were not involved."

"Yes, Colonel, that would be best. But it's quite impossible. Teplov cannot be convinced of it."

"A mistake, an accident!" He literally wrung his hands. " 'As ripened wheat to the mower's blade/the soldiers bowed.' " So true. Perhaps nothing could save the soldiers now.

"Remember, Colonel, whatever happens, you are a Soviet officer."

With a moan of anguish Florinsky left the room. He didn't salute.

"Colonel! Return, please." Looking exactly like a hound, he came slinking back for his kick. Belik demanded a salute, and returned it. "Keep your boots polished, soldier. And close my door."

"Yes, sir."

Belik swiveled around in his chair. The great thing was to remember that he had done nothing worse than come off badly in a skirmish. He was watching the hills go blue with evening when a telephone call came through. "Hello, yes."

"Gorkin here. I have a projection estimated time of 1600 hours on Thursday."

"So soon! Gorkin, you are a genius." Belik could have embraced the huge man. This was quite a reprieve. Surely Teplov wouldn't be able to put his riposte together in forty-eight hours.

"The readjustment of the antenna leaves is proceeding more quickly than I thought possible."

"There will be an Order in this for you, Comrade Professor."

"Right. I'll ring off now. I'm very busy."

Belik put down the phone. Like blood rushing back into his veins, his self-confidence returned. "Colonel Florinsky!"

The colonel burst through the door as if a battery were firing at his back.

"Please initiate the retiming of the Operational Directives to a Thursday 1600 projection.

Florinsky's face did not change. He was too involved in his own fear to realize how good the news was.

"I want a copy of the Integrated Operations Phasing Sequence on my desk in the morning." It was important that the Strategic Rocket Forces and PRO-Antirocket Defense Forces time their activities exactly to coincide with the Black Magic program. Lapses in their schedules simply could not be tolerated. The Main Military Council's Overall Strategic Directive was clear: "You will allow no more than two American warheads to impact Soviet territory. The full resources of the Antirocket Defense Forces, including the land-based Proton Beam Weapons, will be committed to your command for this operation."

Belik was not only responsible for inducing the firing of the American missiles, he was equally responsible for ensuring that they caused as little damage as possible.

Florinsky was staring at his superior officer as if seeking some sort of reprieve. "Thank you, Colonel. That will be all."

"Yes, sir."

He was a soldier; let him get used to the idea.

Belik's window beckoned him, the last shadows. Soon the moon would appear over the mountains, making the weir-snow glow with heartbreaking light.

He punched his intercom. "Bring up the car."

The important thing was to keep following routine. Teplov probably knew already of the rescheduling and would maneuver accordingly. Belik must do the same, and that meant going to Ludmilla Semilovna at the usual hour and in the usual way.

In his car he thought long and carefully on what he knew about her and why Teplov might have visited her. He would have been foolish not to consider the possibility that she was reporting to KGB; certainly someone in his entourage did so. Possibly more than one of them.

Did she figure in some plot against his life? Ludmilla? She was just a girl, innocent, flighty, and foolish . . . and very much in love with the luxuries that went with being General Belik's mistress.

And with the general, too. No woman could pretend a love like Ludmilla's. Such an actress had not yet been born.

The reception room was dark, filled with a rich scent of roses. He saw her figure in the center of the room. As if activated by his coming, she opened her arms and started walking toward him.

Her face glowed; her body was inviting. As she came near him he was enveloped in the scent of perfume and the rustle of linen. Ludmilla was a genius of appearances. As in so many other Russian women, there was within her a deep vein of the exotic, as if the shadowy mystery of the land itself hid in her spirit. At one moment she would be sweat and cabbage; at the next her Tatar eyes would flash. It was impossible not to crumple one's cap in one's hands before such a combination of simplicity and majestic beauty.

She was his secret princess, and this was her hidden palace. There was music just at the edge of hearing, coming from her dayroom. He opened his arms to her, and she came in and leaned her head against his chest. They kissed then, and as always it amazed him to find such pleasure in so familiar a person. "That music is wonderful."

"The new RCA digitals got delivered this afternoon. Four months. I think it's the longest wait so far."

"Things are getting very difficult. There are riots, you know. And strikes, dozens of them. I think that the Ural miners are going to walk out soon. Right here at home."

She walked a little away from him, tossed her black hair. "Well, they ought to be given a treatment. Stalin would never have stood for what our government tolerates." She twirled around. "See my new skirt? Straight from Bloomingdale's."

"In a few months I will be able to take you to Bloomingdale's personally. The Trade Cooperation Agreement will encourage it. The way it's being structured American merchants will welcome the International Ruble."

"Assuming you win your war." She came to him, took his hands. "Oh, Valentin Ilyich, I know I'm not supposed to ask, but I do so want you to win." She embraced him, kissed him with girlish fervor. The smallest of bells rang in his mind. She should not have asked such an indiscreet question. She had never done so before.

"All is well, don't worry yourself about it."

"You've been sleeping poorly. Tossing about."

"Naturally so, on the eve of battle."

She went to the kitchen. He heard the snap of a beer being opened. In a moment she was back with a tray in her hand. "Sit down and take your beer and caviar. 'Brenya' is on." She turned on the lights and put the tray on the table before the television set. He liked to watch the Moscow news, minimal as it was. A practiced mind could learn much about the leadership from listening to what it chose to tell the workers.

Tonight he sipped his Dortmunder and watched absent-mindedly, thinking of the duel with Teplov. He really preferred to be the cat. Too bad Teplov's quick thinking out on the road had forced him to the defensive. Like it or not, he was now the mouse.

"That's the last of the beer, by the way."

"Tell them at Voyentorg."

"I've been telling them for a month. 'Not coming in the way it used to' is their constant refrain. 'There's Czech beer.' "

"Dog piss. Everything's falling apart." He stared at Brenya. Riots in Chicago. Air crash in Jakarta. Brilliant track-laying achievement in Siberia. The hell. "One-winter tracks," they were called.

The thought of the pitiful tracks filled him with a desperate sort of pride and made him hate all around him that was not Russian—the German beer, the Japanese television, the lamps, the chairs, the couch. He wanted a plain Russian room, plywood and oilcloth and his woman in a flowered dress. He wanted the smell of borscht and the sweet passion of Russian music. And a portrait of Lenin in cardboard on the wall—why not?—and two kids in the Young Pioneers. He wanted the innocence and the enthusiasm of being a party activist, the sense of service. At this moment, he thought, he could not feel more truly alone.

"You look so sad, Valentin Ilyich." She sat beside him, filling his nose with the smell of her French perfume. She turned off the television and drew his head into her lap. "Now, that's better, isn't it? You don't want old 'Brenya.' It's all so stupid."

He closed his eyes. How he longed for a love of which he could be absolutely sure, like the kind they had in the long blocks of flats where people lived who were so insignificant that they could afford to trust one another. The thought of it was like cool water on a burn.

Her hands caressed his face, twined his hair. He kissed her fingers one by one, then looked up into the proud face. Her eyes sparkled, They were remarkable, the color of the mahogany doors in Two Dzerzhinsky Square. "Quit that staring, my Valentin Ilyich. I think you need to dream."

"I haven't got time for that."

"You're heroic, then."

"I'm a worker. Son of a worker."

She laughed very softly and laid her palm on his forehead. Lying in her lap, he began to feel curiously at her mercy. It was quite an unpleasant sensation. Why must he be so suspicious? In this way, at least, power had certainly corrupted him.

Teplov's visit to this place could not have been innocuous.

"Did things go badly today, Valentin?"

"They went very well."

"Then it's me. You must be unhappy with me."

"No, not at all." He rose up and stood over her. This was much better; he did not like to lie where this woman could plunge a knife into his throat.

She closed her eyes, reached up, and tried to take his hands. No. He could bear this no longer, this freezing distance. He grabbed her by the shoulders and lifted her to her feet, held her tightly against him. For an instant she pressed against his chest, then let herself be taken. Tighter and tighter he embraced her, locking his arms together. When she raised her face it was red with the pressure. "Valentin—"

"He came here! The Executioner!"

She nodded. Tears were popping from her eyes. There was terror there. That was dangerous, that emotion. If people like her ever killed, they did so because they were too terrified not to.

When he relaxed his grip, she slipped quickly away from him. With shaking hands she took a cigarette from the case on the table and lit it.

"Why did he come, Ludmilla?"

She said nothing.

"Ludmilla!"

She returned to him. "Valentin, I want to tell you something."

At last! She was his after all.

"You are my master."

"Yes, and?"

"Just that I want to dance for you. I want to dance naked for my master!"

He was astonished. Never had he heard of such a thing.

"Very well," he said, still lost in wonder.

"What music, master?"

"You sing well."

"But what, my lord? Please command your song."

"Whatever you wish!"

He did not watch her removing her clothes but rather went through the flat turning on lights, until every corner was bright and the windows were black with what lay beyond them.

After Elena's funeral he had gone to the Hill of Farewells—now called Victory Park. It was still the Poklonnaya Gora then. He had watched Moscow glittering in the night, the domes, the spires, the swollen Stalinist monoliths. They had courted there, and he had paused on each station of their courtship. Never for an instant had he had to question that woman's loyalty.

"Valentin Ilyich, are you weeping?"

"Where is my dance?"

She looked gravely at him. She began to hum and clap, the rhythm, the words, the wildness of the dance called the Virgin, dancing around and around, her perfect flesh reflecting the light like ice. It thrilled him to his depths, this fabulous surrender, and he forgot all his questions.

He grabbed a bottle from the table where they were kept and drank vodka from its mouth. "Faster! Come on!" He clapped with her and danced with her, around and around, kicking finally, the bottle sloshing in his hand. He fell to the floor, taking another long pull. "Oh, no, don't stop," he shouted. "Go on!"

She danced into the night, her eyes shining, her arms smooth and sinuous, the sweat rising on her breasts and forehead, shimmering, her feet pound-pounding like whispered thunder on the thick English carpet. As he watched her he felt in himself an emotion so rich that it could only be love, so cold it could only be fear; it was a bottomless depth into which his heart was forever falling.

The telephone rang. She danced over, grabbed it up, then danced away, laughing. "I thought they were calling you away," she gasped out happily, "but it was only a wrong number, a wrong number!"

11

THEY HAD TAKEN CATHERINE to a building she knew well. The Morgan Brush Company was famous in Clinton because nobody worked there, and yet people came and went all the time. She had passed it hundreds of times on her way up Eighth Avenue to the subway, never dreaming its true purpose.

Now she stood naked in darkness in the Morgan Brush Company and listened to her own heart thundering. How could you be this alone so close to home?

"It's too dark in here!"

Her own voice made the room feel even larger. She waved her arms, wanting to find the walls. She was afraid; they were going to hurt her.

That's me crying. That's my own piss I'm standing in. It stinks in here! Dark, and it stinks.

Then rhythmic rustling. "Who's there?" Wave your hands all around you. "Somebody's there!" Oh, back up, back up against the wall, back up—*no!*

"I've got her. Hold still. C'mon, hold still!"

Powerful arms came around her waist, hurting arms. She

flailed in self-defense, found herself grabbing something soft and fleshy—an ear.

"Good *God!* Will you give me a little help over here?"

"Sorry, Maxim."

"Hit the fucking lights, she hurt me!"

Dazzle, like walking into a spot. Then she was being yanked, thrown from one man to two men. They were in a big storeroom; she saw fluorescent fixtures overhead and a great pile of stuffed Misha bears from the 1980 Olympics against the far wall. Closer was a long, black table fitted with straps.

"Let me go!"

"My ear!"

The small gray man had blood splashing down the shoulder of his blue suit. Had she actually done that? His ear had torn like a dry sponge.

I'm naked, I don't like this!

There were people looming forward now, gathering around the table, men and women, creatures at their feast, eyes upon her, complicated, frozen faces—and hands pushing, pulling—a hand in my hair! "Aaahh!" Back, lie back; and now the black straps strapped, cold across belly, arms, and legs.

"Please!" I don't want them to scar me. There are so many, so very many. Six, seven. It's like some kind of crazy dance the way they keep coming and going. That woman, she has, she has—

It was a thing of wires. She was like a surgeon of some kind, only dressed in jeans and a sweat shirt. She could have jogged here. "For God's sake, what is that?"

"How the hell—it's all tangled up."

She's fumbling. She doesn't know the first thing about it!

"Please, you might make a mistake." Her own voice touched her heart. This was the way it sounded when she wasn't acting, the melodic twang of a Virginia girlhood.

"Boris, get Nevetsky on the phone. I'm not trained to work this thing. How they expect me to use it I don't know.

Look here, the insulation's coming right off the wires. It's a mess!''

Oh, God.

"Wait a minute, here's the booklet. It was in the bottom of the box. Anyway, it's brand-new; maybe the wires are supposed to be like that.''

"Don't you believe it.''

"Plug it in. You ought to get a line feed indication.''

"The light's red if that's what you mean.''

Catherine tried to raise her head enough to see them, but somebody was behind her and pulled her hair again. Next a thick band was yanked around her forehead. Now she was really stuck, straps and bands keeping her absolutely still.

"Open the table; I don't want her pissing all over me,'' a voice said. Somebody did something between her legs. Pissing. I couldn't piss again if it meant my life!

"Read the damn thing, Boris.''

"Make the initial entry through the temporal fossa behind the left ear.''

"OK, I'm doing that.''

A piercing whine seemed to shatter Catherine's left ear. She tried to turn her head away, could not. Then the pain came, the crashing pressure of the worst migraine imaginable. Her whole skull was alive with vibration, her teeth jittering, her vision blurring with the shaking and the agony.

She realized that they were drilling a hole in her head. "Oh, God, save me! God God God—'' This was no operating room; it was filthy, and they were drilling into her brain! "Please, please, I didn't—''

"OK, now you put the needle in.''

The woman moved beside Catherine's head. "How the hell far?''

Pages were turned. "Whoever heard of an instruction manual with no index, eh?''

Catherine saw the device in the woman's bare hands, a long, gold needle that looked as if it could go through her head and come out the other side. "Please, just listen a half a minute. I have money. I'm rich. I come from a rich family. I'm telling you my dad will never—he will *never—no, keep that out of me!*"

"OK, it's in as far as the black line."

"Put the seating grommet around it and plug it in. Then you just turn the rheostat. The more voltage, the more she'll respond."

"Who has the questions?"

"They got a whole list together; it's here somewhere. Hey—"

It was in her, she could feel it, a tight radiating pain just behind her ear.

"Where the hell are they, Boris? Come on, you people can't be that stupid."

"Wait a minute, dear love. Remember, please, who acquired this little package."

"Those questions were from Red Wind!"

"In that case you should have reviewed them yourself."

"Oh, crap."

Catherine listened with desperate avidity, trying to understand, knowing only that they had done surgery on her without so much as washing their hands.

"Wait a minute. Here they are—in *your* purse, Emilya."

"Just give me the filthy things. But first, isn't there a test protocol in the instruction booklet? We've got to be sure the thing is working. I certainly don't want to go through this twice."

"It's not—oh, yeah, here it is. 'The rheostat is to be moved to the level-two setting. If the probe has been inserted correctly, the subject will feel a tingling sensation in the tips of fingers and toes.' "

Someone came and sat at the head of the table. Catherine recognized the voice of the woman. *"Can you hear me?"*

"Of course! And please don't yell; I'm not deaf."

A swarm of pins and needles came into her palms and fingers, making her clench her fists.

"Feel that?"

"Yes. Listen, this is all totally unnecessary. I'll tell you the truth. You can put me on a lie detector. I'll tell you the truth!"

"We'll start with something simple. Who is your case officer?"

"My what?"

The pins and needles spread up her arms and thighs. Her hands and feet began to feel hot. "Reply, please."

"I don't have any case officer! You think I'm on welfare or something?"

The heat became hideous, radiating down her arms and legs. Catherine tried and tried not to scream, but she couldn't help it. Huge, raw bellows burst from her throat one after another. From the distance, the depths of her mind, she felt absolute terror and, oddly, great compassion.

Were they injecting something under her skin? Pressing hot irons against her hands and feet? She struggled but could not see.

"I will repeat the question one time. If you fail to answer I will turn this device to full power for three minutes. I assure you, Miss Harris, this display of bravado is futile. Now, who is your case officer?"

"I told you, I don't have—" The agony made it seem for an instant as if she were tumbling head over heels. She saw stars, then she smelled the burning of her flesh and felt the meat of her hands and feet going crisp and cracking.

Then it stopped.

The group of them withdrew to the edge of Catherine's vision. The woman's furious whisper drifted back. "I'm telling you this is no job for a nurse! It's horrible, I can't bear that screaming."

"Emilya, you're a KGB officer!"

"You do it, Boris. All you needed me to do was drill the hole. You ask the questions; I'm going back to the residence."

"Emilya, these orders are from Pyotr Teplov himself. If

you walk out now, you'll end up getting recalled. And you know what that means.''

When the woman reappeared, she wiped Catherine's face with a piece of Kleenex. For an instant their eyes met. Catherine was surprised to find that she was embarrassed for her torturer.

But only for a moment. ''Who is your case officer?''

''I don't have any case officer.''

Fire. Burns being rubbed with sandpaper. Agony.

''You know, don't you, that the pain will eventually give you a heart attack?''

''I know, oh, I know.''

''Then answer, Catherine. *Please* answer.''

''I can't answer! I don't know!''

Hot blades sizzled up her arms and legs toward her heart, piercing deep, sensitive flesh.

''Have you reported to your case officer yet?''

''This is insane! I haven't got a case officer, I haven't reported—oh, God God God, help me, please. You *bitch*, stop it! *Stop it!''* Her insides were frying now, just as if she had swallowed molten lead; she could hear the pop and bubble of the heat, could feel the roil of steam in her throat. ''God, I am sorry . . . heartily sorry . . . I confess . . .''

''This woman is too strong for Teplov's machine!''

There was a whispered convocation. Catherine knew only that it would never stop, this raw suffering, never until the night after the last day, never even then—

''Because you've been stupid I am going to leave the adjustment at level four. We're going for a coffee; we'll be back in half an hour.''

Level four was a hot blue flame in the middle of Catherine's guts. Level four ate at her flesh and her sanity. The worst of it was that she couldn't even move her head to see if they were making scars. She imagined her flesh cracked with red fissures in black, wisps of blue smoke rising. She was utterly miserable in her helplessness. Then the thought came that she was certainly going to die if this kept up, and she commenced struggles as fierce and forlorn as those of a mink in a trap.

"Come back!" She would lie, would make things up to satisfy them, say anything, and why hadn't she thought of this before? "Co-o-ome back!"

Silence millennia long. Echoing sobs and gasps and squirms, the hammering pain of the needle through the skull, the subtle roaring as if in an empty theater. If only she could *see* just for one second what this was doing to her, she would be able to endure it a lot better. If she could see the extent of the scarring, could know then the degree to which her career was being ruined.

This just wasn't going to end. If she hadn't been tied down, she wouldn't have been able to stand thirty seconds of this. Not twenty, not ten! But here she was, and the minutes were becoming hours—and her flesh must be peeling off by now, that's what it felt like, peeling, and the dry flakes blowing like ashes.

At last footsteps clattered on the floor. The nurse came again, her sallow, blandly pretty face all cow-soft, the Kleenex in her hand. "Now please, I beg of you, Catherine, answer my questions!"

"What do you want me to say?"

Pain.

It took only a few minutes to lose her. He had been standing at the newsstand in the lobby when the group of men had crossed with the woman huddled among them—the woman in the flower-printed dress from the thirties. Catherine, of course, despite the brown wig that had been jammed down on her head like some zany crown.

The men had pushed their captive into a gray Dodge Aries.

Paul looked frantically for a cab but could find nothing. He had to run down the middle of the street to keep the car in view, forcing himself to a burst of effort every time the lights went against him.

In New York traffic a man on foot has some slight chance against a car. Paul kept the Aries in sight until it reached 55th Street and turned north. He loped up the block, air cold in his throat, finally giving out at the corner of Eighth Avenue. Leaning against a parked van, he had looked dismally up the avenue and seen the car pulling away from a large, nondescript factory building, the Morgan Brush Company. There was nobody in it now but the driver.

This was Teplov's way of controlling Paul Winter. Very effective. He felt as if he were descending level by level into hell.

He had no intention of abandoning Catherine. He had always stuck with his people . . . even with that crowd of smugglers CIA had wished on him in Laos.

He caught his breath and continued on.

The whole area was under surveillance. There were cars at both ends of the block and at least one individual on the roof of the building, which was disused but not at all rundown.

The building was heavily guarded. Paul had always heard that the New York *residentura* maintained a safe house in Clinton on the mid–West Side, but he had not expected so large a building. God only knew what they had in there— possibly an armory, certainly a prison.

As long as he was not recognized, he had the advantage. It would be natural to assume that he was a good deal farther behind. He decided to flank them. To do this he walked down 55th to Ninth and then up to 57th, then back to Eighth. He couldn't risk spending too much time on Eighth since he probably wouldn't recognize any of them, but they would all recognize him.

At the corner of Eighth and 57th was a Whelan's drugstore where the old Crest Cafeteria had been. In Crest days there had been a back door to the alley. Paul entered the store. It was fluorescent bright, smelling faintly of perfume and patent medicine. The aisles were almost empty. The store would close at midnight, half an hour away.

The back wall was covered by displays of hairbrushes and combs. But not completely blocked. The door was there all right, marked with an exit sign, behind a rack of Harlequin paperbacks. *Velvet Love, Love's Strongest Heart,* all of that, the dreams of the women of the streets, their sweetly sentimental hearts. And behind the dreams, the door.

In an instant he was through it. No eyes followed him; he was quick by habit. He found himself in the inky-black alley. It smelled, incredibly, of Asia.

For a moment he was back in Vientiane, amid the hiss of fish being cooked and the reek of sesame oil.

There was a Vietnamese restaurant roaring its exhaust into this alley. Paul passed it—white tablecloths, waiters in red jackets.

He went carefully forward, staying close to the back wall of the Morgan Brush Company so that he would be invisible to anybody looking down from the roof.

Quite invisible. Unless, of course, they were also posted on the roof across the alley. What would they do if they saw him?

Let him get in, of course, and take him there.

Ever so faintly a sound came to him. It was audible only because the street noises were muffled by the buildings. It could have been the tinkle of a windbell but it was not. He recognized a woman's hysterical voice, high and frantic, leaping to shrieks of extreme suffering.

Catherine, don't make that noise! They are not torturing you, they can't be. There isn't any reason, you see, so you're wrong—oh, shut up, shut up!

No. It just goes on and on. They're torturing her all right. He was staggered by the thought of it. And the poor woman was in the worst possible situation: she could not relieve her pain with answers because she didn't know enough.

Paul closed his ears to the sound as best he could. He had come here with the simple intention of extracting her from the trap. He still intended to, but he was going to do something more now. He was also going to kill whoever was doing that to her.

Buildings were not often proof against him. The second-story windows of this one were unbarred, for example. He climbed hand over hand up the grating that blocked the street floor and peered into the blackness of the second. A large room populated by warehouse pallets. Storage. Good and quiet. He wrapped his handkerchief around his fist and punched a neat hole in one of the old windows. Then, with his forearm against the inner wall as a lever, he fulcrumed himself onto the sill. He was now twenty-five feet from the ground. Not terrible for a man who had once been in better shape. Living on rice and rotten fish in Laos had done him a lot more good than harm. He had left Southeast Asia a creature of wire and he was still thin.

Inside, the screaming was more distinct, the abandoned howl of a despairing animal.

Now what? He couldn't fire a gun because of the noise. All he had in his pocket was a book of paper matches. Wits, then, would have to suffice. He took off his shoes and tied them to his belt, then moved across the storeroom. There was no door, and in the hall was an empty desk. Beyond it windows overlooked Eighth Avenue. He could see a hardware store opposite, and in front of it one of the typical *residentura* cars, a green Chevrolet. The hallway was floored with wood and the ceilings were high. There was about this place a distinct sense of the past. A hundred years ago men had worked here beneath flaring gas with quill pens. Two dollars a week was probably good money. Simple old past; how could the present possibly be its child?

Paul descended an iron stairway, going always toward the sound of the screams. The voice was hissing and cracking now, reduced to bursts of gasping anguish. It reverberated in Paul's ears as he went down the stairs, activating his guilt and making him hunger once again for what he now recognized was a conceit of martyrdom.

The temptation was great, but he must not allow himself

to get so sloppy as to succumb to it. The appointment in South Dakota must be kept; the effort Teplov was making to draw him off proved its importance. A true professional would already have abandoned Catherine Harris in the interest of the mission.

For years Paul had known he did not have the heart of a true professional. Too humane, to put it simply. It had been his private curse and his pride. They had never known it; they had fired him for other reasons.

The screams grew closer and louder, careening off walls, each one bursting in Paul's mind to cutting slivers of guilt.

Was there going to be anything left of her?

He came to a small black door with a window in it. Beyond was another storeroom, but in the center of this one bright light shone down on a table. The tableau was of some medieval surgery, the doctors lounging about while the patient writhed *in extremis* on the bed.

She was strapped around arms and legs, waist and head, totally immobilized. Her mouth was opened, her eyes tightly shut. Her fingers kept scrabbling against the tabletop; her toes were curled tightly. A woman sat beside her in jeans and sweat shirt, her hair stylishly cut, her face as fixed as plastic. She was pretty in a dense Russian way, perhaps thirty. In her manicured fingers she held a green box. The box was attached by a series of extension cords to a wall socket.

Paul almost cried aloud when he saw that it was also attached to Catherine's head. They had drilled a hole in her skull. They were doing something to her brain.

It took every grain of courage he possessed not to burst wildly through the door and pull that evil machine out of her. They were far beyond the intricacies of the old cold war game. This was something worse even than the horrible devisings of Lavrenti Beria, the sledgehammer to the head, the nails torn out, the mass starvings in the Lubyanka, the slow death mining Kolyma gold.

He placed his hand on the doorknob. In the room beyond

her could see six people. The torturer he ignored; she would not notice him. The other five must be *residentura* types, guards and officials. All eyes were on the table.

Paul tried the door. He was just opening it when the woman rose from her seat. He stopped. As if guided by some uncontrollable force, she turned toward this door and began marching forward. He ducked below the level of the window and crawled to one side so that the opening door would momentarily block a view of him. She came out, slammed the door behind her, and at once doubled over, retching. Her face was streaked by tears. She shook and gasped as she vomited. Paul stepped up behind her and put his hands around her throat.

Where was his compassion now? In an instant he had become an engine of hatred. It felt so very good to tighten his fists against this struggling creature, to feel her frantic efforts coming to nothing.

The windpipe collapsed with a jerk of the neck and a little whistle through the nose. Her struggles grew more desperate. It hurt to suffocate, but not nearly so much as this creature deserved.

The thing went limp. "Emilya," called a voice from beyond the door. "Emilya?"

Paul dragged the thing to the stairway and jammed it under the stairs. Its face stared blankly from a tangled mass of limbs and clothing. He started to kick the face. Then he saw its softness, the girl still clinging to the woman's creases and defeats. He hesitated. From the thing there came a slow, gasping wheeze. Paul touched the bruised neck.

Very unprofessional.

"Emilya?"

Paul trotted to the far end of the hallway and drew himself into the shadows. Soon somebody appeared, a trim little man, the kind the *residentura* sends to UN parties. He hurried off up the stairs, calling the thing's name, never seeing her.

There was silence at the top of the stairs, then footsteps started again, clattering on the iron.

So there had been a guard up there after all. But where? Then Paul knew—in the washroom, no doubt to make sure that poor Emilya didn't try to escape through the filthy little window. When the guards must guard the guards, they're bound to get short-handed.

"Emilya!" The guard leaped down the last few stairs. A responding clatter of feet started in the storeroom. Two more men came bursting out, followed by a slower third. Excellent. Catherine was now attended by exactly one admirer.

"This is impossible!"

"Winter! Has to be!"

"Then he's here?"

"Of course—upstairs, he must be!" Of course. All they had to do was turn their heads to the right and they would see Winter in the shadows. But they did the predictable thing; they began to rush up the stairs. The moment the last foot disappeared around the landing, Paul went into the storeroom. The one remaining guard waited a moment too long, trying in the bad light to be sure that Paul wasn't a friendly.

The guard absorbed a good right and sank into a fairly satisfying uppercut. Then Paul confronted his harmed duchess.

He stuck his face into her field of vision. Her eyes widened, she drew a deep breath—and he covered her mouth with his hand. "Be quiet! We've only got a few minutes."

"Unstrap me, for God's sake!"

"Whisper!"

There was some sort of brain probe in her head. He could not risk removing it. Instead he pulled out its wires so that it wouldn't drag against the weight of the control box when she got up. Then he unbound her, more than half expecting that the thing had paralyzed her.

"Can you move, honey?"

She popped up off the table. "Get me out of here!"

"Get dressed."

Her clothes were ragged; her face looked as if it had been assaulted by an army; she was shaking as if withdrawing from a drug.

He took her directly to the front door. There was no point in going to the alley even if the downstairs windows hadn't been barred. The alley didn't open to the street, and Whelan's door was a one-way affair. He hoped that the guards outside had not yet gotten the alert.

The front door opened easily enough from the inside.

"You've got to get a doctor. I'm burned!"

"Look at yourself."

She looked down to the smooth perfection of her limbs. "My God."

"Do you feel OK?"

"No, I don't feel OK! I thought I was being burned to death. That's what it felt like."

"That thing in your head. Come on, we can't waste a second."

As she moved along beside him, he noticed no telltale foot dragging, no confusion. No overt signs of brain damage.

Nearby Roosevelt was a good hospital, but like many other New York emergency rooms it had a standing rule that if there was no blood showing you waited on the folding chairs. The usual crowd of doubled-up, semicomatose people groaned and wailed there. New Yorkers knew that the only way to deal with this situation was to look as sick as possible. Thus the sinusitis victim held his head and rocked, and the man with a sprained knee seemed about to lapse into a coma from the pain.

And they waited.

Paul cut the crowd with a loud shout: "Help us. Brain injury. Brain injury. Help us!" They did help, doctors and nurses at a run, eyes widening to see the wires protruding from the swollen hole in Catherine's head and she standing there just famous enough to make them think they'd seen her on TV.

"What the hell happened?" A man was showing Paul a shield as Catherine was wheeled away.

"Unbelievable! You know the Morgan Brush Building?"

"Yeah. You next of kin?"

"Fiancé. She hasn't got family. She's Catherine Harris, the actress."

"Jesus, what the fuck's a light socket doin' in her head? Some accident!"

Paul was eager to follow her, to wait out the surgery, but this had to be done. "The people who did it are in the Morgan Brush Building. I think it's some kind of cult. Satanists. Some kind of total crazies. They drilled a hole in her head—"

"How did you find out about it?"

"She got away from them—obviously."

The cop ran his fingers through his hair. "This is nuts."

"It's nuts, that's for damn sure. But it happened."

"Morgan Brush? We'll check it out."

Paul went past the cop and down the long green hall, following a hurrying doctor to the operating room where Catherine had been taken. Through the door he could see a chaos of activity around a table, but this time there were olive-drab oversuits, rubber gloves and gauze masks, and eyes full of humanity.

Paul waited. He wished that he could have the pleasure of seeing what was happening in the Morgan Brush Building about now. That was one safe house blown.

A vivid flash of memory shot through him—Emilya. He should have killed her.

No.

His college ring had a hair under it. He removed the hair, dropped it to the floor.

While the minutes turned into an hour, Paul fought himself to get up and go on his way. But he wanted to be sure about her. If she was dying, or going to wake up crippled, she would need somebody.

Anyway, with Harmon dead he couldn't move without

173

making contact with CIA. He had to figure out how to go about that, exactly whom to call. The trouble was, if one didn't know about ELF, Paul's claims would sound like the weavings of a madman. Old operatives were known to go senile in exactly this way, getting lost in mazes of traitors imagined and secrets hiding secrets. "Yeah, Paul, sure, we're checking that out." The smile, quick, dismissive as hell. "Good thinking, though. Wish you were still aboard! No way I can make lunch. I'm about five feet under!"

One viable contact. A man he hadn't seen in five years except to resign to. Nevertheless a good man, a conscientious one. He had read Paul's memoranda on ELF and had questioned him closely about it. One good man.

A doctor appeared. "You're Paul?"

Olive-drab surgical fatigues, mask down around the neck, face grave. "Yes."

"It's out. What is it?"

"Some cultists—weirdos—captured her and put it in her."

"She said Russians. Said you were a CIA agent."

Paul shook his head, trying to dismiss the idea without suspicious vehemence. "Is she going to be OK?"

"It was a very small insult. The main danger is infection. We're keeping her here for observation and we want to run antibiotics intravenously. But I don't think you have anything to worry about. You have no idea what it was?"

"None."

"She says it made her hands and feet feel like they were on fire. They were torturing her with it."

"Doctor, when can I see her?"

"She'll be in postop for half an hour. After that."

He waited in the sullen bright hall, listening to the calls for Dr. This and Dr. That and the chimes that mean something to nurses. A cadaverous aide in a smeared uniform came for him at last, and he followed her squishing sneakers to Catherine.

They had put her on a ward where everybody's head was

in bandages or plaster. She was one of the few without a white cranium. Her wound was small, discreet. She was lying with her eyes closed, her body very rigid. She was not asleep.

"Catherine?"

She sighed, opened her eyes, looked at him. "I guess you got your wish. I'm not going back to the play for a while."

He took her hand, knelt down by the bed. There was no chair. "I'm sorry, Catherine."

She nodded, the tears welling in her eyes. "It hurt."

"It was supposed to."

"I couldn't tell them anything, that was the trouble! They were asking me something about my caseworker. Can you imagine? It was crazy. They thought I was on welfare."

"Case officer. CIA field agents report to case officers. They assumed that you were CIA."

"I should have been! There must have been lots of nice girls in the CIA who were interested in you, Paul Winter. They would have known what they were getting into at least." She pulled her hand out of his, started to roll over onto her side, winced, and lay still. Paul was aware of the hiss of the air conditioning, the steady moaning of a patient across the ward, the clatter of a tray of instruments, a nurse's urgent voice. A hospital at one A.M. is only a little quieter than noon.

"They won't bother you again, if it's any consolation."

"No? Why not?"

"I'm shifting my operations to South Dakota. They'll follow me there."

She was silent a long time. "I love you," she said finally. Her tone said more than her words. She loved him, but that wasn't all. She had started to hate him too.

"I love you too. I'm so sorry."

"Good."

"When I heard you screaming in there—"

"Shut up! Don't *ever* talk about that!"

He shuddered, remembering. It was a hard, hard moment. For her certainly worse.

He stood up. "Catherine, I'm going now." She nodded, said nothing. On her face was an expression too complex to read. His heart was filled with hurt and love. He stood, unable to turn away from her.

"Paul, will you come back?"

He couldn't deliver the cheerful lie. He could not leave her with a lie. "I doubt it. But not because I don't want to."

Her eyes sought his. "Good luck."

That was a little funny. He smiled, let her think she had encouraged him. "I do have one card left."

"You always have one card left."

"There's a man in CIA who knows a little something about ELF. He was Wiser's boss. I think I can probably get some help from him."

"If Wiser is any example of the kind of help they give—"

"Wiser was trying. He couldn't afford to be too obvious about it."

The corners of her mouth turned down briefly. She had disliked Wiser from the beginning.

"With Harmon dead and you in the hospital, CIA will at least check out my story."

"Dead?"

Paul nodded. "It's a brutal profession, Catherine. What can I tell you?"

"Profession, you call it!"

"It's been mine." He turned to make good on his promise to leave.

Her hand came out. "Not just yet. I want us to kiss, Paul."

In an instant he was leaning into her face, contacting her lips, kissing them gratefully.

"You saved me," she whispered. "Paul, I was *so glad* when you came. I just couldn't believe it. I was trying to pray, Paul, but it was like a nightmare. I couldn't remember the words or anything. It was horrible. I was so alone."

"The words don't matter really, do they? Wanting to— isn't that most of it?"

She smiled at that, softly. "You came."

"And now I'm going."

"Call me from South Dakota."

He shook his head. "No further contact. Too danger- ous."

For a minute he thought that she wasn't going to let go of his hand.

"I'll leave a number at the Sequoia."

"That is definitely a lie."

He could not disagree.

She closed her eyes. "My body still aches," she said. He slipped quickly away. Next stop Washington, then on to South Dakota. Not alone, he hoped. Surely he could get a small scratch team for the few days it would take. He could count on at least that much, even from Omar Jones.

12

THE *RESIDENTURA* WAS GOING to go mad now. They would dispense with secrecy; they would shoot him the instant they saw him. He had to break the cordon around him or not live through the night.

He got in a cab and returned to the Excelsior. A certain maneuver of escape possible only from there might extract him from the net. On the way back his thoughts returned to Catherine. He had not known that the heart could hurt this much on behalf of another person. It was not only that what had happened to her was his fault, but worse that his own survival had remained so important to him even while he was saving her. If it hadn't gone as well as it did, he suspected that he would eventually have left her behind.

The hunger for martyrdom in her defense was a lie. And yet, at the same time, he loved her with a passion that amounted to desperation.

If a man in a deadly profession clings to life too much, he becomes a kind of monster, capable of any betrayal, even murder, to preserve it. In such men there exists what could be called an ideal of violence. They kill to avoid death. Their humanity dissolves like old snow beneath a red sun.

He still had his key to the room in the Excelsior. He went up to wait for his visitors.

As he expected, they were not long in coming. He had already surmised that the people chasing him were not all professional clandestine officers. The *residentura* in America were nowadays peopled by computer specialists, economists, and such. Their main advantage so far had been numbers. To retain the asset of his own greater skill Paul had to keep putting them in positions where experience counted for more than bodies.

They first announced themselves by a long scraping sound outside the window. He knew that one of them was sliding along the wide sills of the old hotel, some foolishly brave soul armed with a silenced pistol. It would certainly be a pistol. By now they would have given up on the more sophisticated weapons. Men at extremes trust the familiar most, and the New York *residentura* must be at quite an extreme.

The scraping drew closer. The attacker was going to experience a moment of vulnerability when he arrived on this sill. Paul positioned himself before the drawn curtains. This close he expected to hear the scuffle of their arrival. In that they surprised him.

With a great clatter of glass and rip of curtains two men burst through the window, the force of their bodies slamming Paul back onto the bed. If it hadn't been for that bed, he would have been knocked breathless to the floor. That helpless moment would have been his last.

Too much self-confidence this time—and promptly rewarded. They were on him, both of them. He rose up and managed to throw off the smaller. The other one had him around the waist, was positioning to deliver a disabling kick to the groin. Paul relaxed the muscles of his torso and pushed downward as hard as he could against the back of the man's head while bringing his left knee up with all the force he could generate. There was a loud pop and the attacker became a sodden blanket of loose flesh.

"That's enough, Winter!"

An accent, not usual among the men of the *residentura*.

"Who're you, the code clerk?"

The pistol was indeed silenced. The hands holding it did not waver; he knew his ordnance even if he wasn't practiced on it. Only someone skilled with a .45 would fire it while holding it in one hand. This man held it in two.

Paul tried the trick of looking suddenly beyond the man's head. No luck; his eyes didn't flicker for the instant that Paul needed.

"Boris," the man said. "Boris!"

"Boris is going to be asleep for at least an hour."

Reinforcements would arrive momentarily; Paul had to get away from this pistol fast. He tried another in his inventory of tricks.

He dropped heavily to the floor, lay with his eyes open, holding his breath.

"What the devil?" His captor came a step forward. "Get up, you!" Paul took the kick like an old mattress might. The little man frowned. Was he deciding to get assistance? Yes. Good, good, go to the door, take your eyes off me for a second.

"Emilya, come in here!"

Now! Fists the little man never saw slammed into both temples. He dropped, his eyes staring blankly. Paul took the pistol from slack fingers.

Quickly he left the room. The woman he should have killed was pounding down the hallway waving a PPK. Her face was distended with hate and pain. He could hear her agonized, whistling breath. Must have creased her windpipe. Damn fool for not choking the life out of her.

He ran up the stairs and ducked into a broom closet full of dust and filthy towels. Her feet rattled past. Paul jumped out and backtracked. In a few more seconds she would catch the simple maneuver.

No, she already had; she was on her way back down. Paul would be only one flight ahead of her, which meant that she would certainly see him go through the door to the basement. That was most unfortunate. He hadn't expected to be followed into the tunnels. He didn't have enough running in himself for that.

It happened as he feared. He was just closing the basement door behind him when he heard more than one pursuer clatter out of the fire stairs and start running past the startled desk clerk. She had acquired reinforcements on the way down.

The basement was stinking and dim, but Paul remembered its twists and turns well enough. As a young man he had come to the old Cellar Club to listen to jazz. About a thousand years ago.

Here was the room, the chairs stacked atop the little round tables, the stage covered with dust, an empty milk carton its only occupant. Seeing a stage, Paul thought of Catherine. Every moment without her was painful. He could not help but worry.

He crossed the cellar and went through the little door beside the bandstand. The kitchen it led to was not lit even by the dim bulbs that illuminated the rest of the basement. Paul struck a match. At first he was confused, then he realized that the room was empty because the valuable kitchen equipment had been removed. He went through to the back. Before him now was a remarkable vision, a ghost town sheathed in dim light. As recently as the sixties the Excelsior Arcade had been a bustling strip of shops. No more. Nearby stairs led up to a rough cinder-block wall. On the other side would be the lobby of the hotel. Paul walked between the gaping, ruined arcade shops, Stillman News, Metro Lunch, Adorna Shoe Shops—names from the lost past. Paul had often lunched at Metro back when he was a green Treasury Department officer assigned to wire frauds.

He didn't want to think about that now; it reminded him that he was not nearly as young as the people behind him. At the end of the arcade was a mesh gate, long since sprung by vandals. Paul went through it and down the three steps into the pedestrian tunnel—a long, empty death trap with pursuit this close. There was an alternative, though. The Sixth Avenue subway ran directly beneath this walkway. He would open one of the escape hatches and drop onto the tracks.

No, he wouldn't, there wasn't time. They were already crashing along the arcade. To the right the tunnel extended about twenty yards to the 34th Street station. He ran past the WNEW Radio and Purdue Chicken posters, vaulted the turnstile, and hurried to the far end of the northbound platform.

Far behind him the token clerk was shouting angrily. Paul jumped onto the tracks and started walking the ties as fast as he could without risking a slip onto the electrified third rail. He was looking for one of the escape hatches to the surface. As a boy he had more than once used a hatch—and been taken to the old Centre Street Police Headquarters for popping out between the legs of a blue Irish the last time he tried it.

He had been an untamable kid. He avoided the reformatory only because he was the son of a senior vice-president of the International Guarantee Bank.

What the hell had the escape hatches actually looked like? He couldn't recall, not under these circumstances.

Silhouettes were appearing against the light of the station behind him. There was no hope of hitting anybody at this distance with a silenced pistol, but he got off one shot to slow them down. It didn't. He could hear Emilya coughing and cursing as she ran. Why did she hate him so much? For sparing her life?

There didn't seem to be an escape hatch around here, at least not one that Paul could see. He plodded on, marshaling his strength, forcing himself to breathe easily. Ahead he could see the 42nd Street station. Soon he would also have the problem of being silhouetted against lights. Were any of his pursuers carrying unsilenced weapons? If so he stood a good chance of getting hit.

To confuse them he hopped across the third rail and onto the southbound track.

A train was ahead in the 42nd Street station.

Next to diving off Spuyten Duyvil cliff, snagging a train in a tunnel had been the ultimate dare of his boyhood. He heard it start, fought to remember the technique. Everybody told of boys who had lost hands or feet or worse snagging trains. You put a lot of money on it during those long summer afternoons. A guy might make a dollar snagging a train, if he neither went yellow nor wound up at Bellevue.

The headlights of the train began to flicker, which meant that it was in motion. Now which side was best, right or left? There was more room on the left between the tracks. The horrible thrill of doing this came pouring up from the past. The train's noise rose, the rattling, deafening roar that was so familiar and yet so awesome. Paul stepped out for a moment into the tracks so that the motorman would see him. The horn blew three times, the warning code. Maybe the motorman would brake a little.

The lights grew closer and closer, the train pounded louder, became a shrieking wall of dirty silver. Paul looked up at the passing windows, down to the lethal, sparking tracks.

Then he was surrounded by panting, staggering people with guns in their hands. He reached up and felt a passing guardrail slam against his palm. Wind rose around him, and then he was banging against the side of the train, one hand jammed into the guardrail and the other flying free.

The 34th Street station appeared, and Paul was able to pull himself up between cars. He crouched there and did not leave the train until 23rd Street. He could have shouted for joy. There was no way he hadn't broken their cordon now. He stood on the platform dusting himself off.

It was terrible what this sort of thing did to good clothes. By now he must look worse than a Bowery wino.

There was no time to worry about it. Too bad the filthy suit made him conspicuous in this part of town.

He had to try for Omar Jones at once, despite the lateness of the hour. The cordon was broken, but that wouldn't last forever.

He went to a phone booth and direct-dialed Langley. A female voice answered. "Central Intelligence."

"Omar Jones, please."

"One moment."

It was one-thirty A.M., but Paul hoped that what he had to say would at least get him Jones's home number from the duty officer. "Mr. Jones's office."

"This is Paul Winter. Daisy?" What was she doing there so late?

"Mr. Winter, it's so kind of you to remember me. It's just terrible, isn't it?"

"Terrible?" Daisy had been Jones's chief secretary for at least ten years. "What's wrong?"

"You mean you don't—"

Paul felt sick. "What happened to him?"

"Oh, Mr. Winter, it's been in the papers! He was killed in an elevator fire with Harmon Wiser."

For a moment Paul was too stunned to speak. "Daisy," he said at last. "Daisy." He put down the phone. He must have missed Omar's name in the *News* list. But then he hadn't exactly been looking for it.

The Soviets considered themselves at war or they would never have killed a man as important as Omar Jones.

For the first time, alone on that street corner, Paul found himself really thinking that he was up against too much. He was going to lose.

The thought tightened his chest, made him gasp. ELF tuned correctly could make people into cheerful zombies.

There were swift night clouds passing through the sky, sheathing the top of the Empire State Building uptown in ghostly mist.

The tower, which he had always loved, now loomed horrible. An ELF installation up where King Kong had climbed would completely take over the wills of millions of New Yorkers. The Field would spread north and south, and this city would enter dreamy submission, the freedom of its citizens intricately and secretly devastated.

And not only New York. They would spread an ELF system across the whole of the country, a system of dreams and terrors. Every single citizen would be affected.

He had never really been in love with the country before now, but seeing the streams of cabs, the buses loaded with people, and imagining all the bright cities so gloriously tall and as delicate as leaves made him desperate beyond desperation not to lose his war.

The sequence was deadly clear to him.

They were going to use Jamshid in a weak Field in South Dakota to fire a few Minuteman missiles at themselves.

Their retaliation would destroy Minuteman and SAC.

Washington, thinking it had all started with an American accident, would be desperate to contain the destruction and negotiate.

That would amount to surrender. And then the black ships would come and the antennas would be emplaced.

The dream would begin, and it would be forever.

Paul fought his heart, his breath. Thoughts like these brought panic unlike anything he had ever experienced. If he believed it would help, he would have gone down on his knees in the middle of the street.

"God help me," he muttered, looking wildly for a cab. When he finally found one and slumped into the seat, he started shaking so badly that he could barely force himself to say his destination.

"Marine Air Terminal," came the gasping, trembling words.

The cab started off. He closed his eyes. OK, Mr. Winter, get yourself back together. You need the old cool head now. Come on, calm down, man! That's it, breathe deeply. Good man. That's it.

Now use your mind. Think this thing out.

He could be reasonably sure that he was no longer in the net. He'd be safe for a time. They didn't have the manpower to pick him up in a city this big. They would redeploy in South Dakota and hope that would do it.

His best chance—his only one, in fact—was to move so fast that they stayed off balance.

He'd take the indirect approach, charter a plane to Bismarck and drive to Rapid City from there. Landing at the Rapid City airport would be suicide.

Once there he would have to come into contact with them to obtain the location of their installation, but he had to do it on his own terms.

At some point, he realized, he was going to get himself killed. There just wasn't any way around it. But please, by all that is good, let me win my war first. The cab crossed the Triborough Bridge and soon slowed for the airport exit.

Pan Am's Atlantic Clippers had once set out from the Marine Air Terminal on their journeys to Europe. Now the terminal was one of the city's primary centers of corporate aviation, its tarmac crowded with Gulfstreams and Learjets. Around the lobby rotunda were old murals depicting the early triumphs of aviation, culminating in the ascension of a huge flying boat.

Paul went to the Butler Aviation office. Finding a charter this late at night was going to be difficult.

"You want to go to Bismarck?" The clerk looked him up and down. "Take the bus."

"It's urgent. I can pay."

"With what?"

"Credit cards, checks—"

"For you we'll extend the privilege of cash. To get from here to Bismarck on a Lear will cost—lemme see— $1,628.40, plus twenty-two percent overtime and a fuel surcharge of $344.50. Altogether that'll be $2,331.15."

"Do you take American Express?"

"Mister, not from you."

"My card is as good as anybody's. Better."

"You're dressed like a bum, you're unshaved, your clothes are filthy, and Howard Hughes is dead. Therefore I must conclude that you are a garden-variety bum with somebody else's credit cards."

Paul retreated to the lobby. In desperation he called Northwest Airlines and found the accuracy of what he had suspected. There were but three flights a day and the last one had left at eight. The earliest he could get another was at seven-forty tomorrow morning. By then they would be completely and totally ready for him.

He would have to get help, somebody more reliable-looking to do his chartering. That was all the reason he needed: he rushed to a pay phone and called her.

"Paul! Where are you?"

"At the Marine Air Terminal trying to charter a plane and failing. I need a famous actress's kind of clout, baby."

"You want me to get up out of my hospital bed and hold your hand while you sign the papers?"

"You've got to, if you're physically able."

"Well, how shall I put it? I'm obviously insane but I'll be there in thirty minutes."

He waited with a cup of coffee in the cafeteria, wondering whether or not the *residentura* was watching the hospital and if he had given them a chance to pick up his trail again by getting her to come out here.

He sipped his coffee and thought of Catherine. He was going to take her right back into danger if he allowed her to come along with him. He could tell himself that she was safer with him and that would be a lie, or he could tell himself that he just couldn't bear to be without her at such a hard time in his life.

That would be the truth.

"You look like a wet dog that just got a whipping."

"You look great! How did you get here so fast, and how did you get those clothes?" She was in a fresh blue dress. Except for the bulge of gauze behind her ear she looked more than perfect. When love is so great that it usually hurts, a painless moment—such as coming together again—has extraordinary impact on the lover.

For Paul it was like that, and he thought perhaps for her too. Nothing was said about it. Their joined hands spoke for them.

"I had my things sent over from the theater, and Jenny loaned me her limo. Her chauffeur, Edward, is a very fast driver."

"Rent me my jet so you can go home and get some sleep."

"Yeah, right, Paul. We've got to hassle together a little first, I see. I'm going with you, obviously, and you know it."

"I don't know it."

"Otherwise you wouldn't have called me. Now come on."

Charlie had taken care of the plane. It seemed that Jenny used this place frequently. Her movies as well as her plays were hits, so why not? The clerk didn't flinch when he saw Paul coming over with Catherine Harris, nor when he signed the passenger manifest Mr. and Mrs. Howard Hughes.

"Reports of my death have been prematurely exaggerated," Paul muttered.

"What was that all about?"

"Never mind. Let's be on our way."

The plane was a small piece of pretty clockwork, blue and white in the stony sodium vapor lights of the runway and inside all leather and wood. The pilots, disheveled and one of them somewhat bleary, came hurrying across the pavement.

It did not take long to get a clearance for takeoff. The terminal isn't busy at two A.M.

The interior of the plane was cramped but luxurious, equipped for moving the super-rich from colony to colony. Catherine snuggled down on one of the two facing couches and closed her eyes. Paul found the bar and poured himself a finger of Black Label. Not a terrible Scotch, but a definite bite for someone with a taste for the better single malts.

"We'll be arriving at four-fifteen A.M. central time, sir. If you want to make any calls, the phone is on."

Paul nodded. As soon as the copilot closed the door to the flight deck, he took up a vigil over Catherine. He could not leave her side. From time to time he would lean over and kiss her cheek. She did not stir.

After what she had endured, most people would be in a state of panic for days. Yet she slept with the easy peace of a child in this roaring little airplane, calmly oblivious as it pressed on, deep into the night.

Let him think that she was asleep; maybe it would calm him down. As he hovered beside the couch, she could sense his desperation and fear. From time to time he would kiss her cheek, and a wash of alcoholic breath would remain behind.

She thought of the teary face of her torturer, the nurse who was being forced to do a dirty job. She thought of the pain, the almost unimaginable agony, so intense that it did not seem completely real even while it was being administered.

When she had seen Paul's gentle, haunted face appear above her, she had experienced relief and love unlike any she had known before. The fact that he had managed to reach her raised him to the level of hero. She had understood even through her urgency to escape how strong he really was.

But just at the moment he seemed more like a buzzard as he loomed over her, boozy and miserable. Something had scared him to death.

Would he ever tell her what it was? Did she even want to know? She intended to stay with him because she loved him. She didn't need courage for that, only loyalty.

He loved her too, but what he knew about his private war had made his heart into a machinery of fear.

His picture of himself was pitifully wrong. He believed himself weak, and yet was better and purer than any man she had ever before known.

Courage was so much a part of him that he didn't even believe in it.

Catherine suspected that he assumed himself a coward.

She understood that he was going to face an incredible test of some kind in South Dakota.

Could this thing he called ELF actually be that bad?

Seeing his eyes, she knew that it must be.

She wanted to help him. Her motives were as simple as love and also as complicated. Her part of their love was to hold him when he faltered and to push him forward when he needed it.

But there was no time for love now; such tests as this do not come into their lives often, and they must be treated with the highest seriousness when they do.

She remembered his hilarious, innocent courtship of her, just as winning as it would have been fifty years ago. She would help him, of course, yes, no matter the danger, no matter the bandage on her head and the suffering.

"You're not asleep anymore, Catherine. Please—"

Naturally he would be able to tell. "I was."

"Only for a moment. You're lying there wishing you'd never gotten tangled up with me, and I can't stand it."

"If you want to demean yourself, go ahead, but please don't insult me in the process. Actually I was enjoying those kisses you've been giving me."

He lurched in the small space, hugged her hard. He was shaking, finally overcome by the emotions beneath the surface. "If you stay with me you might get killed."

"Don't you think I know that?"

His answer was silence.

"Has it ever occurred to you that I feel the same way about you as you do about me? I went through hell after you left, Paul, wondering what was happening to you. We were meant to share things, you and I. That's a fact and neither one of us can escape it. You waste yourself worrying about it. Just accept it.''

He looked at her. "You're wise. That always amazes me about you. Twenty-four and wise.''

She did not say what came to mind: that his lack of wisdom at age forty-eight was equally amazing.

Even though they said nothing more, just sat on the couch in each other's arms, she sensed that she had at last caused him to test his feelings. He leaned his head against hers, and she drew it down into her lap. They remained quiet together.

As they landed in Bismarck, the little jet was buffeted by wind; somewhere to the west lightning guttered, flickering the dark interior with blue. Dawn was just coming, and there were storms about.

Catherine was surprised when they rented a car; she had thought that such things were easy to detect.

"For the police it'd be easy, but remember that we're dealing with the KGB. They can't exactly demand cooperation from Hertz."

She slept on the drive southward along Highway 83, stirring only to the crash of thunder. For a little while she watched the landscape passing, the glory of space revealed in the lightning flashes, the windswept little towns with names like Strasburg and Onida and Pierre; the road following the land's stately march.

When she awoke and thought to take a turn at the wheel, dull light filled the car. The radio was playing softly, the sort of old dance music Paul favored. He drove with his head leaning against the window, one hand on the wheel. The other lay on the seat between them. She covered it with her own. "I'll drive."

"Too late. We're here."

The land was becoming spotted with houses, and soon a glowing little city began to be visible from the road's higher elevations.

"The Black Hills are to the west. We're right in the middle of the Eighty-third Strategic Missile Wing. There are Minuteman silos all around us.''

Catherine looked toward the jagged line of hills silhouetted against the rising gray sky. They were not gentle like her home hills of Virginia. In the gray light the emptiness of the land made it seem sinister. But there was no sign of missiles.

She loved the hotel in Rapid City, an impeccably restored old place called the Alex Johnson. The lobby was all beams and wood, with an enormous stone fireplace.

They were shown to a room that looked toward the Black Hills through spacious windows. Day had arrived, and the world outside was rich with sunlight, the morning's storms in abeyance. After so many months of New York, Catherine was awed by the luxuriant space, the sky, and the twenty-mile view. Their room was large and sunny, with a painting of an Indian on the wall above the bed and a wide green-carpeted floor.

After the bellman departed, Paul went into the big bathroom and started taking off his clothes. ''God, how disgusting. Do I smell as bad as I look?''

''Don't ask.''

He sent his clothes to the laundry and they took a long shower together. Afterward Paul showed her a pistol encased in blue metal. ''This is a silenced .45 automatic. It will be our first, last, and only defense against the person or persons who will shortly arrive at our door.''

A cold, cold thought came into Catherine's mind. She knew what Paul was going to ask her to do.

The face of the torturer appeared before her. She jumped back, so real was the hallucination. Paul took her, held her close to his naked body. She looked over his shoulder at the huge sunlit view. The predawn grimness of the morning land was gone. Now it was all light and joy. ''I don't want to kill anybody, Paul.''

He buried his face in her neck. ''You're so precious to me, Cath.''

She decided that they would make love and began to kiss him. He was shaking with desire when she quit. They went together to the bed and lay awhile, touching. He seemed almost like the sunlight now. For the moment that haunted look was gone. There was the most delicate joy between them as they took their pleasure; it seemed to Catherine almost a prayer of bodies. He was fierce and yet gentle, pressing her to the bed, probing and then entering with his hugeness, making her forget the pain, forget the fear, in the happy sweating, pumping pleasure of their love.

He sank down on her, this wonderfully lean old man with his sleek, hairless body and shudderingly hard muscles. They shared a long silence together. Perhaps it was the pressure they were under that made it so, but this seemed an unusually blessed moment.

Paul was the first to break the silence. "We can't afford this. We have to make some plans."

Not just now, my dearest one. She cast about for something to preserve the beauty of the moment. "Look at the hills. They really are dark. They're wonderful."

"They're covered with pine. The contrast with the grasslands makes them seem like they're in shadow. But that isn't what we need to discuss."

It was over. So be it. Paul was right to keep to the business at hand.

"They're going to find us soon. I want them to."

She shook her head, not understanding.

"We have no other way of getting to their installation. They've got to tell us where it is."

"And they will, I suppose. Just like that."

"Don't get scared. I don't need you scared."

"You should talk, you who were sweating it out last night in the plane. I *am* scared and I don't mind admitting it."

"I got over it, Catherine."

The doorbell rang. "Room service."

"You don't even have any clothes to wear."

Paul went to the door. "Now I do."

"Half an hour? I don't believe it."

"A good hotel and a good tip. The combination has been known to work wonders."

Despite everything, Catherine was beginning to feel a sense of competence. In deep, important ways, she knew that she was helping Paul.

He became lighter and more brisk, and when he demonstrated the pistol to her, showing her how to unlatch the safety with her thumb and how to aim at the middle of a man's chest, his voice was soft with confidence.

"There won't be many of them because they'll want to remain as inconspicuous as possible in the hotel. It's one thing to gang-rape somebody in a big New York hotel, but in a place like this the least thing out of the ordinary will be noticed by the house dick."

He explained to her how to shoot and said that she was going to have to start shooting the moment their pursuers entered the door. "They'll ring the bell, demand entry on some pretext. The second they're in, fire. I'll take care of the rest of it."

"What rest?"

"There'll be an officer behind whoever comes through the door first. The officer is the one we're going to want to have a chat with."

"I suppose he'll tell us everything we want to know."

"He'll tell us."

She didn't care for his tone. Catherine had absolutely no intention of participating in any torture and killing. Then she felt the pistol in her hand. What did she expect to do with it, if not kill?

Her heart had already made the decision. She would kill for this man. She loved him that much.

"It's worth the sacrifice, Catherine." Paul stood facing out the window. "We have an incredible responsibility. You understand that, don't you?"

"I suppose I must."

He turned suddenly. His face was radiant, a sight so unusual that Catherine must have looked astonished. He burst out laughing. "Let's have ourselves some breakfast. Eggs, bacon, O.J., about a gallon of coffee."

She dialed the coffee shop. Ten minutes passed and the food was there, big fried eggs and thick bacon, fresh orange juice and coffee with a solid, newly brewed aroma. "This looks wonderful," she said. "I hadn't realized how hungry I was." They ate in silence.

"I'm going to get some sleep," Paul said afterward.

"Sleep, after all that coffee?"

He lay down on the bed and was soon breathing heavily. The frightened man of the small hours had indeed disappeared completely, to be replaced by this creature of studied ease. Excessively, dangerously calm. She lay on the double bed beside him and watched him sleep. Every time she decided that she understood Paul Winter, another aspect revealed itself.

Morning grew old, and afternoon came. There were sounds of light traffic outside. Catherine slipped away on a dream, and in her dream soared out the window and down a wide, quiet street to the Richmond of her girlhood. She sat on the porch beneath the wisteria vine and cried, it was so beautiful. She had known even then how youth ends, in these fearful commitments.

At first she did not understand what had awakened her. Then she realized that Paul was on his feet, motioning her to get up and take her position.

The doorbell had rung.

13

Amir Pakravan lay on his bed smoking a cigarette, staring at the dim ceiling. He kept the curtains tightly drawn; he did not like to look out at Rapid City.

Captain Kislitsin, the GRU's local chief of station, came in quite suddenly. He tossed his briefcase onto the foot of the bed and sat on the edge, drawing his long, aristocratic fingers around his knees. "Would you say that this is Paul Winter?" He dropped a small photograph of a man standing at the hotel's registration desk onto Amir's chest. Pakravan fumbled for the bedside lamp.

"So he's here at last. He looks a wreck."

"He's vicious. He wounded a woman in New York. A nurse! Can you imagine it?" He stared away toward the door.

"Winter is a weak man. I know him."

"Oh, yes? If he is weak, then our own people in New York must be hopeless."

"Quite possibly."

"In any case checking into this hotel was his great mistake." Kislitsin rubbed his hands together with exaggerated glee, then betrayed his nervousness by fumbling for a cigarette.

"It wasn't a mistake. He wants to negotiate or he wouldn't be here."

Kislitsin crossed the room, a marching cat. "Negotiate? What the devil does he have to trade?"

"Nothing. Of course." Paul's voice came into Pakravan's memory, that intense, droning softness.

"Then we kill him?"

Had Paul gained any weight or lost any hair? Pakravan got up and swept the curtains open. The sun burst into the room. "Where is he?"

"A suite on the top floor."

"Paul likes small rooms. The suite must be for the benefit of his actress." He was living better now. And why not, with all the money he was rumored to have made in Laos? Certainly in Shah days he had always enjoyed luxuries. Paul was elegant, that was the word for him. An elegant bastard. "He helped me extensively when I was in the SAVAK."

"Then you know his ideas, his methods."

"Nobody knows Paul. Not even Paul. But I can predict one thing—unless we act with cunning we won't get him."

"Perhaps we should play a bit of chess with him—"

"We have no such orders! Our orders are to kill!"

Pakravan turned the latch on the window and raised it. Sweet, hot air came into the room. He breathed deeply. He could not tell Kislitsin that they had only until two A.M., when the Field was to be cast. No, that was not the good Captain's department. His specialty was the monitoring of the SAC base and its missile wings. This station had carried out its prosaic duties until Amir and his team had arrived last week.

Kislitsin was forceful and quite good at his job. He was running a major agent in the public-affairs office at the Air Force base. All Kislitsin's man had to do to get information was hang about with the intelligence officers in their headquarters upstairs from his office. The easy camaraderie of the Air Force made it possible to obtain enormous amounts of data.

As effective as he was in his prosaic way, Kislitsin was not close to the equal of a Paul Winter. Pakravan even had doubts about his own ability to defeat Paul, and he had known him for a long time.

"Have you reported Winter's arrival to New York, Captain?"

"Yes, sir."

"No response?"

"I would have given it to you immediately."

"Yes, of course you would." Pakravan wondered what Kislitsin's real orders regarding him were. Was he scheduled to be terminated along with the rest of the Black Magic team? Probably so.

Well, never mind. One lives a long enough life of deceit, and the end of it comes to seem a relief. Sometimes he thought of death in exactly the same way that he thought of slipping away into a good hot *korsi* on a cold January day.

"Winter aside, you've got to have your team in place to terminate Black Magic tonight." Although he knew that Kislitsin would get his orders concerning this from New York, he could not resist saying it. It was as fascinating as ordering his own execution.

"I know."

The two men looked at each other. When Pakravan realized that Kislitsin was standing there worrying about whether or not the mysterious colonel had orders to terminate *him*, he nearly laughed aloud. "Perhaps, Captain Kislitsin, we will be toasting the end of American imperialism by this time tomorrow. You and I together."

Kislitsin did not answer directly. "I hope that they keep making American cigarettes. I couldn't live without them."

"You know what Pyotr Teplov once said about the plans for the United States? He said, 'We think of it as an empty tablet.' But perhaps they will be able to make cigarettes even on an empty tablet."

"Teplov isn't in power yet."

Pakravan said nothing. He knew from the coding on Teplov's cable traffic that he was in Sverdlovsk. That meant that he was trying to take Black Magic away from the soldiers. Certainly this must not be discussed with Kislitsin, a military intelligence officer.

"What do you think we should do, Captain Kislitsin?"

"Put together a force of ten men. Rush the door, break it in, and kill them both."

"Our team will be caught."

"Winter will be dead."

"But the murder will be a local sensation. When American intelligence hears about it, they will pour into Rapid City. We'll end up blown." Even as he spoke he wondered how true it was. Did he not, perhaps, have a little touch of love for Paul within him, even now?

Paul at the Intercontinental bar ordering that horrible Scotch of his . . . Paul saying, ever so gently, "There are ways of interrogation that don't involve torture, Amir" . . . Paul's profound moral conflicts . . . his childish idealism . . .

Paul Winter was deeply human, the kind of man Persians much respect. Sometimes he had seemed to Amir as otherworldly as a *mullah* of the best kind. A rare man.

"We must kill him quietly, Captain Kislitsin. Quietly and with no fuss."

"You will be responsible?"

"Of course."

"Good. My orders specifically prohibit me from engaging in acts of violence except in self-defense."

"I know that. You're not Directorate V."

"I'm glad you realize my position."

"Just keep your surveillance net spread. Especially the comings and goings at the base and the civilian airport. If Winter has support, we want to know about it as early as possible."

"Very well."

Pakravan turned his back on Kislitsin. The captain waited a moment, then Pakravan heard him pick up his briefcase and start for the door.

"Captain."

"Yes, sir."

"You'd better start breaking yourself of American cigarettes."

Kislitsin did not laugh, but at least he left, and Amir was glad to see the back of him. It made him uneasy to feel this disloyal love for Paul in the presence of another officer. One never knew what another might notice about oneself.

Here he was, a gamesman capable of commitment to any side, being asked by his current side to murder the man he most honored in the opposition. You didn't do that; it wasn't playing by the accepted rules.

He looked down toward 6th Street. It was as usual quiet, the hot pavement almost empty. A woman with two small girls crossed at the corner; a Ford passed the hotel. All quiet, all well.

Soon after the destruction of SAC all this would change. The military part of the war would create minor damage in Rapid City. The citizens would see flashes to the north tonight and feel shocks as the tiny Russian warheads devastated the missile fields. Twenty miles south there would be no hint of war.

Four days from now the local ELF antenna would arrive and be erected in the Black Hills. Its Field would dominate the whole of the northern plains, swamping the weak Field now being projected from Russia for Jamshid's use.

Long before the new antenna came, Amir was to kill Jamshid. Nobody wanted his sort around anywhere near a really powerful Field.

It was designed to affect the emotional life of its victims, not to provide a vicious creature like the boy with living toys. It was designed to create a paradise of happiness. Worker joy.

In the depth of his belly Amir Pakravan felt a curious stirring. To know the future of others was an unforgettable thrill. To see the face of one who does not know that he has been condemned is an experience beyond pleasure. ELF. As terrible a condemnation as man had ever invented.

The girl in the halter, the children with her, would they dance to the joy of Teplov's tune? To hear him explain it, they would. And the rancher passing in the pickup truck, and the lawyers in the office building opposite? They too.

And me?

It was time to gather his force and go to Paul.

He dialed 2235, waited through a ring. "Viktor Ivanovich, come, please, and bring Constantin Feodorovich with you. Please wear full equipment." His force was spread through this and the Imperial Motor Hotel, one and two men to a room. Altogether there were twelve. With Kislitsin's group the Soviet Union had thirty-three men on this station. While the other two made ready and came up, Pakravan began composing a "read and destroy" cable for Teplov. He consulted his routing codes and finally addressed it so that it could be transmitted directly from Washington to Sverdlovsk.

He withdrew his scrambler from his suitcase beneath the bed and inserted the telephone into the black plastic device. Then he made a call to the Washington *residentura*'s forwarding number in Los Angeles.

He listened as the high-pitched whine of the forwarding station came over the phone. Then he began to press numbers into the scrambler. It was a simple system, with each letter of the alphabet assigned a number. But the scrambler reassigned all the numbers on a random basis after obtaining timing information from the forwarding station. All Soviet codes in the United States changed hourly. The big Honeywell computers at the embassy and in Moscow generated the random changes and kept track of them. It was as perfect a system of coded communications as had ever been developed.

His message was simple: "Winter in Rapid City. Attempting immediate execution. Will advise soonest."

Pakravan glanced at his watch. Three P.M. Two o'clock in the morning in Sverdlovsk. So the bad news would wake the monster up. If, that is, it ever slept.

The information shattered Teplov's sleep as if it had been an explosive charge. Paul Winter had made it to South Dakota.

He rose from his cot and ordered the watch officer who had brought in the cable to leave the room. No soldiers wanted here, please. He scrambled for the New York *residentura*'s last note. Yes, here it was. "Winter contained. He will be dead within the hour."

"Somebody's coming home," he shouted at the stuffy little room. "Somebody's getting shot!" Be careful, man, don't shout so loud. This place is made of paper and spit. Even the concrete bulkheads of the Black Magic installation were in places turning to powder—and in other places bulging ominously. In the quiet of the night it groaned.

He grabbed the phone. "Moscow Center!" He had to get through to Andropov at once. "This is a coded call from Red Wind to Black Fox."

A silence followed. Even though the call was scrambled, there was no assurance that NSA couldn't unscramble it. Since the shuttle had started they had placed some phenomenal new satellite equipment in orbit that could monitor every electromagnetic communication in the entire Eastern bloc. Signals officers joked that it wouldn't be long before NSA had succeeded in bugging every telephone on earth.

Whenever he picked up a telephone, Teplov felt obscurely outdone. It made his claws come out.

"Black Fox here." The scrambler rendered voices unrecognizable, making Andropov sound like a frog in a tin box. There was a new device, however, that was supposed to solve this security problem.

"Test, test, test. Is that sufficient?"

"Forget it, Pyotr. The voice identification system won't work until the people from Mitsubishi get finished with the French job and come back here. The goddamn French job."

A curse upon the Director; he sounded filthy drunk. What a wonderful Marxist was the Director. A real inspiration, the swine.

"I have cable traffic strongly suggesting that we have a traitor in the New York *residentura*. Maybe more than one. I want to recall Boris Panin and hold him under house arrest pending an investigation."

"Yuri Panin's boy? Never."

"He cabled me that Winter was contained. Three hours later I get a cable from Pakravan that Winter is there! In Dakota!"

"Yuri Panin's boy is a patriot."

"Oh, hell, maybe he's just slipping, but I want him out of the picture for a few days. Send him to Bermuda on rest trip if nothing else."

"I'll cut the orders in the morning."

Teplov almost wailed. "Cut them now!"

Andropov came back with a low, satisfied chuckle. "Hot enough for you yet, my dear *Colonel?*"

Teplov rang off. If he managed it all the way across this hideous Black Magic tightrope, he was going to do much more than just retire Yuri Andropov. That one wouldn't end up in a Zhukovka dacha, no indeed. He would experience the fierce justice of the proletariat. He would be condemned to live outside the Field.

Teplov began to pace. He couldn't dream about Andropov's punishment now.

Winter must be a ghost! "I could have killed you in Laos, you swine." But no, that was not allowed. Winter was CIA support for General Dong, and the good general was exporting tons and tons of raw opium to Singapore for processing into heroin for the U.S. market. "Officers will not take any action which will interfere with drug traffic into the

United States and will assist and support this traffic whenever possible.''

So Paul Winter had lived, the innocent who thought that General Dong was a Lao patriot loyal to Souvanna Phouma. He wasn't even Lao; he was overseas Chinese. And Winter wasn't assisting him to "disrupt the integrity of the HCM trail" as the fool believed; he was assisting him in running the opium.

Winter was a man who could do that and deceive himself into believing that he had not. A good man, certainly, but susceptible to delusion. Like Homer's heroes, he was heroic precisely because he did not understand his flaw. He was not like a scientific socialist, who could observe flaws through the microscope of dialectic and ruthlessly eliminate them in himself and others.

How ironic that the crazy delusion that he could stop something as massive as Black Magic was enabling Winter to threaten to do that very thing!

Teplov held his head in his hands. It banged and throbbed, a horrible headache beginning to blur his vision and make him sick. He sank onto his cot, buried his face in the greasy little pillow, and gave vent to his terror and rage, bellowing until his throat hurt.

Then he sat up. He took a deep breath of the fetid air. It didn't help much, and the half-empty vodka bottle on the desk would help even less. He was a man under too much pressure, and he was beginning to think that he might simply fly apart.

Pressure. If there was too much, then some must obviously be relieved. Obviously, obviously, but *what?* He could not call Ludmilla Semilovna. No, that would expose that plot to the GRU. There was nothing to do there but hope that she had followed her orders.

And as for America, everything he did seemed to have negative consequences for the situation here.

Walking the tightrope, step by step. Were circus performers also made to feel this way by the multiple possibilities of falling? No, he had seen their bland, concentrated faces often enough to know that theirs was just a job.

Angrily he dismissed the imagined tightrope. The thought of its swaying threatened to nauseate him. He tried another favorite comfort.

"To be in Dombai now, in the high last snow with a bottle of *petrovka* under my arm and a bag of freshly plucked mushrooms." He shut his eyes tightly and vowed never to open them again. "Dombai, Dombai, Dombai." When he breathed it was the rich scent of Dombai air, the crispness of wild pines and wood smoke from the dachas down the mountain.

It changed to the smell of concrete and sweat.

He had to get out of here.

He burst from the office, startling the guard at the end of the hall. "I'm going up to the control room. I have business there."

"The control room is off limits to nontechnical staff until 0600."

Teplov almost went mad fumbling for his papers. "Clearance . . . of course!" He held out his red leatherette folder. The boy took it and carefully examined the documentation.

He handed back the folder and snapped off a salute. All a mad charade; everybody in this place knows I have a First. Everybody knows I have a First. Everybody!

"Ah, Teplov, come join us!"

Astonishingly, the control room was filled with people. Igor Gorkin was sitting at the control console, a haggard remnant of the huge, dark man whom Teplov had met two days ago. "It's two o'clock in the morning, Dr. Gorkin."

"And you look it!" He laughed, a mirthless roar.

"What—" He indicated the activity with a wave of his hand. Gorkin crossed his lips with his finger.

"Very secret. Not even Belik knows. Should you?"

"Yes, please!"

"If Belik bothered to come out here more often he could know too. But he prefers his mistress to our tomb! Now, look at this instrument. This is an ELF receiving device. Not much more than a radio especially designed to pick up the frequency. And look!''

The needle on its face was quivering slightly.

"You're transmitting and this is picking it up?"

"We are not transmitting. You know who is? The U.S. Navy." Teplov's stomach began to tear at itself. A fist of bile rose in his throat.

"They've been ordered to restart their ELF field in Wisconsin."

"What does it mean?"

"Before they shut it down in 1979, it was running at about a quarter-hertz off the correct tuning. Then for two days last week it suddenly came back on, at the correct tuning. That was what caused our difficulty, not some natural phenomenon as we first thought. Now it is on again, and again at the correct tuning."

"They have it."

"They are just discovering it. We are witnesses."

Teplov could not resist the agony of irony that made him explode with laughter. There were a few answering chuckles. "We've already been through that," Gorkin muttered.

"The Navy? The U.S. Navy."

"ELF at most tunings works as a very high-penetrating form of radio wave. Only at the one harmonic does it affect the human mind. Their original interest was in creating a worldwide submarine communications system."

Gorkin had mentioned that they had shut down their project in 1979. It was in 1979 that Winter was exposed to Hassan's ELF field. His report and subsequent investigations must have had more of an impact than anybody had suspected.

The magnificent window of opportunity that ELF superiority represented to the USSR was rapidly closing.

"If their transmitter is on, will it interfere with our activities?"

In answer Gorkin raised the lid of a bleary eye with his

finger. "Thirty hours of continuous labor caused this and prevented that. We have changed the frequency of our transmission by a few millihertz—not enough to affect reception but more than enough to prevent interference. Their signal is weak and diffuse, oscillating all over the place."

"You're certain that the adjustments have been made properly?"

"I am going on a personal inspection of the ELF array this moment. If it will make you feel more confident, come with me."

They went down a long, flimsy metal ladder past what appeared to be huge leaves of gold so thin that they were translucent. Here and there along the way naked light bulbs shone, but their glow was absorbed by the size of the chamber. When they at last reached the bottom Teplov looked up to a strand of bulbs disappearing into the foggy reaches. There was fine mist falling.

"This is the largest underground room ever constructed by man, Colonel." Gorkin brushed his shoulders. "The major problem at first was controlling its internal weather. We used to have rainstorms in here."

He grabbed an electric megaphone from a rack affixed to the sweating stone. "Anatol! Anatol! Send me the car!"

In a few moments a loud electric hum filled the air and a ski lift appeared, moving rapidly down a spiral of steel surrounding the enormous antenna.

"You want to come?"

Gorkin had correctly perceived Teplov's need to do something, anything, that had the appearance of work. The car was cramped, merely a steel platform with a large electric motor attached. They rose with buzzing protest and a smell of hot wires. "Is it dangerous to be so close to the antenna?"

"Not unless somebody turns on the Field. This close to such a powerful transmission the results would be unfortunate."

Teplov could not resist asking what *unfortunate* meant.

"Our brains would short out like overloaded transformers. Its happened more than once. The victim is left, well—just blank. Nobody home. And nobody ever returns."

Unfortunate.

They arrived at the site of the technical work at the very top of the array. Gorkin inspected several of the leaves, looking at their edges under a powerful glass. "Good work," he said. "Do I need to look at the rest of it, Anatol?"

"I'll sign my report if you will."

"I've got all the geniuses," he said as he scrawled his name across the bottom of the long document. "That's why the rest of the country is in such a muddle—except your Sverdlovsk, of course, Colonel."

Teplov watched as if from a great distance. He had been insane to come down here away from his teletype and his telephone. And yet something within him had been fulfilled by the journey. It was deeply fortifying actually to be in a place of real, physical Communist achievement. The largest underground chamber on earth, Gorkin had said. Altogether an antidote for a pounding head and a tired mind. If the workers could do this, he also could do his duty.

The car started off with a jerk and careened back to the floor of the chamber barely under control.

At first the climb up the ladder was a matter of little consequence. Then it became difficult, then an ordeal. By the time they had again reached the control room Teplov was trembling, his whole body wracked by the pain of the effort. Gorkin seemed hardly to notice. "I didn't need to go down either, Colonel. But it reassures me too, just seeing it. Knowing that it's really there."

"Yes."

"I knew just what was in your mind the moment you appeared in the control room."

"Thank you, Comrade Director."

Gorkin paused a moment, seemed to sink into thought.

Then he spoke more softly. "Don't mention the American signal to Belik. If the General Staff found out about it—"

"Of course. I understand perfectly."

"Ah. Then no more need be said."

No, my dear Project Director, no more.

Teplov returned to his office and, as the teletype was for the moment silent, began to review his American antenna placement schedule. He found no flaw.

Catherine knew the moment she heard the doorbell who it would be.

She took her position opposite the door, the pistol in her hand. She was going to kill. She, Catherine Harris, was going to pull the trigger of a funny-looking gun and somebody was going to face the final mystery.

She felt confident of her own survival. Paul's rehearsal had been careful and the plan was clever.

From the door the men entering would see a woman pointing a pistol at them. The trouble was, the woman they were seeing would be a reflection in the mirror on the back of the bathroom door. She would be across the room. If they had a chance to fire at all, it would be in the wrong direction.

She felt the gun in her hand, its heft, the wetness of the sweaty steel. She nodded to Paul. They exchanged a glance. Paul spoke.

"It's not locked, gentlemen. Come on in."

The door clicked and swung open. Just exactly as Paul had predicted, two men entered. Both of their faces turned toward the bathroom door and Catherine pulled her trigger twice, aiming as best she could. The silencer reduced the shots to two inoffensive-sounding pops.

But they had a shattering effect. One of the men flew up like a surprised rabbit, then dropped on his back with a thud that shook the room.

The other just stood there, staring in wonder at the mirror. Paul pushed past him and in an instant was dragging a third individual in from the hall. But Catherine took little notice of this. She was transfixed by the spectacle of her second victim's death. His head sank to his chest and he started to sway. A continuous ripple of words came from his lips; Catherine thought that he might be praying in Russian. His shoulders slumped and his hands fluttered at the end of slack arms. As Paul brought the third man to the center of the room, Catherine's victim sank to his knees. His hands, now touching the floor, made a sound like roaches clattering in a bread box. A thin cry came from his lips. Dark red blood spread across the bowed back of his cheap suit.

It was as simple as that, and as huge. Her feelings surprised her. She was not scared or disgusted so much as awed by how important the simple act of pulling a trigger had been.

The silenced pistol had made only insignificant clucks when she fired it. She looked at it, quite warm now, as warm and as rigid as certain flesh. The hand that held it had given such pleasure to the strange race of men. They had kissed those fingers.

Once Jenny had said, "It exhausts me to be at the center of so much longing."

Paul was embracing the third man. Catherine saw tears on his cheeks. "Hell, Amir, why did it have to be you?" Astonishingly, they were friends. Their community must be like a nasty little city, its inhabitants condemned to search the dark, bad streets forever.

Amir hung his head like a naughty child. Catherine saw his pistol lying on the floor, another exactly like the one she was holding. She picked it up. Neither of the two men took notice of her.

"Paul, you got me."

"You were easy, Amir. You forgot everything I ever taught you."

"Maybe so."

"And maybe not, eh? There's room for you on this side, Amir. We'll take you in."

Amir shook his head. "It's much more complicated than

that. You never really understood me, Paul. You see, I was always KGB.''

Paul embraced him as a father would. "Don't talk about it now. And don't assume that I didn't know.''

As Paul had instructed her, she began to fill the bathtub with water. "We'll get a little of our own back,'' he had said. "You'll see.'' Exactly what that had to do with the tub he had refused to say.

"I don't need that water, do I?'' he was saying as Catherine returned from the bathroom.

"Paul, my old friend, obviously you need it.''

As if struck a blow, Paul turned away from him. "I'll do my duty, Amir, you know that.''

"Would you expect less of me?''

Paul shook his head, suddenly brought Catherine into full participation in the situation with a long, searching look. "Take the belts off the other two, tie his hands and feet, please, darling.'' His voice was husky; he was embarrassed. "I've got to drag it out of the poor jerk.''

Although it made her shake almost uncontrollably to touch her dead, she managed to carry out his instructions. When she turned back, Amir was wearing only underpants. "I don't want to get my good suit wet.'' He grinned quite horribly. His brown skin had acquired the waxy pallor of fear.

She bent down and drew one of the belts around his ankles, fastened it tightly, then did the same with his wrists.

"Come on, Amir, give me a break.''

"That is exactly what I cannot do.''

"OK, Cath, let's put him in the tub.'' Paul took him under the arms and Catherine lifted his feet. He had fine, delicate feet, beautifully arched. His toenails, though, were cracked and misshapen.

He sat in the tub, his face in curious repose. "Paul, do you appreciate this?''

"Amir, for God's sake reconsider. I'm going the whole way if you don't.''

"No, you aren't, Paul."

"This time I have to."

"So get started then. I'm waiting to see you harm a fellow human being."

Paul looked suddenly a great deal older. Then he leaned over the tub and pressed Amir's shoulders until his head was beneath the surface. For a long time Amir remained absolutely still.

Catherine tried to be revolted.

"Hold his ankles."

"Right." I sound so calm! But why does that surprise me? I feel calm. What we are doing to this man is horrible, but necessary. And *they* did worse to me. There might be consequences from it yet.

The face beneath the water was twisted, distorted by diffraction into a pinched lizard face leaking a few bubbles. Then more bubbles came out, and finally a cataract of bubbles.

Catherine was jolted by a sudden burst of kicking. She managed to contain it only because Amir was in such an awkward position, his knees bent almost double.

With a heave of his strong shoulders Paul pulled his old friend from the water. "Where's the installation, Amir? Ten seconds!"

A gasped breath and down he went again.

Catherine had never seen such agony. The pinched face opened, the eyes bulged beneath the roiling water, the mouth distended, and a frothy gob of bubbles came out. Urine began to discolor the water. Her hardness turned out to be fragile. She was not calm now. She wanted this to be over!

"Where, Amir? Next time you will not come up."

"The hi-ills . . ."

Then down again. "Paul, he said something! Please, he *said* something. Oh, Paul, look at him!"

The face was gray, the eyes showing only white. Paul hauled him up. "Where in the Black Hills?"

"Don't go. You'll never make—never make—"

"Where, Amir? Come on!"

"You can't kill Jamshid Rostram, not even you! He's way out of your league."

"Cath, soak down a towel, will you? I can't let him get any more water in his lungs; he won't be able to talk even if he wants to."

She did as she was told and Paul laid the towel over Amir's face. It ballooned faster and faster but Paul held it tightly. Finally, in sharp outline beneath it, the mouth opened and a faint hiss began as a trickle of air was sucked through the soaking cloth.

"Where, Amir?"

Cloth removed, gasped breath. "Out Ninety to Piedmont, then you take a ranger road in toward Nemo two miles. Then you walk in another two miles."

"What heading?"

"North-northwest. It's a rough hike."

Paul went limp with relief. "That's all I need. You stupid jerk, I never liked what you did in Iran, but I respected you. I still respect you."

Amir began to cry; not weep, but cry, and loudly. His sobs were eerie, like the calling of a loon.

"I've gotta kill him, honey." Paul looked more desperate than she had ever seen before. "Oh, Lord, Amir, please, you understand. You'd do the same."

When Paul looked at her again she was afraid that he was going to ask her to do it. But he was stronger than that. He took the gun from her and laid it against his friend's head.

The crying got louder and a splashing, miserable struggle began. Amir's eyes rolled toward the nosing weapon and he kept jerking his head away.

Paul fired.

A stream of blood came out like water from a tube, splattering on the floor and in the tub. The body sank down.

One eye was partly closed, the other opened. The mouth also was opened, the lips poised as if to spin a last web of words. Here was another life, fully as true and singular as her own, ended. So now she had seen death close. She looked at Paul's hunched shoulders and heard the smothered rack of his sorrow. The pity was automatic, the reaching human and less; animals comfort too.

Something immense had been lost, but also something gained. Paul became suddenly much less a mystery to her. He was a soldier, but not a professional soldier. No, the dead men around him were professionals. Paul was that rarest of the men of violence, an artist. His idealism, his romance, the constant insecurity, and the seeking for truth made sense in this light. Even the personal elegance.

He turned to her, his gray eyes as desolate as an arctic sky. She dropped the pistol firmly into her pocket, to say to him that she accepted him.

He understood; it was Paul's kind of gesture. "It's time to make the next move," he said.

"What about these people?" she gestured.

"Leave it for the brass to sort out. We have a mission to accomplish." It was like him simply to ignore the tears on his own face.

She realized why, and his bravado made her love him all the more.

He blinked. "Let's pick up some hiking clothes and head for the goddamn hills, to coin a phrase."

In the distance a bell was ringing. Some church somewhere, marking Vespers.

14

As V. I. BELIK made frantic, wheezing love to her, Ludmilla thought again and again of the phone call.

Wrong number. Tonight she had to kill Valentin.

Automatically she writhed and squirmed beneath Valentin's powerful thrusts. She touched his face with trembling fingers, slapped at his chest, and tossed her head from side to side. One, two, toss the head; three, four, gasp his name; five, six, grab the hips. On and on it went. She counted the thrusts, watched the face. Afterward he would need to use his inhaler. Very well, it was on the bedside table.

Wrong number.

The intensity of the thrusts rose. Ludmilla began a series of little cries. She shook so that her breasts bounded beneath his chest. He moved faster and faster, his face hanging slack, his eyes avid, then glazing, seeking middle distance. Bang bang bang, here he came, and sank then upon the cushion of her body, lay in his sweat, wheezing out her name.

"I love you, my dear, dear Ludmilla."

So you do.

"Was it good for you? Was there enough time?"

"Oh, yes, Valentin!"

He rolled off her and lay beside with his head propped on his hand. With one finger he traced along her breasts, touching each nipple in turn. "Yes, it was good for you." He had a theory that a woman had come to climax if her nipples were erect after lovemaking. She swept her hair out of her eyes and reached for his inhaler.

"Open your mouth, Valentin."

"I don't need that now."

"You're wheezing. Come, now, open up." She gave him a puff of the mist. Soon the awful whistling subsided. At least now there would not be that constant undertone of struggle for breath that made her so nervous.

"Let's drink some cognac, Valentin."

"Love, cognac, and you."

As she poured she found that she was wishing that she had better orders than those provided by Teplov. It was far safer to have such things in writing. Of course there were security problems; it was a sensitive matter.

Should she, perhaps, try for some sort of confirmation? If there was a mistake she would be shot. Quite simply that. Pouring the cognac into the glasses, she very seriously considered how much that mattered to her. She had just finished making love with a handsome man who loved her dearly, and that had mattered hardly at all. Did the rest matter more—or was the urge to live only a biological side effect?

Teplov was trustworthy, of course. She could not disobey him without also disobeying her role as an instrument of state and history.

She found herself privately confronting the most fundamental questions of loyalty and love while sipping cognac and smiling at Valentin's sweet words. His ardor was boyish. He made her twenty-eight years seem like eighteen. The fascination of Valentin had always been the way he combined great power with great love. She had heard that he drove his subordinates like *chernomazy,* but he was never harsh with her.

Kindness was the word for what Valentin showed her. He had been kind to her. In her life this had not been a frequent experience. And why should it be? She was the third generation of Communists in her family. At school she had been a *zvenovoi*—an informer—from the first, and an Octobrist, and a Young Pioneer. At home always the presence of the state was felt, kind, firm, and fierce with love for Communists. She had read the stories of the Revolution and leaned for hours in the sunny kitchen window, dreaming that she might have been a woman against the Whites, that she might have dashed across the marble floors of the Winter Palace with a torch in her hand, leading the way of the brave Bolsheviks.

All of that and a life of fives (except fours in English), and the wonderful day when her father had taken her by the hand to District Headquarters and enrolled her in the Komitet.

At twenty she began working her way through Moscow University by doing political observation for the Second Department of the Surveillance Directorate. She followed foreign students and filled in weeklies on them, and even learned a little of the ways of the outside world.

That knowledge was useless now. There were no outside models for a Russian situation like the one she was in. Should she just act and make an end of it, or continue to examine the traitorous shades of the thing?

It had been a long time since he had spoken. She looked toward the bed, realized that he was asleep. In the dim light he seemed somewhat at peace. The cognac was on the table, his inhaler lying beside the glass. She went to his closet, reached behind the rack of uniforms for the small metal case that contained his pistol.

It was locked. There was no point in searching his drawers for the key; she took the box to the kitchen. It was a personal item of army issue. She could trust it to be flimsy. She laid it on the kitchen table and turned on the light. The box was green, and his name was stenciled on the lid. She took a knife to it and it popped open almost immediately.

The gun lay before her. She had seen several executions, but she had never killed before. She did not think that it would be particularly difficult. "General V. I. Belik," she whispered. "Please be only that to me." She moved cautiously through the kitchen, turned out the light, and crossed the silent parlor. From the dining room there came the smell of his roses. His? She had cut the orders that had gotten them fresh from Rumania. She inhaled their perfume. The moment Belik died, all this opulence would cease. Where would she be sent? Perhaps to Moscow to screw more attachés, or perhaps abroad. Yes, abroad. They would want to get her out of the way for a while after this.

She approached the bed, paused to cock the pistol. Then she placed the barrel against Valentin's temple.

It was a desolate moment.

"So you are the one."

"Valentin!" She almost jumped back, regained control of herself just in time, then spoke more firmly. "I am performing my assigned duty, Valentin. It's nothing more than that."

"I ask you not to." There was black misery in his voice.

"Valentin, you would do the same in my position."

He uttered a bitter laugh and she pulled the trigger. His head jerked violently as the kick of the pistol jolted her.

It was a powerful weapon, too powerful for this duty. The side of his head was a crater shooting blood in half a dozen places. Slowly his legs came up to his chest—and then went limp.

For a moment she was panicky, thinking only that he knew, had known all the time!

He had been executed by the one he loved. Was that a good or a bad death? His laughter echoed in her mind. A very bad death.

There was nothing now to do but follow instructions. She

fitted the gun into his hand, drew on her robe, and went to the telephone. She dialed 35-35, the number of the KGB's central HQ at the Institute. "Valentin Belik has committed suicide. Please come at once."

"I'm telling you, Colonel Teplov, she shot him! Captain Semilovna *shot* Belik!"

"You are absolutely certain of this?"

"Powder marks on her hand. Yet she was quite composed when we arrived. Not in the least upset. She was astonished when I arrested her."

"What a catastrophe this is for the KGB!"

The young security officer nodded sadly. "A first-rate scandal."

"She must be an American agent."

"The flat was full of American items. Her name is at the bottom of all the order slips."

"In this case, it is sufficient proof. Have you the document of custody with you?"

The young officer handed Teplov the papers. "Remanded to custody," he wrote. "What's your name, Captain?"

"Rastutin, sir, Anatoly."

"Remanded to custody Captain Anatoly Rasputin—"

"Rastutin."

"Excuse me. It's very late." He paused a moment over the next words, thinking ruefully of what a magnificent woman she was. "For the imposition of the penalty of execution to be carried out according to War Orders 1678-84, 'The Ruthless Elimination of Spies and Agents Provocateurs.' "

He signed the document. "I want her dead within the hour. We're officially on a war footing and she is an imperialist assassin. Is this clearly understood, Captain Rasputin?"

"I will telephone you with confirmation of the execution."

* * *

The cell reeked of sewage and vomit. It was so small that she could neither stand up nor spread her arms. She sat on the edge of the pallet, prim, careful lest she be bitten by a rat. What a stupid, formal little rat of a captain had put her here. Rastutin. She shouldn't be surprised, though, that one posted this far from Moscow would be an idiot.

The door shrieked rust on rust as it was slid open. "Come."

"Thank goodness, I thought I would be here all night. Is this the usual thing?"

The guard, a young private, was more than a little drunk. He looked at her with an ugly expression.

His first slap stunned her for a moment. As she sputtered in surprise he did it again. "Captain," she managed to cry. "Help!"

"You're first," a voice said. She lifted her head. A man with the bland, pinched face of a minor *apparatchik* dropped his pants to expose an erect organ.

It hurt. She shut her eyes tightly, tried not to scream. When she did there was general laughter. Strong hands held her arms and ankles. The smell and power of these bestial men surrounded her. It was hard to believe that she was actually in the Soviet Union. This was a terrible infraction; these men should never have been allowed to get liquor on the job. "You must come to your senses! You will receive long prison sentences if you—"

Another slap, this time followed by a moment of dark. Then pain in her loins and the cracked plaster ceiling reeling above. She was being dragged by her feet down the hall. By her feet!

"You got the papers, Anatoly?"

"Yeah."

Somebody put a tag on her ankle, fastening it with wire. They did that to people destined for execution. Oh, God.

She realized at last what she had refused to see even when they were raping her, the ugliness of Teplov's betrayal. To seal the secret of Belik's assassination he had painted her as a murderess.

"Here, it's all signed and sealed."

"OK, listen, we've got those coffins down in the storeroom where they keep the old bicycles."

"There aren't any coffins in there."

"You look, you'll find them; they're behind the bikes. There are three or four. Bring one up, and make sure it doesn't have any holes in the bottom. I don't want a lot of crap leaking out when we take it upstairs."

She looked from one of the men to another. Each averted his eyes. They were not without souls. "This is tragic. A tragic mistake. Yuri Andropov will not forgive you. You see, I am his favorite. Yes, it's quite true."

"Then why are you here?"

"I have always been a Communist. Since I was an infant! They let me draw Lenin in art class when I was eight. Eight!"

Three men came back with a black tin box. It looked like something you might keep the oilcloth curtains in during the summer. The thought came to her that she was going to spend more time in there than she had on earth thus far.

She screamed.

"Stand her over on the newspapers. She's going to get crazy if you don't hurry up."

The pistols went off like an atomic bomb in her face, dazzling white fists of silence. She was astonished—and then so free.

"Come on, get her in the coffin before her bowels go!"

Dead, poor woman. Teplov sat staring at the telephone, unable to prevent himself from wondering if she had understood the need for her sacrifice.

So he was sentimental about Ludmilla Semilovna. He accounted himself guilty for that. But never mind, there was no time to lose in dreaming and hanging about. He had a coup going now and he must concentrate his authority at once.

He left his office and hurried along the corridor to the control room. "Heads up! I have a tremendous shock. V. I. Belik is dead. His mistress has been arrested for murdering him."

Exhausted men, slumped on chairs, some sipping tea, others hunched over test instruments, raised their heads. Teplov banged on the window to the aiming room and motioned to Igor Gorkin, who reluctantly came out.

"Belik is dead. Murdered."

Gorkin's face was swept by calculation. "Ah. Is General Sukovsky going to assume command?"

"Naturally not. In due time the General Staff will appoint a new military commandant. Meanwhile all orders will be routed through me."

Gorkin nodded and returned to his work.

Teplov was mildly disappointed. He thought that he had established rapport with these people. Apparently not.

"Just so you understand, I will repeat: no orders except through me." He left the room. His next task was going to be more difficult. He had to establish himself with Belik's staff officers. And he had to obtain the command control documents and codes or he would not be able to deliver coherent directives to the various groups supporting Black Magic.

But first he must examine his cable traffic. More grim news, of course. The message was brief. "Pakravan dead. Winter escaped. Awaiting orders. Kislitsin." Wonderful. Who the devil was Kislitsin?

He telephoned the Registry and Archives Department in Moscow, identified himself, and read off his authorization code from his papers. "Kislitsin. A captain. At present stationed in the United States."

There was a wait of fully five minutes. Just as Teplov was about to try another office the clerk returned to the line. "Kislitsin, Yevgeni Ivanovich, Captain, GRU, presently stationed Rapid City, South Dakota. Acting Commander of Station for eighteen months."

Teplov hung up the phone. A GRU officer, of course. All the SAC bases were covered by GRU. That meant the added complication of another level of command interface, unless this Kislitsin was willing to take his orders directly from KGB for a few days.

Teplov looked up the routing for Rapid City, wondering if matters weren't now so unsettled that even he must consider delaying the project.

But it couldn't be delayed, not with the U.S. Navy working on ELF. The Politburo would sooner or later get that piece of information, and when it did Black Magic would be sacrificed to caution and canceled forever.

"Teplov to Kislitsin. Captain, my regrets. Please assume full command of Black Magic field operation reporting to me. Place a *cordon sanitaire* around the Black Magic team, recalling the rule that there is to be no contact between team members and your command. Please keep the advisories coming."

The reply took fifteen minutes to appear. "Kislitsin to Teplov. Colonel, I do not have authorization to assume command of Black Magic nor can I violate the Black Magic Regulations, section 14–323, part 4. Please advise."

Teplov furiously referred to the Green Book, which contained the orders and regulations governing management of the U.S. part of Black Magic. "Soviet personnel will not defend Black Magic foreign operatives from hostile interference in such a way that the involvement of Soviet personnel might be in any manner deduced by hostiles or by the foreign operatives themselves."

He had written the Green Book, and now it was going to haunt him. There was no way to coerce from this distance. Teplov had no choice but to surrender to his own regulations.

And let some leaden fool defend Black Magic from the genius of Paul Winter.

He slammed his fist again and again into the desk.

"Teplov to Kislitsin. Your reading of regulations appears to be correct." Were all soldiers stupid and destructive? Judging from his purges, Stalin had concluded so. Teplov now concluded the same.

He was forced to ignore America and continue with the next phase of the coup he was engineering here. It was actually a relief, simply because he could control it directly.

He telephoned Colonel Florinsky, whose voice was flat and demoralized. Good.

"Colonel, you will report to the installation at once with your technical documents. Please be prepared to manage Black Magic from here, commencing immediately."

"Yes, sir."

Sullen, too. Did he know how certain he was to die or end up in prison? Probably so.

Through the half hour it took Florinsky to come, Teplov watched his teletype and listened to the silence of his telephone. Nothing happened. He expected Moscow to be calling and a stream of reports to be coming in from America. He should be getting the traffic even if he couldn't act on it.

The sudden silence could mean only one thing.

With Belik dead, Andropov must be starting to protect his own position. Was this his first move, cutting off Teplov's access to the American operation?

It might be, but there was at the moment no way to find out. He loathed being left in ignorance. Not knowing was going to act on his mind like acid. He looked at his watch. Four more hours to the soldier's part of Black Magic. The beginning.

Florinsky stepped into the room. "Good morning, Colonel Teplov. I would have knocked." He hefted two large briefcases onto the desk. "This is Black Magic."

"Let's begin, Colonel."

"Very well." Manicured fingers opened the first of the cases. Inside were thick masses of orders and operational directives, all on the red paper upon which "must read" material had been written since the days of STAVKA in World War II. In the Soviet system people reacted when that paper appeared in their boxes. Teplov was no exception. The very sight of it created in him a sense of urgency.

"I had no idea that it was this complicated."

"Altogether, 4,728 pages. Perhaps you should just read the summaries."

Teplov had not been exposed to this sort of military terminology to any great degree. "You'll have to translate, Colonel. Remember that I'm a civilian."

"I haven't gotten any orders about you from General Sukovsky yet. I don't know how much assistance I can give you."

Here it was, in this quietly spoken sentence, the attempt to reassert soldierly authority. "I am your commander. You will give me every possible assistance or face the consequences. Your part of Black Magic is minor compared to mine. I was always overall commander."

"If you would put that in writing—"

Teplov scrawled a note and signed it, thrust it at the beautifully dressed colonel. "Put that in your pocket. But please remember that there will be no court of inquiry if Black Magic succeeds. And if it fails, details like this will not save you."

"Written orders are required by protocol in a case like this."

"You have them. Now what the devil does all this mean? How could you possibly need five thousand pages of orders for a half-hour missile battle? My whole operation, involving thirty ships, tons of antenna equipment, and thousands of technicians, is covered in a hundred pages."

Florinsky explained the careful steps of the military operation. The weapons were incredibly complicated, and their use required the highest levels of proficiency. Despite himself, Teplov was somewhat impressed.

He knew the overall concept, but these details had never been revealed to him before. As military commander he would be responsible for coordinating the whole affair from a headquarters he hadn't even known existed before.

"Where is the HQ?"

"I don't have clearance to tell you."

Teplov drummed his fingers. He was up against another difficult obstacle of the security system. Even though he had clearance to hear the information he wanted, he couldn't get it from Florinsky because the colonel wasn't cleared to reveal it. "Very well. I assume that you'll make certain that we arrive on time."

"Yes, sir. It's not a long drive."

"I presume from all this that you concede that I will be responsible for moment-to-moment coordination with the supporting commands."

"That's correct."

Teplov said nothing, felt no triumph. He was thinking that he might well have presented himself with an impossible task. The job he would be doing in another three hours would require great exactitude. The worst of it was that he didn't know the technical language.

"You will give me support."

"As you wish."

Condescending swine. "You *will* give me support, Colonel! I cannot be expected to do this without a great deal of it from you. If you make a damn bit of trouble, you will end up facing a charge of treason to the aims of the state!"

"We ought to get over to HQ. You'll want an orientation on the maps and communications equipment before the countdown gets too hot."

The HQ was only fifteen miles from the Black Magic installation, but because of four security checks it took better than thirty minutes to reach it. Because of what had happened to Teplov himself, KGB were now operating under a revised war-warning directive requiring them to search all cars, code transponder-equipped or not. And because of the nervousness surrounding the Belik disaster, the military had undertaken procedure tightening of its own. Black Magic could easily sink into a bog of security. It had happened to more than one crash program.

"The HQ is attached to the Eleventh Military District, redesignated the Sverdlovsk Front, by the way, for the duration of the operation."

"That makes sense." The redesignation of the district as a front put it on a war footing, exactly as if battles with hostile armies were being fought here, and greatly simplified the chain of command. It explained why Belik could issue his war warning with such ease.

Their car pulled up in front of a low, weather-beaten building and was at once engulfed in its own cloud of dust. A few kilometers distant the tall smokestacks of Uralmash belched steam and soot into the air. Because of it the once-white structure was discolored to yellow. Inside, it was stifling and dim after the bright morning sun.

Yet again a full security check took place. Finally they were ushered into a large lift. The grate rattled closed and they dropped into the earth. Teplov watched the frayed cables passing the open sides of the car.

Conditions changed the moment the grate at the bottom of the lift shaft was opened. Gone were the dim lighting and the atmosphere of decay. Here was a bright, modern headquarters of the first class. The walls were painted a soothing green, and cool light poured from ceiling fixtures. A young major sat behind a desk that contained a single red telephone.

Another security check.

When it was completed, Teplov was amazed to see an entire wall begin to move. It was actually a huge six-foot-thick door. Beyond it another door, smaller but as thick, was opening. This was what the military called a "hardened" HQ. Compared to it the Sovmin bunker outside Moscow seemed built of thatch and wattle.

Beyond the final door spread the most magnificent communications and command control center Teplov had ever seen. There were five rows of consoles, and in front of them a massive electronic map of the world ablaze with twinkling lights. It was an arctic projection showing the United States and the USSR facing each other across the polar cap.

It astonished Teplov to speechlessness when he realized that not only the military part of Black Magic was displayed on that map, but his own operation as well. There, winking just outside American territorial waters, were blips that could only be the ships containing the antennas. And the pulsating purple light in South Dakota must represent Jamshid Rostram.

The planned locations of all the ELF antennas to be installed in America were also designated. New York, Chicago, Los Angeles. All the others.

This was no missile control center. This was a Black Magic control center.

He remembered his little Lada being sprayed with bullets. The bourgeois murderers had come so very close.

"Comrade Teplov?"

"Yes, Colonel."

"I was telling you that this is the command post. From here General Belik could control the whole operation."

"Everything, right? Not just the military part."

"Well, theoretically, yes."

"You can contact my ships, for example, can't you, without going through KGB Center?"

"Again, in theory—"

Teplov threw back his head and laughed. He could not help himself. Various officers looked up from their jobs, but he stifled himself quickly.

The soldiers had unwittingly given him everything he had always dreamed of—total and absolute control of Black Magic. He could do exactly what Belik had been planning all along and use this center to circumvent his own commanders.

Good-bye KGB Center.

Good-bye, Politburo.

At last, freedom!

15

JAMSHID SPREAD HIS ARMS to the dark and threatening air. The storms of morning had returned at nightfall, bringing rain and thunder and angry wind hissing through the pines.

Black water had gurgled beneath the cabin during one of the downpours and a rat had come squeezing up between the floorboards. Jamshid had watched it move about the room, sniffing first at the sleeping Kajenouri's beard and then climbing across Ismail's chest. When it had come to Jamshid and perceived that he was awake, it had gone still, its black eyes watchful. Jamshid saw how full of wrath the little creature was; if rats were only larger, they would kill human beings for pleasure.

He had wanted to catch the rat, but despite his own stillness it had not come close.

For a quarter of an hour it had watched him, only its whiskers revealing that it was not a waxwork.

Jamshid finally decided that the rat was another portent. It was here to warn him that he was soon to be under hostile eyes.

He looked at his two Muslims. How innocent they were

with their hopes and their empty prayers. There was no Allah; Muhammad was a complete fraud. As the rat watched him, he watched Kajenouri and Ismail. Poor Ismail. He was shattered by the truth of his own love.

But why? Have I no right to be loved?

Kajenouri had always accepted what was in his heart. Loyal, simple old man. He would die before the moon rose.

Jamshid stroked the face of Ismail. The rat moved slowly off, attracted by the food stench from the larder. Ismail stirred, turned his face toward Jamshid. Asleep it was blandly innocent, self-satisfied. "What if I told you," Jamshid whispered, "that I am a much greater destruction than you know? If I told you that the Brotherhood was a myth and you were working for the Russians?" He stroked Ismail's face again. "You would go off into the hills, and Kajenouri would kill you."

He wished that Ismail was awake enough to hold him. The cabin was so lonely. The trees outside were growing sullen with menace as the sun set, a final grace among towering clouds, the reborn storms of morning. Ever since he had been inside Pyotr Teplov in Kabul, Jamshid had understood perfectly the plots and reflections of plots in which he was tangled. Teplov had claimed to be a German named Rudolf opposed to the U.S.-Jewish world hegemony. But within himself he cradled a secret: his name was Teplov; he was a Russian and the Muslim Brotherhood was his lie.

It mattered to Jamshid only in that Russians helped his cause even more than his Muslims did. They were powerful in the world. Without their help the entry into America would have been far more difficult.

He had seen inside humanity, had touched the happinesses and pleasures of others. They had no right to such joy when even one among them was as deprived as Jamshid.

When they were warm and pleasant he had been licking yogurt skin from the sides of tins, plucking undigested beans from offal, going like a rat in the world of the rats.

By his tenth year every shadow of happiness had passed

him by. He knew only the lusts of men and could read by their eyes which ones pitied and which despised him. He learned the furtive looks of the ones who wanted him, how to make the gesture of the hand, the wisp of smile, that would bring them down the alleyway . . . and there to give the pleasure and get the money.

It was always the time of mourning within him. He had a catalog of hatreds in his heart. Allah was at the top of the despised hierarchy, then Muhammad and Ali, and below them the others, Rumi and the poets, Mullah Nassir Eddin even, the heart's fool. Then the males of the species and then the females, the woman-things; then the beasts that served, the horses and the cattle and the mules, and the loathsome beasts, rats and hogs and dogs.

"And all must bare themselves to my justice. I am more than Muhammad, more even than Allah. I give the world to Russia because Russia is so cruel."

His own words made his heart a little lighter. He began to feel ready for this night's confrontation. For some days he had suspected the finality of it. His friend the rat had confirmed it. At age sixteen he had reached his life's ultimate night.

"Up," he shouted, and clapped his hands. "The sun leaves the tops of the trees, or have you heathens forgotten how to pray?"

"How is this that you are so eager to awaken? Usually I roll you out of the covers."

"Pray, Kajenouri, for tonight you prove your strength."

They unrolled their rugs and placed their prayer stones. Kajenouri intoned the First Sura of the Koran aloud, his voice quivering with devotion. Jamshid bowed his body with the others, but in his heart he spat. Each time he heard that prayer he was seized with venomous hatred. He wanted to throttle the devout, to hurl the muezzin from the minaret.

And he would! With the United States gone, Russia would hound the lands of the faithful, and the muezzin *would* be cast down and the *mullahs* left to dissolve in dungeon darkness.

"Come, let us begin. Ismail, get my things." In the dark cabin Ismail could be heard scuttling about, the sorcerer's apprentice. When he came close, Jamshid was not surprised to see the terror in his eyes. He took Ismail by the hand. "What troubles you?"

With a toss of his head Ismail returned to his work, wrapping the other implements in the traditional patched cloak that Jamshid would wear on the Circle. Although Shazdeh Hassan had believed otherwise, Jamshid knew that the trappings and rituals of the sorcerer were necessary. Hassan had been a fool. For all his wisdom, he knew nothing of the Master's ways.

"Come and stay with me awhile among the trees," he said to Kajenouri. "Ismail, go down to the Circle and wait there."

He watched Ismail's back disappear into the shadows that blanketed the way to the Circle. Then he led Kajenouri in the opposite direction, to the top of the rise behind the cabin. From here the fastness of the hills piled to the west. Eastward was a jumble of steep gullies and ravines. Haze hung over the ghostly prairie beyond. The distant horizon was purpled. Here and there lights marked isolated human places.

"Kajenouri, my enemies are coming tonight. I want you to range along the ridges above the road and watch. Kill them if you can."

The old man drew himself to full height and put a huge hand on one of his daggers. Kajenouri needed no other weapon; Jamshid had seen him split a dog's head in half at a hundred paces with one. Pistols he found laughable. Larger guns he scorned as dishonorable. Of bombs, probably, he understood little.

Suddenly the great brute was overcome by emotion. He grabbed Jamshid and embraced him, drawing him close to his ugly troll's face. Even in the shadows Jamshid could see

232

the intensity of the love in the eyes. "I am the sheath of the sword of God," Kajenouri said. "The sheath of the sword says to the sword: 'I will preserve thee forever.' "

"The sword is unsheathed, old man."

Kajenouri went off down the ridge, his form soon disappearing among the rocks and the trees. It would be horrifying to meet such a creature in the wilderness. He was so big and yet so quiet.

Jamshid followed him as long as possible with eyes and ears, then he went down past the cabin and along the path to the Circle. Ismail waited there, squatting beside the heap of ceremonials as humbly as the woman who lived in his heart.

"Dress me," Jamshid said. Behind him Ismail stirred himself and came forward with the patched cloak of tradition. Such a cloak, cloth of black with brown patches on each shoulder and in the middle of the back, had been worn by Xerxes' wizards, and before by those of Babylon and Akkad. Next Ismail sprinkled the rosewater on the cloak.

"*Rashan, arshah, narash.*" The ritual began.

Ismail drew the cowl over Jamshid's head.

"*Ashhadu inna la illah illa Allah!*" He let his voice ring through the wilderness.

Ismail began to beat time with two wooden blocks. *Click,* they went, *click click click,* as soft as the snapping of a beetle. Jamshid let his thoughts drain from his mind like water from a vessel, drain and sink away into the earth beneath his feet.

"By the name and power of Suleiman, son of David, prince of magicians, may the angels of the darkest house breathe upon me!" His cry could not have been more deeply felt. It echoed as if taken up by the hills. "Angels of the darkest house . . . the darkest house . . . darkest . . ." He closed his eyes as the Master came within him, laughing and dancing like a baby with fresh-baked *nane shirin.*

"*Divs* of the wind, crack your whips!" They cracked as he had been sure they would, and the pines roared fair. Dust rose from the Circle, and broken boughs slapped his cheeks.

The wind passed with a great bellowing and mourning into the starry sky.

"Is the Field up?" Ismail asked in wonder.

"No."

"Then how—the wind—"

"Look at me, Ismail, look closely at your lover!" He thrust his face into Ismail's.

A sharp scream silenced the crickets and the night birds. Ismail's eyes grew small with loathing. He backed away.

"What do you see, Ismail? Tell me what you see!" Off at the edge of the Circle Ismail was coughing and groaning. Jamshid could hear wings flapping about his head. Rising from the center of the Circle he could almost discern *huma*, the bird of dark regions. Jamshid in that moment knew all the loneliness in hell, the sorrows beyond counting. "Tell me what you see!"

Ismail's voice, quivering like the voice of the reeds, barely crossed the distance between them. *"Audubillahi min ash-Shaitan er-Rajim."* The incantation against demons. There came to Jamshid the sensation of something crawling in his stomach. He doubled over, covering himself in the folds of his cloak. The words Ismail had uttered were like a filthy mist that came within, filling his nose with the stink of sickness.

When the fit passed, Ismail was close beside him, his face barely visible in the dark, pinched with terror.

"Tonight you must give up your life in my name."

"I must give up my life, Jamshid, I know that."

"Let us begin."

Ismail clicked his wooden blocks together once, then again and again, and this time nothing interrupted him. Jamshid danced around and around the edge of the Circle, danced until he was one with the emptiness within, danced in the rising moon, until his body sweated and his heart swooned and the red moon over the prairie stared like the eye of all-seeing, the great eye of evil itself.

* * *

As night gathered and the neon came out, Paul drove toward the Black Hills. They had stopped at a sporting goods store for jeans and shirts and shoes. Five minutes was all they had dared allow. Paul's boots were too loose, and his shirt too big, but they were better than a suit and broughams for this hard journey. He had Catherine watching their back; they must not drop their guard, but he hoped that Amir's death would place his troops in at least temporary confusion. To confuse further he was not taking the direct route out the Sturgis Highway, but a more roundabout approach across the rolling prairie to the east of Rapid City.

Despite his reputation, Paul had never before today taken life. Perhaps he was only being sentimental, but it seemed as if a great deal had changed today.

"You want to know a secret, darling?"

"Not especially, to tell you the truth."

"I'm going to tell you anyway, because I think you deserve to know. We both killed today for the first time. Amir was my first."

He prepared himself for a reaction.

She touched his shoulder in a concession to comradeship but did not even interrupt her vigil out the rear window. She was probably right to give it that little. He had been trying to prove to her that he wasn't a blooded man. But killing wasn't the whole of violence.

"I think we might have a tail," she said. She was laconic, concentrated. He had known professionals more easily rattled. It was no longer possible to ascribe Catherine's courage to ignorance of consequences. She had experienced the worst of the consequences.

"We'll turn off Ninety at Box Elder. If they follow us, we'll know."

The exit appeared, and they left the main highway for the less-traveled state road.

Behind them the floodlit bulk of Ellsworth Air Force Base's ramshackle old main hangar could be seen, and beside it a tall line of B-52 rudders. How much longer would the base even exist?

"I wonder what it'll be like," Catherine said.

He would not give the whole answer. It was better that she not know what it would be like if the USSR managed to construct ELF antennas in this country. He understood the odds against him. Catherine might well have to live under ELF control for the rest of her life.

"We'll encounter some sort of resistance in the hills. That much is certain."

"But what'll the war be like—if there is a war?"

"There won't be. That's why we're here."

The silence that followed this statement lasted so long that Paul turned in his seat and looked directly at Catherine. He saw a face waxy with anger, disgusted and frightened.

It was torture to see her like that and he almost cried out at her to stop, almost shook her to rattle her back to sense. Catherine slipping beyond the edge of terror was a shattering thing to witness.

She laughed, crisp and mean. They loved each other, yes, but there was also this violence, this corroding anger beneath the love.

The thought of it changed Paul's mood to bitterness. She was damned right to see him as an angel of death. He had been seduced by it a long time ago, maybe even before he had grown up, when he had seen geese dropping from the dawn-touched skies of winter and listened to the fine barking of the spaniels and the spatter of the guns.

"I'm not being inhumane, Catherine. I still love you."

"I love you too." The pain in her words was difficult to bear. He knew what made her hurt: to a dying man there is absolutely no difference between his own individual extinction and the death of the whole world.

He wanted to shout at her, to scream out his insight, to convince her somehow that their duty was to risk death so that others could live—and that it made a great deal of difference. But he knew what she would say, so he did not. Catherine was too alive to believe that there could be such a thing as a noble death.

She began watching behind them again. They were now passing through the rolling grassy country east of Rapid City. It was full night. The horizon was beginning to glow with the light of the rising moon. Paul opened the windows and let the smell of grass in. The night was warm, as dense and sensual as southern dark. It was a night for love, not for the hard adventure that confronted them. Far to the west the Black Hills were a dark, craggy line. In all their length not ten lights glimmered. The scene was reminiscent of the Zagros. The image of Hassan and Jamshid and the scientists standing in his car lights as he left was strong in his memory.

Jamshid. He would never forget the way that sensuous, curious mind had entered and dominated his own, And the way the Field itself had affected his emotions. All they had to do was tune the thing to get the emotions they wanted. They didn't even need a Jamshid for that.

"The road is empty."

"More accurately, there are no lights. There won't be, not if our esteemed tail has any sense. He'll be running dark."

"Then how are we supposed to find out if he's still there, if I may ask?"

"Patience, dear. Wait until we get to the crest of the next rise."

As they mounted it and began to descend, Paul put on the brakes and stopped. "We're going to listen, since our friends won't be using lights. Come on." The car was just far enough over the crest that their motionless taillights wouldn't be seen by a pursuer. To the east there was a steep dirt road cutting an embankment. On the cliff above, the dismal ruins of an abandoned Anti-Ballistic Missile site loomed into the sky. Paul and Catherine scrambled onto the trunk of the car. "Cup your hands behind your ears."

At first Paul heard nothing. He was just deciding to relax when Catherine's body stiffened. "You hear that?"

"Barely." Far off a powerful engine was guttering. It grew rapidly louder. Its pitch deepened. The driver had stepped on the gas. Cresting a rise, he had discovered that he could no longer see the lights of this car.

"Let's go." Paul gunned the motor and put Catherine to work on the map. Too late it had occurred to him that it had been foolish to choose a road without any major intersections. He was dealing with an unbroken fifteen-mile stretch, entrance and exit only. If the other side was lucky, they might just have a car available to block the far end.

He watched the speedometer creep upward. The car toplined at eighty-five. That was the consequence of having to settle for a rental.

"I see them. They're about two miles back. I can just make out the car against the road. It's coming down a hill."

Two miles! Eighty-five was not going to be enough. There was an alternative, a very dangerous one. But the only one. "Hold on, dear." He dropped the car into low. There was a protesting roar from the transmission, but it got them down to fifty. "Brace against the dash; this is going to hurt." To stop without the telling flash of brake lights he began popping the emergency brake, causing the car to halt in a series of violent jerks. Then he allowed it to roll off the side of the road and into the tall grass. He turned off the headlights, let the roll continue until they were well away from the road.

"Paul—"

"Just keep your head down. If they pass us we're going back the other way."

"If they stop?"

"We make some new friends."

The thunder of the engine grew and grew until it filled the night. When Paul saw it, the car was doing easily 130, its tires sighing in the curves. The windows were closed, the interior dark. It was a Buick, dark blue. It did not slow down. The trouble was, they must know exactly where Catherine and Paul intended to go. Destinations always lie at the end of funnels. All they really needed to do was wait there. Paul's hope that his move would be too fast for the leaderless army had been futile. Evidently KGB's command control had suddenly improved.

He started up the engine.

"Paul, no!" She grabbed the key. "Don't you hear that? There's another car."

Thank God for her hearing. It was coming more slowly, this one. A backup to guard against just this maneuver. Clever, and very, very professional. This group was showing more skill than the New York *residentura*.

The car moved into view. All the windows were open. A flashlight was playing along the roadside. "Say a prayer if you've remembered any as yet."

"Get us out of this, God!"

"Great. Now we're doomed for certain."

But the car passed by. Paul gave it time to disappear over the next hill, then he turned around and headed back to the road, the high grass hissing against their doors.

As he drove he wondered whether they would draw a perimeter around their critical site, or if they had the manpower to do that and chase him as well. Considering his alternatives, he began to feel beaten. He had only the vaguest directions. He was facing the best intelligence organization on earth. Except for Catherine he was totally unsupported.

And they knew a great deal more about the operation than he did: its exact location, for example; its defenses; and above all when it would be used.

They reached Highway 90. They could turn left and continue the mission or right and drive straight through to Minneapolis. Within hours they could be on their way to some safe country.

"We have a critical decision."

"I know. I can figure odds too."

If she wanted it, he decided that he would quit. "Well?"

"Paul, you're being an idiot. We've gotten this far, we've got to see it through."

239

He turned left and accelerated into the sparse traffic. "Keep watching, especially for any cars pulling into the road from unlikely places like behind signs. If I were them I would have left a picket along this road."

"You aren't them. They're good at this, but not as good as you."

"KGB has more technical people in the U.S. than clandestines nowadays. They can take apart a computer in the dark, but they aren't good at this kind of thing. Too old-fashioned."

"You know this for certain?"

"Their planning is very professional but the execution stinks."

"You're just trying to build up my confidence."

"Could I?" He hoped so, but she didn't answer the question.

"A very proficient-looking car just pulled out from behind that McDonald's back there."

"Could be routine. They have the odd customer."

"Making a U-turn and crossing the divider? I doubt it."

Paul accelerated. That blatant U-turn was sheerest amateurism. If they got him, it was going to be because there were so many of them.

He floored the accelerator and felt the car drop into passing gear. They went around a semi. The Loop 90 exit was just ahead. "That's the way to the business district, right?"

"That's the way."

Paul took the exit. "I suspect that I'll turn out to be the better driver. Hold on." As the density of traffic built, Paul increased his speed. Sixty. Seventy. Eighty. He leaned into the turn where the divided highway became East North Street. Catherine was hanging onto the back of the front seat.

"They're still on us."

"Right."

He was going to have to leave the road. That had worked

well once before, in Vientiane. "I believe there's some open country around here. Take a look at the map."

"Roosevelt Park coming up on the left after you go through a long curve. Beyond that there are fairgrounds the other side of East Omaha Street."

The park appeared, fenced but with the main gate still open. "Here we go." He pulled at the wheel and almost spun out turning into the park drive at high speed. But it was necessary; if he had slowed down, the brake lights would have served as a beacon. Catherine had fallen against the door and then onto the floor of the car. "Stop watching and get strapped in. This is going to get wild."

"What if we pick up a cop?"

"He'll take the last car in the line first. That won't be us." Ahead Paul could see a small lake, and off to the right the lights of another street, no doubt East Omaha. He left the road and began roaring across the beautiful, moist grass.

"Somebody's going to hate us."

"I suppose so." Again the low stone fence topped by iron spikes appeared. Paul angled away from it back to the road. That hadn't helped much; he needed more space to do this right. "Close your eyes and pray." Without even slowing down he crossed Omaha and sailed the car onto the shoulder—and saw his chance. A railroad track stretched along Omaha, and on it was a long freight train. Paul wheeled into the right-of-way and began following the tracks into the center of town and toward the front of the train. He caught sight of lights behind him in the rearview mirror. The right-of-way was gravel, and it made a thunderous racket cn the bottom of the car as they passed hoppers and flatcars and boxcars, finally coming parallel to three diesels under full power.

The train was probably doing forty, close to its top speed with such a big consist. The next maneuver would contain very little margin for error. Paul accelerated until he was parallel with the first engine, then dropped back to match its speed. The lights in the rearview mirror started coming up fast. "Hunch down. If they're aggressive we're going to take some shots."

They were aggressive. The first bullet hit the rear deck with a subdued thud. The second penetrated both windshields. It must have passed no more than five inches from Paul's head. Wonderful; one of them was a good shot.

As Paul had expected, the car pulled up beside them. The driver brandished a pistol. A man in the backseat showed another one. The engineer of the train started sounding his horn, three short blasts repeated. He was warning of danger on the right-of-way. The flashing lights of the 5th Street crossing appeared ahead. Paul was parallel to them. He saw some barbed-wire fencing at the roadside. He hoped it wouldn't get tangled in his axles and tear up the brake drums. "Here we go."

Simultaneously jamming on the gas and turning a sharp right, Paul got the car onto the road and into the path of the oncoming train. Its powerful light blazed through Paul's window, dazzling his eyes. The ground was shaking, the big diesel's horn screaming. Then the crossing guard was snapping across the hood and they were at 5th and Main. Paul wheeled onto Main and proceeded west again.

Behind them there was a long grinding sound so loud that it carried even into the closed, speeding car. Their pursuers had been hit by the train. Their car was becoming sparking, crumpled metal beneath the lead engine. Paul saw the engineer in his cab clutching his hair in his hands, his eyes bulging as his train ground the Russians to generalized meat.

Black smoke was rising from beneath the engine as they lost the scene around a curve. "I think they didn't make it."

"I think not."

Her heart was thundering; her left knee hurt from being slammed against the floor. He was slowing down now, thank God he was slowing down. His hand came over, sought hers. She gave it a quick squeeze and withdrew back into herself.

She didn't want him to know the black, surging fear she felt within, and the coldness of her skin might reveal it to a man sensitive to such perceptions. All her skills as an actress were being used now. She was determined to maintain the cool, laconic front that he seemed to need from her. When those men had been not ten feet away from her side of the car, waving big pistols at her, she had almost lost it, and again when Paul drove in front of the train and that blazing light had filled the car.

But they were here, and alive, and there was nobody behind them.

"Tell me," he asked cheerfully, "is there an alternate route to Nemo? Pakravan said to go two miles in from Piedmont toward Nemo. I'd prefer to go to Nemo first and do it backwards. We might actually get away with it."

"Green Mountain Road. Stay on Main past the Sturgis Highway."

"Done."

Was he really as calm as he appeared to be, or was he acting too? She wished that there were some way to find out. It would be awfully nice if they could just drop fronts and be scared to death together.

They were passing the western limits of Rapid City, rising into darker country. Ahead of them the Black Hills glowed in the light of the full moon, pine forests silver gray. Beyond the hills to the east lightning marked the passage of the night's storms.

"Hold my hand again, Paul." She had to let him know. Acting was a joy on the stage, but it tormented her now. She had the feeling that Paul was afraid too, but that the emotion was for him so powerful and so potentially destructive that he couldn't even allow himself to feel it. When it contacted hers his hand was wet and hot. It told little.

Around them the world seemed to crouch down. These hills were hard country. How they were going to negotiate them on foot at night Catherine could not imagine. But they _were_ going to do it. Would there come some point out there where Paul would meet and fail some terrible test? She wanted him to acknowledge his fear, at last to face his real, human feelings honestly. Otherwise she might well lose him to panic just when she needed him most.

She felt that, but didn't know for sure. Couldn't. "Paul, how do you feel?"

"Like we outflanked them."

"I mean inside."

"Before we get into that, I think we should talk out some more practical problems. For example, have you ever been hiking?"

"I used to do a lot of it back home."

"The Blue Ridge Mountains can hardly be compared to the Black Hills. This is not tame country."

"I'll pull my weight, Paul Winter. Don't think I won't."

"You're scared?"

"I'm a normal human being. The only thing I really know about what we're getting into is that it's bad. So I am indeed scared."

"You're good at concealing it."

She decided to try to pin him down. "Not as good as you."

He smiled. "Nemo. Big little town."

Paul was not an easy man to crack. She attempted a more direct approach. "I think you're scared too. Scared to death."

For a few minutes he drove in silence. When she looked at him she saw compressed lips, a rigid stare. "Goddamn it, Catherine, you are astonishingly ignorant of human psychology for a supposed method actor. We'd be fools to start screaming this out of our systems right now. Of course I'm scared! I might even be more scared than you because I know more about what might happen tonight. But I don't have time right now to go on the analyst's couch about it!"

"You intend to keep it stuffed away inside with all your other feelings?"

"Damn right. Until we're sitting in front of a fire together drinking hot toddies and remembering. Then you'll see Paul Winter afraid. I'll be able to spare the time for it.''

She suspected that moment would never come. Paul was as far into himself now as he would ever go. She had chosen to be with him because he was a truly extraordinary man. In making that choice she had also, it seemed, chosen to be alone in some painful ways. There were things that Paul simply could not afford to face and still be what he was.

She watched the little town of Nemo pass behind them, Exxon station, a line of motels, the sound of music from some festivity.

Parties had always bored her and loud music hurt her ears, but right now she wouldn't have minded a little oblivion, a night that moved from Xenon to dinner at Regine's to the Mudd Club and breakfast at the Empire Diner. Sausages and eggs and those big mugs of coffee, a little drunk, a little high, and lovely sex with Paul at sunrise, then a day in bed, ordering in flowers from Wadley and Smythe and drinking Bloody Marys.

The air in these hills smelled wild. They were on a dirt road with pines towering up on the left and emptiness on the right. Paul had slowed the car. He cut the lights. ''Oh, Jesus, look up there.''

She saw the briefest twinkle of a brake light ahead.

''Brace!''

The car lurched horribly, pine boughs slamming against the windshield. Then it dug into the steep grade and began to nose over. Catherine was slammed forward and then back hard. Her hands flailed, suddenly found the ceiling in front of her. There was a tremendous crash, then silence and the stench of gasoline. They had gone down the shoulder of the road; only brush prevented the car from dropping over the cliff.

She was hanging in her seat belt, facing straight down through the windshield. Ahead she could see lights. It took a moment to realize that they were the headlights of cars on Highway 90 far below.

"My God, Paul!" She could not help sobbing, didn't even bother to try.

"Get out very, very carefully."

"How?"

"Get a grip on the cross strap of your belt with your right hand and unbuckle it with your left. You'll swing free. Go out through the window and climb back up to the road. Use the trees as handholds. There're plenty of them."

"You?"

"I'm going to get the car over the cliff."

That wouldn't be difficult.

She did as instructed, gripping the cross strap and then unbuckling the belt, which released with a loud crack and sent her lurching harder than she had expected against the door.

The window was up and the crush of trees outside held the door closed. She began to unroll the window.

As Paul got out, the car shifted and settled. The lights beyond the windshield gyrated wildly. "Catherine, move!"

A groaning and sighing started, began to get louder. Catherine worked with the window, rolling it painfully, slowly as the car's angle got steeper and steeper.

"Hurry!"

She wasn't making it. "The window's stuck!"

Suddenly his hands were there, grabbing her shoulders and pulling as a foot slammed again and again at the safety glass. The car was dragging her now, and him with her, his hands under her arms. He was grunting and cursing—

The car tumbled out into silence and she clutched him, dangling in the scrub pine.

From far below there rose a solemn roar. Flickering light colored the coarse trunks of the pines and cast shadows on the sloping forest floor. The car had exploded among the rocks.

"Come on."

She was shaking so hard she could hardly move. She

didn't want to follow that gruff voice; she wanted to be held, just for a second to be taken in kind arms.

"Catherine, you're better than that. Now come on!"

"To you better means less human! I'm human and I'm scared to death!" Maybe, but she found that her own voice sounded a lot stronger than she felt. She started climbing toward him. Together they reached the road.

"Very, very quiet. Let's take it easy." He went on hands and knees at the edge of the pavement and bent down.

"No vibration." Now he looked up and down the visible stretch of the curving road.

"OK, consider us cleared to cross. Keep low, move fast, and continue into the trees until you're well away from the shoulder. Go!"

Night had transformed what must have been a beautiful woods into a dark and sinister forest. Beneath the tall pines no breeze moved. There were clicks and sighs from the trees and a steady drone of insect life. Farther up a fitful glow indicated a moonlit clearing.

"Lie down. Quick!" She sprawled flat. Back on the road she could hear the hiss of tires, then the squeak of brakes and soft Russian words. Doors opened and closed, and there was a tapping of leather-soled shoes on pavement. At least they were worse equipped for hiking.

"They're investigating the accident," Paul breathed. "If I did my job right they'll think we're goners."

His job? That meant the car crash had been planned. "Next time give me a little warning when you decide to risk my life."

"Keep it down."

The clicking of footsteps was replaced by the sound of people rustling the brush at the edges of the road.

Paul's hand grasped her shoulder and squeezed, then slipped up her neck and lifted her head. She got the message intended and looked forward.

At the edge of the clearing stood a huge, bearded man in a

flowing robe. He was very still. Paul had started breathing hard, as if in shock.

The man began to edge back into the darker woods, moving with the supple grace of a retreating snake.

Beside her Paul moaned. She had wanted him to reveal his fear.

Now she wished he hadn't.

16

"WINTER HAS BROKEN THROUGH the cordon around the Iranians."

"Give me that cable! How dare you read—by all the holies!" This was terrifying. "Do something, Florinsky!" The colonel was sitting close behind Teplov, and he could sense the swine's glee.

"What can I do?"

"How much time left until we project the Field to Jamshid?"

"An hour and twenty-one minutes."

"You're lying. You must be!"

Florinsky pressed some buttons. The computer confirmed him.

"We have to advance the count."

"The cable said Winter might have died in his car—"

"Forget it. He's a ghost! I saw him in action in Laos. Advance the count."

"It isn't possible."

"Oh, no? Just listen." Teplov regarded the forest of switches before him. "Turn on the general intercom for me, Florinsky."

"I'm not authorized."

"You accepted my command! Now turn it on or you'll be shot in half an hour!"

Florinsky flipped two switches and gave Teplov the headset. "Attention, all battle managers. This is Black Magic command. The count is advanced thirty minutes. Please adjust your plans accordingly."

He removed the earpiece to avoid being deafened by the outburst of voices. Down at the Rocket Forces control area there was a flurry of activity. A heavily decorated officer pulled off his headset and began blustering up to the slot. Teplov had heard of General Sitnikov, the fierce, superefficient commandant of the elite nuclear arm.

"Colonel, you are forcing me to violate specific articles of the Black Magic Protocol approved by the Politburo. The Protocol is clear and I am quoting. 'No less than ninety-five percent of SS-18/4 missile delivery systems shall be at firing readiness before the ELF field is cast.' If we advance the count the cast will occur when I'm at a readiness level of below fifty percent. The result could be catastrophe."

"You will continue as ordered."

"I don't take orders from colonels!"

"My command authority is absolute. You throw the Protocol at me, I throw it back at you. The moment Belik died I became commander in chief, and I will remain so until the General Staff replaces him. If you wish me to file a complaint of cowardice—"

"I'd kill you with my own hands!"

"General, the count is advanced thirty minutes. I suggest you waste no more time. Begin revising your schedules."

The general delivered a glare incandescent with hatred. Then he turned and walked stiffly back to his group.

Teplov called through to Gorkin and told him to be ready to cast in exactly forty-nine minutes.

Next he contacted his ships at sea and ordered them to start proceeding toward American territorial waters.

Oh, this was luxury, to be able to command as fast as his

mind could move! He called Kislitsin via a direct satellite link. Voice to voice. This time Kislitsin was going to take his orders. Sheer force of will would overcome his resistance without the impersonality of the teletype to insulate him.

"This is the commander in chief of Black Magic. I'm assuming direct command of your forces under war emergency orders. Do you accept?"

A short silence.

"War emergency orders, Captain. Disobey me at your risk!"

"Very well."

"How far is Winter from the Iranians?"

"Not far. Perhaps a mile."

"And your group? Where is it?"

"On the road perhaps five hundred meters from Winter."

"And you're not giving chase? You must be mad, man!"

"One of the Iranians is just a few meters from him. If we chase we reveal ourselves."

Teplov considered. His impulse was to order Kislitsin to kill both Winter and the Iranian, but that might have unpredictable consequences. No, Kislitsin's conservative stance was correct.

"Florinsky, advance the count another ten minutes."

Down on the working floor General Sitnikov slammed his fist into a chair, knocking it against a wall where it broke to pieces.

A well of silence was moving through the darkness. Crickets would stop, owls cease their hooting. "He's nearby," Paul said, "shadowing us." They had passed through the clearing and were now in dense scrubwood. Underfoot the soil crunched with ash. A season or so ago fire had destroyed the old trees along this particular slope. Paul kept angling upward. Their adversary would want to beat them to the high ground if he could.

Beside him Catherine was limping and breathing hard.

Her right knee had been hurt in the car and she was favoring it more and more. But when he tried to support her with an arm around her waist she gestured him away.

A limb cracked. "Sh!" The sound had echoed through the woods, coming from the dense growth farther ahead. The man from the clearing had achieved his advantage. He was above them now.

"We've got to spread out. See that thicket to your left?"

"Yes."

"Get down in it, down deep. Be ready to use your gun."

"Paul, I haven't got my gun! I must have lost it in the car."

"Great. Then keep as quiet as possible."

Her hand came around his wrist. He could sense the stiffening of her body, hear a sharp breath. Then he saw why.

The man was easily six five, and he must be a master woodsman. He had come upon them in total silence. Even now he was moving, and there was not so much as the crunch of a leaf beneath his feet.

He was slipping through the scrub like a ghost, working toward some sort of position. But why? A gun could easily be fired through the leaves and branches that separated him from his quarry.

He must be a knife man.

It was not brilliant to deploy a knife in an area choked with obstacles to the thrown dagger. "Let's move up the hill."

"He's right over there—"

He pulled her roughly to make her follow. "Trust me," he said. As quickly as possible he entered the deeper scrub, moving in the direction from which the crack of the limb had come. This was a choking forest. Their adversary had made his sound here to trick them into heading toward clearer territory.

Despite his temporary advantage Paul felt no safer. The man's silence in the woods was a disturbing sign. No doubt his skill would soon overcome the minor obstacle of his victims' keeping to the thickets.

Paul had tried to keep going generally in the correct direction. It was going to be difficult enough to locate the installation without getting disoriented. Fortunately it was a clear night and the moon was visible through the trees.

Ahead the scrub diminished. Between the matted branches Paul could see gleaming black rock. They had reached the top of a ridge.

"Wait here. I'm going to reconnoiter ahead." He slipped as quietly as he knew how through the sparse growth. A dangerous spot, but with a good view of the terrain. To the west other ridges rose to sharp crags. Northward the land ascended more gently, then dropped abruptly into a huge draw. From the top of the draw there would be an unobstructed view of the entire Eighty-third Strategic Missile Wing.

There was a stunning richness to this night. Paul's senses were strained to hypersensitivity. He experienced the shadowy world around as a single, seething creature made up of trees and moonlight and insects, and the dark man of the woods, too.

The man meant that Jamshid was very close. His first line of defense. Jamshid of the golden eyes. If Paul managed to get past this guard, what would then happen? Surely this was not all. No, he would be a fool to expect such an important creature to be guarded by a single knife.

The cat-eyed things that belonged to ELF might be here too.

No, that was crazy. They were hallucinations.

They know only the dead, and soon they will know you.

He heard the dry rustling of their fingers in the wind and felt the light of their searching eyes.

A frantic scream soared through the silence. In reflex Paul threw himself to the ground. The scream grew louder and louder, undulating through the night. Pistol in hand, he scrambled to his feet and ran to her.

* * *

"Ismail, be silent!" A sound was marching up from the jumble of draws and gullies below them. It was a scream of extreme human terror.

"A woman."

Jamshid's body felt almost as if it were floating, such had been the intensity of his dance. He was working toward a new state of communion with the Master. There would be no failure this time. When the moment came, the mind that rode the Field would be at the summit of its power, sweeping the wills of the missile crewmen aside as leaves of winter.

"Kajenouri must have killed a woman."

Was that all? A woman? The darkness seemed to oppress Jamshid, as if watchers were surrounding him. The woods were beginning to seem full of menace. There should not have been a woman's scream. Perhaps Kajenouri had been tricked.

He wanted physical contact. He opened his arms. "Please love me, my friend."

Ismail hung back. He too was afraid, but not of the screaming creature in the hills. If matters had not already gone so far, Jamshid would at this time have killed Ismail. He was hopelessly weak.

He dropped his arms. There was no further sound from the dark. The moon glowed over all, indifferent to all. Far away the music that had been playing in the little town stopped. The lights of a great jetliner swam in the sky. Overhead a nighthawk caught a cicada and rose, calling softly its triumph. There was gentle motion in the close woods. Jamshid's dance having stopped, the deer were returning.

"Ismail, the time?"

"One o'clock."

"Soon, Ismail."

"Soon."

"Let us begin again."

* * *

254

Catherine had not wanted him to leave her, had sensed that it was a mistake. When his form had disappeared into the shadows, she had hunched as far down into her thicket as she could.

It was strange to be so intimate with the ground, the beetles and the gnats and the ants. There was a dense, rich smell of pine sweat and earth. All around her insects were living out their tiny, spectacular lives in utter secrecy.

She became aware of large movement nearby. It did not seem possible that a human being could be so close and yet so silent. She began turning her head very slowly in the direction of the motion. Surely it would be a deer or some other forest animal, surely not—

A long, knobby arm was reaching through the pine branches, the fingers of the hand extended and questing to twine in her hair.

She plunged in the opposite direction, scratching herself on the stiff tangle of twigs and limbs. Then she felt a shattering jerk; she had not been fast enough; the hand was gripping her thigh. It was so impossibly large that it contained her hip like an apple. She called for Paul, trying not to be too loud. She didn't want to scream and risk being heard from the road. Anyway, Paul was close; he would hear. Even as she struggled, beating at the hand with her fists, digging her heels into the dirt, she felt herself being dragged by a ruthless strength.

She was ripped through the branches so fast that her shirt caught and shredded. The twigs dug deep.

Then she was out of the thicket and being grabbed by the hair, lifted bodily by a great, dark figure. "Paul!" Her voice was sharp, still controlled.

He came bounding through the brush. Suddenly he stopped, raised his arm. The pistol made its silenced thud. Catherine was hurled to the ground and in that moment she saw a most terrible thing.

The creature's face was visible in the moonlight, a twisted old gargoyle with heavy brows and goggling wet eyes. With a long hiss from between its cage of teeth it moved into the woods.

"Catherine, run!"

She went furiously across the little clear patch and into Paul's arms.

There were screams echoing in the hills, back and forth, dying their eerie death among the hard crags. She recognized her own voice, but she hadn't even heard herself doing it.

Paul dragged her behind a stand of pine. There was a loud *thunk* and the tree she had just leaned against shook. She jumped away—something sharp had stuck her through the bark.

It was the tip of a knife, driven all the way through the trunk by a powerful throw. A somewhat thinner tree and it would have done far more than scratch her.

"He—did you see—"

"I hit him in the chest, honey. A .32 in the chest is going to slow any man down, no matter how big he is."

The terror of it all caught her again. She doubled over, feeling her stomach contract with sudden nausea. When she managed to rise to full height again he embraced her for a moment. "You're doing fine, Catherine. Better than you can possibly imagine. Let's go."

She was sweating now, and she was glad when they reached the crest of the ridge. Here there was a fresh breeze up from the east.

From far down the hillside came the voice of a fiddle. Catherine recognized the last few bars of "Amazing Grace" before it faded away.

"Thirty minutes mark. Counting."

"Tracking radars operational."

"Rocket Management confirms. We have your feed, Tracking. We will begin aiming calibration in thirty seconds. Begin count—now."

"This is AH-8 Antirocket Battle Management coming online. Do you read us, Black Magic?"

"Black Magic reads you," Teplov said. He felt that he was getting used to this job already. If one refused to be intimidated by the jargon it all became very logical.

"SideNet Radars available to you, AH-8," Teplov said. He was even doing well with the soldier's jargon.

"All right, all right, Black Magic, relax. We'll get to that."

He let it go.

"This is an SS-18 fail-safe point," Florinsky said into the auxiliary headset. "Report any failures, please."

"Launcher A-28N is not operational due to nonfunctional silo blast doors. We will be firing one silo attached to 678 Strategic Rocket Group as backup."

"Do you want to interrupt the count, Rocket Forces?" Teplov kept his voice as neutral as he could.

"We do not," came the sullen reply of General Sitnikov.

"Do you want a prior firing of that 678 silo?" Florinsky asked. To Teplov he explained, "The 678th is attached to the Thirteenth Military District. Their missiles are far to the south. To keep up with us they'll have to fire early."

"Won't it reveal our intentions to the Americans?"

"Sitnikov must weigh that danger."

There was a conference going on at the Rocket Forces console. General Sitnikov could be seen pointing his thumb back toward the slot. Some of his officers were shaking their heads, disagreeing with him. Finally the voice of their battle management officer returned to the comm net. "No prior firing."

"So noted," Florinsky replied.

"ELF installation reporting. We have successfully completed the half-power tests. We are ready to cast when ordered."

Teplov had been sweating earlier. It started again. If it weren't for all this intricate military nonsense the cast could take place right now. He hated the feeling that Winter was getting closer and closer to Jamshid Rostram. Snap the bud and kill the flower.

"Would you like a handkerchief, Colonel?"

Teplov would not take even that simple assistance from the decadent Florinsky. "No, Comrade Colonel. I have my own."

"AH-8s ready for SideNet data transfer test."

"We will input Games-1544 targeting data to you. Please arm with the proper coordinates."

"This is Sovmin interrupting for a general comm check. All report to Sovmin, please." That was the Politburo's underground command center near Moscow. There would be a full assembly there today, which would hear that the voice of Black Magic was now Pyotr Teplov's voice. Let Andropov swallow that.

"Black Magic Central Control hears you," he said. The other commands followed, right down to the crew leaders of individual missile squadrons and radar stations. It was considered essential that Sovmin have communications in depth. The principle of centralized command was, in the case of the nuclear and secret forces, taken to its penultimate limit. The Politburo could speak directly to any missile-firing officer, General Staff be damned.

After the commands had been confirmed, Teplov looked a long time at the console. Finally he was forced to ask Florinsky a question. "Is it possible to route Sovmin through this console?"

"Illegal."

"Is it possible!"

"You reconfigure the communications net by switching out all the overriding circuits. Then Sovmin is cut off."

"Do it."

"Colonel, I will point to the switches. You will have to turn them."

Teplov cut off Sovmin. It was insane to trust decisions like these to a committee. Russia had too many committees. It needed one or two strong men.

One such man.

The satellite radiophone warbled. Kislitsin!

"The woman with Winter has apparently been killed."

"And Winter himself?"

"No information."

"You imbecile! How dare you waste my time with prattle!" He slammed the radiophone back onto its hook.

The room lapsed into silence. Teplov, embarrasssed by his outburst, stared at the computer information streaming across his video screen.

He sank miserably into himself. Eighteen minutes left to Black Magic. Eighteen minutes for Paul Winter to do mayhem. "If only I were out there on the spot," he said aloud.

"If only you were."

He would have told Florinsky to go to the devil if he had been able to spare the energy. If Pyotr Teplov ever got to the top, Colonel Florinsky had better get himself a nice coffin. He and that pompous self-defender General Sitnikov and a few million others. All the plotting, antisocial swine—anti-Leninist provocateurs, revanchists, outright criminals, the secret bedfellows of the American imperialists. The fiery wind of the workers' wrath would blow them to tatters. They would be buried with their criminal brothers from America. All of them, every one.

"Florinsky, is there anything at all we can do to speed matters up further?"

"I'm afraid not. The Rocket Forces are already well behind the count."

Teplov ran his fingers through his hair, rested his head on the edge of the console, closed his eyes.

Quite a horrible image appeared before him. At the moment it was startlingly real, but after he opened his eyes again it seemed only a dream. What the devil had it been?

The rocks that Paul and Catherine were crossing were full of caves. From time to time Paul could smell their stuffy dampness, the odor of the grave. There had been nothing more from the knife, but Paul would not allow himself to believe that a single shot had stopped that giant. Certainly it was possible, just not very likely.

He looked at his watch. Nearly two. "We must be close." They had climbed as high as possible in order to see what might be hidden in the land. From here its secrets were less dense, the moon hanging over a dark green ocean of swarming, windswept pines.

There was, however, no sign of hidden construction, no square shadow in the moonlight—nothing at all, in fact except the rough hillsides and the prairie below. They were only a few hundred feet beneath the main ridge of the Black Hills, and the twisted trees around them sang with sharp, cold breeze.

Catherine's hand came into his. "Look. Is that him?"

The shadow flitted like a bat or blowing paper. "It's him."

"He looks hurt, the way he's moving."

"My shot must have done something."

Too bad he was still alive. Paul chose not to share the matter of his one last bullet with Catherine. If he missed she was going to have to experience the full terror of that man.

"He's stopped."

Easily a hundred yards off, too. Paul stretched out on the ground and took aim. The shot was still too risky. Paul's own pistols could have made it, but not this miserable thing.

There was a sudden movement from the figure. An instant later a clang broke the quiet and a stone flashed sparks in Paul's face. The knife skipped on the rocks and hummed past his head. When he looked again the man was much closer. If the throw had been intended to cover a rush it had worked.

Eighty yards. Was it still too far? Paul rested the pistol on the rocks, got the chest of his attacker centered in the sights. "I'm going to try a shot. If I don't make it, run."

"In other words, it's your last bullet. I thought it might be."

"You're too smart."

The man stopped again, raised his arm. In the moonlight Paul could see the gleam of the blade. Now. He squeezed his trigger. There was a flicker and the silencer's peculiar thud. Simultaneously he felt a shattering pain in his left shoulder.

Dizziness followed, so great was the hurt. He let out a cry and felt Catherine erupt to his aid, then lay with his eyes closed, listening this time to his own scream echoing off into the hills. In anger more than sadness, he prepared to receive final blows.

From below there came the singsong of prayer. Paul was confused to hear it, but his own agony obscured the question. He recognized the Farsi, the noble words from Sura 32 of the Koran: "The angel of Death, who has been entrusted with your souls, shall gather you, and to your Lord you shall be returned."

"He's hit, he's dying."

"You have a *knife* in your shoulder! Oh, my God, Paul."

"I got him."

"It's in all the way to the hilt!"

"In the flesh, and in my collarbone. You'll have to pull it out. But tear off part of my coat first, get a pressure bandage ready. The axillary artery's in there and it might be nicked."

She pulled and tugged at his jacket, finally producing some long strips of lining. "Ah, silk, good and strong. Grasp the hilt and draw it out as smoothly as you can. And don't mind my scream; I won't be able to help it."

She pulled. He sucked air through his teeth.

"Is it still in?"

A desperate sob. "Yes! It's stuck!"

"It's in the bone, dear. You'll just have to give it a good hard tug."

"I'm scared."

"You've got to do it."

She pulled again and screamed with him, but then she had the knife in her hand. "Don't throw it away!"

"No."

"Is the blood spurting?" It felt like a cataract.

"Spurting? No." A shaking hand felt the wound. "It's oozing out."

"Put on the bandage as best you can. We'll make a sling with my belt."

She wrapped her strips of silk around his shoulder and under his arm. He sat up, closed his eyes and dealt with the inevitable vertigo, then let her get the belt and affix it. She placed his hand in the loop.

"You're very gentle. Any training?"

"Hardly. I was a candy striper."

They went to the Knife.

He was dead, but his prayer had not left him peace. His chest was sheeted with blood; on his face was what could only be seen as a rictus of absolute dread.

Paul wanted to close the eyes, but could not bend down. He had no wish to face another death eye to eye, and yet the stillness of the body somehow provided a sort of comfort. No matter how hard living is, it will have an end. That is the unassailable terror and freedom of death.

Even another confrontation with Jamshid would not be forever. He could almost see the boy's gold eyes, hear his high, sad voice. The most frightening of people would inevitably be the most pitiful.

Catherine's hand found his. "I hear a noise."

Paul listened, but her ears were more sensitive than his own.

"It's a sort of clicking. Rhythmic."

"Can you tell where it's coming from?" He closed his eyes to stifle nausea; the wound wrapped his arm and shoulder in a sheath of fire. He took deep breaths, tried to turn his mind from his suffering.

"Straight ahead, about where the draw widens out."

It was a possibility—the only one they had found. "Let's have a look." He stumbled, she caught him, and they went on.

* * *

In one minute the cast would be attempted. Around Teplov the command center was seething with excited activity. The Soviet Union was going to war, but quietly, carefully, beneath the surface of the earth. Teplov reflected that almost all recent wars had started this way, with one dragon stealthy and the other sleeping.

"Fifty seconds."

"We're only at forty-eight percent," the Rocket Forces battle manager reported.

Teplov responded to that. "Bring them up faster!"

Sitnikov's voice came on, grave beyond rage. "I wish to lodge a formal complaint that the Politburo's Black Magic Protocol is being violated by the slot."

"Thank you, General." Teplov said nothing more. Around him intense activity was occurring. It was as beautiful in its way as ballet, and incomparably more exciting.

"Forty seconds."

"Black Magic control here. We have full generator power."

"SideNet Radars calibrating."

"Black Magic control. We have a live antenna."

"Thirty seconds."

"Tracking radars confirming to missiles."

"Missiles locked to tracking guidance."

"Fifty-five percent ready. Rocket Forces."

"Black Magic control here. We have a Field. Stabilizing."

But would it project, and stay projected? Teplov was shaking.

"Twenty seconds," Florinsky said.

"Fifty-eight percent ready. Rocket Forces."

"That's better than expected," the soldier murmured.

"Of course."

"SideNet Radars calibrated. AH-8s, are you on us?"

"AH-8s confirmed for quick launch."

"Ten seconds."

"This is Igor Gorkin. I am pressing the Field projection button now." Teplov hung on the pause, his eyes fixed to the large clock above the winking, shimmering map. Gorkin spoke again. "I have a stable Field projected."

There was a smattering of applause. Only the Rocket Forces group was silent. Teplov watched their backs, the men hunched and intent, speaking into their intercoms as ever so slowly the number of red lights grew on the face of the map.

"Rocket Forces sixty-two percent ready."

Across the world Jamshid Rostram and his targets were all inside the Field. There was nothing left but the waiting.

Jamshid was dancing with furious precision, the sweat flinging from his face, when he was suddenly enveloped in the most gloriously powerful Field he had ever experienced in his life. It made him shout out in joy; his body seemed to explode into a thousand stars; his mind soared to the sky crying free.

He heard the hearts of night birds and felt the hunger of bats, swept through the velvet mind of a deer and into a coon's sharp terror and on into the night, turning at last toward the fine little light at the far limit of the Field. The Launch Control Capsule.

Yes.

Jamshid's body tingled, the sensation spreading from toes to head in an instant. Around him the *divs* of the wind shook the pines. *Jinn* circled and bellowed. Recoiling from their noise, Ismail almost lost his rhythm.

Jamshid was beginning to float out of his body, to exit each vessel and pore. He came out of himself like smoke from a lamp; his own voice filled the firmament as he laughed at the joy of being so incredibly free. The truth about the *jinn* in the bottle was revealed: the bottle is the body, and the *jinn* the spirit unbound.

Below him the world was shifting and turning. Ghostly beasts swarmed in the hills, poured over and through the huddled, quaking Ismail, flickered in the sky and shone beneath the earth.

Only a moment Jamshid watched, then he was off, flowing down the gleaming trail to the two men in the Launch Control Capsule.

He went quickly along, the distorted reflections of his own self twisting and looming about him. The path into another mind was mirrored with images of one's own.

He sought them; he could taste the tastes in their mouths and smell the scent of their thoughts. Crew R-087 was their designation.

The thrill of contact was almost unendurable, but Jamshid would not be shaken out of his targets this time. He felt himself at once in their tomb with them and at the same time high in the sky, journeying through the warm, still air.

He reached the lap of Satan and the minds of the missile crewmen at the same time. *Divs* and *jinn* fell silent. Dark angels clustered. From them all there descended one great word that set Jamshid's very spirit to ringing with glee. The word echoed across the hills and soared above the prairie, swept the sleeping cities and towns of America, *destruction* whispered and sung and shouted, *destruction* as prayer and pledge, upon the faces of the dreaming child and the wakeful one, the workman and the leader, the saint and the corrupt, on all their houses *destruction.*

I am home. I am so glad. Let me touch you now, my dear soldiers.

This one is Charlie, and that is Dave. Charlie, his is the quieter mind. He likes this work. He is writing out an incident report, waiting for dinnertime. He remembers the moonrise; he has been here two hours. He is acutely aware that men died here last week.

There came, like silence in a storm, a disharmony of voices.

"It's getting louder," said a male voice. A familiar taste to its owner's mind, too.

"Yeah."

265

Who can this be? These voices are here in the hills.

Didn't I heard their death screams? Didn't Kajenouri kill them?"

"Someone's beating a rhythm."

Kajenouri did not kill them!

After all, my enemy has reached me. Now, the last battle.

17

TEPLOV WATCHED THE SECONDS unfold. The subdued voices of battle managers and radar controllers increased tension by their very calmness.

He heard a distant noise, as of a child laughing at the far end of a quiet street.

"Florinsky, do you generally feel echo effects of the Field in here?"

"Of course not. We're miles away and the antenna isn't aimed in this direction. It's aimed downward, into the earth."

"Yes."

Something in here smelled bad, like a rotted turnip. Of all times for there to be a ventilation failure. If this place had been in Sverdlovsk, the workers would have kept it in perfect order.

"It's stuffy. Call for ice."

Florinsky snapped his fingers and whispered the request to an orderly.

Teplov felt something moving beneath his feet. He looked down. His chair appeared to be on a huge, scaly back. He could even see the bulges of enormous vertebrae beneath the skin. The thing's muscles were seething, as if it were just awakening.

He stared, transfixed with confusion and loathing. Only the iron of his will stifled a scream.

The Field burst up in Paul like a great eye opening in the middle of his head. He felt Jamshid's unmistakable presence instantly, the same ugly closeness that had so revolted him in Iran in 1979.

Beside him Catherine stopped and made a short gasping cry of surprise. "Is this—*this!*"

"We're in the ELF field. Now remember what I told you. It's going to be worse than the worst nightmare. Just remember, it's inside our minds. Only inside our minds."

Paul looked off into the dark. He had heard more movement there. Jamshid's first line of defense was down. What would be his second?

Jamshid recognized Paul Winter at once.

Always, as if from the beginning of time, he had been destined to do battle with this man. In the Zagros he had known it, and all his life since.

"Ismail, my great enemy is here. He is coming down the ridge."

"Kajenouri—"

"Dead!"

Ismail sighed and looked wildly about.

"If he gets to the Circle, protect me." He went close to Ismail, offered his face to the soft light of the moon. "Protect me."

Ismail staggered away. "That smell, what is that smell, Jamshid?"

The demons came to strengthen Ismail.

Jamshid heard them calling with soft voices, laughing like children in the woods. Ismail staggered and grunted. "Allah deliver me." The calls came faster now, gentle and kind. A woman and a child stood in the moonlight. "Fatma," Ismail cried, "Fatma! Little Ismail and Fatma!"

He went to them.

There was a roaring struggle. Ismail's body writhed and jerked, and his voice bubbled choked cries of utter desolation.

Struggling like a bird caught by the claw, he twisted off through the dark. As he went his cries changed from sorrow to anger to wild, galloping rage. Ismail was becoming one with the demons. His eyes glowed with their light; his skin stank with their stench.

He was moving toward Paul Winter, across the rocks and through the trees. The tips of his toes scattered dust as he passed just above the ground.

Teplov had to force himself to stop looking at the floor. It was a hallucination brought on by fatigue. It could be nothing else.

"BackNet Radars. No joy." That meant that American missiles had not been fired.

"Teplov to Gorkin. What is the condition of the Field?"

"Strong and holding."

Paul Winter was the only danger. Had he already killed Jamshid?

Somehow Teplov thought not. He suspected, with a sudden burst of the most intricate joy, that he was going to win this one.

He imagined his ships, now steaming through the moonlit waters toward ports with exotic names like Boston and New York and Houston. Exotic, glittering cities. They even smelled American—of automobile exhaust and discarded food. He had not been to America since the sixties, and her cities had become for him a bright haze recalled as lights and cars and confusion.

No more confusion, American workers. Help is coming soon.

His headset suddenly chattered. Behind him Florinsky leaned forward, intent.

There were cries coming from somewhere, desperate and horrible.

The antenna! Something was wrong at the antenna!

"Gorkin!"

A shouted reply, unintelligible.

"Gorkin, what is it?"

The reply was a muddle of voices.

". . . get them out of here . . ."

"What the hell—it's—aaahhh!"

". . . get the fucking thing shut down . . ."

"Gorkin, is that you? You will not shut down!"

A chorus of cries, rising to freezing high tones. Then silence.

"The Field, my God, Florinsky, something has gone wrong with the Field!"

"No, our computers are reading a steady Field. Very steady. And getting stronger."

"Stronger? How could it get stronger?"

"Colonel, I don't know."

Jamshid left Paul Winter to the demons, going once again down the shining path to the Launch Control Center. He ignored the twisting, misshapen images of his own body that curled like smoke around him, concentrating instead on the clear white light ahead.

Crew R-087. Dave and Charlie.

He began to hear their voices as if they were speaking twice, once in their minds and once aloud.

Air War College . . . he can't . . . nah . . . nah . . . "You don't want to go to the Air War College. You wanta get out of here and get into industry."

Bird . . . bird . . . "I wanta be Bird Colonel, man."

No way, he's too . . . turkey . . . "Yeah. You. Seeing is gonna be believing."

Jamshid worked quickly. The Field helped him. It was

getting incredibly strong, a hundred, a thousand times stronger than ever before, so strong it almost hurt the way sun in the eyes hurt. Oh, it was good though, it was so good!

If this is fire, bathe me in fire!

Like a shadow, like light shimmering on an eyeball, Jamshid crept closer.

Charlie's was the quieter mind. He touched its web and watched it shake and quiver, a silken lacework of awareness, so very sensitive.

Hanging in the air before the face, he studied Charlie. The crewman frowned, shook his head as if to clear his vision.

The lights . . . goddamn Air Force . . . "I think we're about to lose our lights, buddy."

"Oh, yeah? Seem OK to me."

"They aren't OK!"

Now Charlie, be quiet. What was your lullaby? "Golden slumbers fill your eyes" . . . yes, Charlie, remember . . . mother . . . "smiles await you when you rise . . ."

Jamshid drew closer, came again to the edge of Charlie's mind and—yes!

—my kitty has funny eyes.

—Mommy, why does Mitzi have . . .

—pie smells good I like *mince!*

—smell the radiator when the car stops don't do that, Charlie!

—get the codes, Charlie, do that, Charlie!

Yes!

"Oh, Paul, something's in my hair!"

"Good God—a frigging . . . here, lemme—shit, they're all over the place, they're goddamn *bats!*"

Not one or fifty but hundreds and hundreds flapped out of the night sky, dulling the moon with their multitudes, their tiny cries magnified by numbers to a single, dizzying shriek.

Paul saw Catherine go down in the swarm. He hit, he grabbed, he tore, but then they were on him too, so many he could see nothing but little bat bodies and leathery wings. He struggled forward one step, then another, then faltered. He was smothering in bats! For an instant he saw Catherine pull free, but more of them came and soon she was a writhing, indistinct heap of flapping insanity.

The stinging was bites!

"Help us! God help us!"

Catherine's hand suddenly found his. She pulled at him with the strength of ten, yanking him free of the mass.

The bats, tangled in themselves, could not follow.

Catherine's eyes flashed in the moonlight. "If this is your idea of a nightmare, fella—"

"Let's go. Mustn't be late for our appointment with Jamshid."

"I should say not."

"Igor Gorkin, answer, please!"

Static.

"The Field is double its registered maximum intensity," Florinsky said. Down on the main floor a man vomited, setting off two more. The smell in the HQ was close to unendurable. Teplov, seeing the retching soldiers, had to fight his own guts.

"BackNet. No joy."

The U.S. missiles still hadn't risen.

Something touched Teplov's shoulder. Florinsky? What the hell—the fingers were long and black, so dry that flakes of their coating were dusting down the front of his suit.

"No!" He jumped forward. Behind him Florinsky was a bloated yellow corpse, the eyes dangling from cords of ooze, the lips fat with pus, the tongue bursting green between the teeth.

"Florinsky!"

"AH-8s preparing launcher readiness test. Thirty seconds to test. Count back—now."

The corpse, the hand, could not be real. Just could not be.

Then he saw his own hands. And he looked around him at the other men.

"Colonel, are you unwell?"

Florinsky's voice was thick from the distention of his mouth. And he stank.

"Field at triple registered maximum now. Gorkin's really goosing it."

Teplov vomited. It spattered onto the console before him. It was black. It was alive.

Begin the launch procedure, you dirty bastards! Begin come on! That's right, give me your voices, your hands! Oh, yes, give me your *voices!*

"DEFCON One alert. Prepare for launch."

"Check. Alert status confirmed."

"Check."

"Launch option select."

"Select full flight."

"Ten missiles selected."

"Check."

Catherine heard them before she saw them. They came hissing in the grass, their bodies sighing across the rocks, their stone-shaped heads darting up here and there.

Paul grabbed one and slung its long, coiling body into the darkness.

"Paul, I hate snakes!"

"So do I, baby!"

They came as the bats had come, in hordes, their rattles buzzing, their bodies whipping as they rushed closer.

As quickly as flowing water one of them reared up and wrapped itself around Catherine's neck. She grabbed its daywarm flesh and flung the rippling muscles away. Venom spattered her face, numbing her skin where it touched her.

"The purpose of venom is to dissolve prey animals from the inside out. It is a digestive enzyme." O'Brien High School, Richmond, Virginia, spring of 1974.

273

"What the hell are you standing there for?"

"Paul, the snakes!"

"Big fucking deal. Run. What're they gonna do, sprout wings?"

She followed his swaying form into the darker forest. In the rocks behind them the rattling died away. "They won't follow us?"

"Damned if I know. Let's just go. There isn't any time to waste!"

Jamshid moved Charlie and Dave at their consoles like two robots. He had never been in a Field this powerful before. It was so strong that it had enabled him to crush out their minds like two little moths in his palm. When he left they would be empty. Vegetables.

"Launch sequence initiated."

"I agree. Signal on. Signal off."

"Missiles ready."

There came a disturbance into the Field. It was voices, thoughts, pouring up from below, roaring and swarming closer and closer, getting louder, men shouting in some foreign tongue, "Gorkin, turn it off, turnn it offf—" And that name again, Gorkin, Gorkin, every one of them thinking only of that name, cursing, pleading that Gorkin would deliver them.

Propelled on the wind of this extraordinary Field, the whole parade passed up and out into the sky. It left only stench behind.

Jamshid was not disturbed; he trusted the Field too absolutely, loved it too much. He returned to his work.

"Unlock code insertion time."

Paul kept his mind fixed on the single object of reaching Jamshid. He forced himself forward, down the rough hill to the earthen circle he was beginning to glimpse through the trees, to the figure standing at the center of it, a thin-shouldered child in a cloak so large it draped to the ground.

Above him the sky cracked. Offal, dead flesh, bits and pieces of human beings fell from it. The stink of corpse gas was overpowering. Big bones and skulls thudded like stones to the ground. Paul saw cracked boots and the tattered shreds of Soviet uniforms, and paper, sheaves and piles of orders fluttering down, all in Cyrillic, and with them intercom headsets and lengths of cable and electronic components.

"Cover your head, Catherine."

He was being splattered with liquescent decay, the wet extremity of flesh.

Like the opossum he had found under his grandmother's house, as dead and oozing as that.

A foot glanced painfully off his wounded shoulder, but the larger objects were deflected by the trees. In moments the whole forest was draped with wires and papers and pieces of flesh.

Christmas among the pines.

Then the forest parted. Before them was only Jamshid's Circle. And Jamshid. And something else, tall, its head bobbing on its long neck, its cat eyes fiery white.

"Unlock code inserted."

So marvelously close now. So very close. Close the hand on the squirming mouse!

"Missiles armed."

"I confirm."

This was it, the final, critical moment.

"Key turn commit time."

"Key turn."

"I agree."

"I'm scared, Cath. I can't face that!" He had seen it before in the Zagros.

It was what came for the evil dead, the truth.

"It won't hurt you, Paul."

Wind started, a deafening, bellowing wind out of the

clear sky, a hot, hurting wind. "How the hell do you know?"

She grabbed the wrist of his good arm. "Trust me."

"What did you say?"

"Come on!"

Paul went past it, past the bobbing head, the steely clatter of teeth, the questing, nervous fingers. He passed through the light of the eyes.

Then there was Jamshid. Catherine bounded up to him and grabbed his shoulders.

Beyond his body Paul saw a long, silver tunnel leading off toward the plain. When he looked down it his face seemed to extend and stretch until he felt as if he had had popped out of himself.

He heard voices at the far end of the tunnel. The missile crew!

"Prepare to press firing button."

No! Don't press it!

A raging panther flew at Paul's throat. Its claws began to tear at his windpipe. No, his hands, his own hands!

Catherine bent down to the body. It was wrapped in a tattered, beautifully embroidered cloak—scenes of death, beheadings and crucifixions, burnings, and ugly symbols, stars, twisted crosses, pentacles.

When she drew the cloak aside, she gazed in open wonder at the strange, delicate creature that lay within. He was in his teens. Paul hadn't told her that. His hair was dusty red, his skin olive, and on his face was an expression of such peace that it almost broke her heart to look at it. He was in a deep trance, completely at her mercy.

This was what she had to kill?

She sobbed aloud.

Her strongest impulse was to kiss those sweet, sleeping lips.

Paul had realized that he was out of his body, that he was actually inside the Launch Control Capsule with Jamshid.

He drifted, he tumbled, he could not keep himself in one place. The Field was like a million tiny wires or a thin, loose net on which you couldn't get a handhold. But Jamshid was running it like a spider, and he was running after Paul.

He has to be killed! How dare he come here, how dare he do this to me! Jamshid reached for him, grabbed his slippery confusion, lost it, tried again.

He had never had this happen before. Master, help me!

From far away there came a huge shock. It reverberated through his whole being, bouncing him on the Field and making him lose balance. "My body, someone is hurting my body!" But he couldn't go to help himself, could not leave the crewmen alone with this intruder. Blow followed blow, and Jamshid began to fade.

"Master, help me!"

The intruder was scuttling about like a confused insect. Roughly, with a joyous shout, it pulled Charlie's hands from the console. No, he's mine!

Again and again she smashed his head with the stone. She wept as she did it and knew that never, ever would she stop, no matter how beautiful Jamshid seemed, until he was dead.

At last there could be no life. She covered Jamshid with his ugly cloak.

There followed an uncanny silence.

"Paul?"

There was a pitiful heap at the far edge of the Circle.

"Paul!" She shook his limp body, blew into his slack mouth, shouted his name again and again.

He was at the bottom of a pit of black sand, and the harder he climbed, the deeper he sank.

Catherine was calling him. Her shouts sang in his mind, drew him inch by inch back from the dark.

"Catherine?"

She grabbed him to her breast, sobbed over him. "I thought I'd lost you!"

He sat up, embraced her, kissed her warm, sweet lips. "No, not that, not yet."

They spent a long moment together, full of the peace of the night. An owl hooted. Breeze fluttered Jamshid's cloak.

"Come on, old man, let's go home."

They went together, leaving the Circle and the dead to quiet.

It hurt so to leave the world. For half of eternity it had coveted the fruitful earth and the blue skies, and the souls.

Now it must wait longer.

But it had the patience of eternity. Men had conjured it before, and they would conjure it again.

Just give them time.

368